D1450925

also by the author

The John Jordan Series
Power In the Blood
Blood of the Lamb
The Body and The Blood
Flesh and Blood
Blood Sacrifice
Rivers to Blood

The Jimmy "Soldier" Riley Series
North Florida Noir
The Big Goodbye

Flesh and Blood
and other John Jordan Stories

Michael Lister

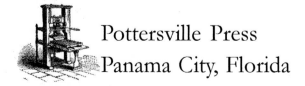

Pottersville Press
Panama City, Florida

Inquiries should be addressed to:
Pottersville Press
P.O. Box 35038
Panama City, FL 32412

Publisher's Cataloging-in-Publication Data

Lister, Michael.
    Flesh and blood : and other John Jordan stories /
Michael Lister.
      p. cm.
     ISBN 1-888146-13-3
    Contents: Flesh and Blood—A Fountain Filled with
Blood—Bad Blood-
    -Blood Bought—A Taint in the Blood—The Blood-
Red Rec Yard Ruse—
      Image of Blood.

1. Prisons—Fiction 2. Prison chaplains—Fiction. 3.
Recovering alcoholics—Fiction. 4. Florida—Fiction. 5.
Hurricane Katrina, 2005—Fiction. 6. Holy shroud—
Fiction. 7. Detective and mystery stories. 8. Short stories. I.
Title.

PS3562.I78213 F44 2006
813.54/21—dc22   Library of Congress Control Number: 2006929974

First Edition - Printed in the United States

Design by Adam Ake

For Pam,
Flesh of my flesh, blood of my blood

Acknowledgments

Though my name is the only one on the cover, this assemblage of ink, paper, cardboard, glue, and stitches is actually the culmination of a collective effort, and I'm truly grateful to the following for their contributions:

For unparalleled support and encouragement, for penetrative insight, for unwavering faithfulness, I'm far more thankful than I can express to Pam Lister, my own personal patron saint.

This book is in existence because my son, Micah, thought it should be, and because he and his sister, Meleah, were willing to endure their mom's reading and rereading of their dad's writing during our many treks down the long, empty rural highways of North Florida.

I'm indebted to Pam Lister, Lynn Wallace, Bette Powell, Ron Kenner, and Jeanmarie Martin for editorial and proofreading assistance.

I'm grateful to Phillip Weeks, Dayton Lister, Terry Lewis, and D.P. Lyle, M.D. for help with the correctional, legal, medical, and forensic details.

I'm also appreciative of Adam "Professor Kisses" Ake for his mad computer skills.

Thanks, too, goes to the following people who have shown great kindness and support to me and to John: Carolann Johns, Lou Boxer, Jon Jordan, Tim Whitehead, Dan Nolan, Fran Oppenheimer, Bruce Benedict, Kevin Dreyer, Jamie Smith, Rich Henshaw, Margaret Coel, Michael Connelly, Dawn Radford, Georgia Anglen, and Joan Bond.

Contents

Introduction
by Margaret Coel

There is a distinct pleasure in reading an anthology of short stories featuring the same character. Each story explores a different aspect of the character's life and shines the spotlight on different parts of his or her personality. In the best of such anthologies, the stories build upon one another, adding layer after layer of complexity and contradiction until the character's inner life—the most guarded thoughts and feelings—are exposed, and in the process, we, the fortunate readers, are able to gain a deeper insight into our own guarded thoughts and feelings. And isn't that the true value of stories? We open an anthology and begin reading, anticipating both the pleasure to come from the reading itself and the way in which the stories will take us outside of ourselves for a brief time and provide a new perspective that can help us to make sense of our own lives.

Flesh and Blood and Other Stories by Michael Lister is that kind of enriching experience. The character whose life opens up for us is John Jordan, a man of irony and contradictions, which make him real, like an old friend we thought we knew who continues to surprise us. He's an ex-cop and an alcoholic struggling to hold onto sobriety and sometimes failing. An ex-cop in recovery, he says of himself, and now a chaplain at a tough prison in the northern gulf region of Florida. He wears a clerical suit and collar, yet finds he has little in common with other men in clerical suits and collars. He navigates the rocky shoals of racial tensions in a place where old prejudices still run beneath the surface of things—"a white man at home among blacks, underprivileged and oppressed. " He's in love with Anna. "The one," he says," and the one who got away."

He's also a superb detective, this John Jordan, often called upon to investigate the inexplicable and sometimes unsolvable cases. Ex-cop and chaplain, he is part Sherlock Homes and part Father Brown. What he brings to the investigations is the combination of Sherlock's powers of observation—the ability to see details others overlook—and Father Brown's openness to the fundamental mysteries at the heart of life. Those are the mysteries that infuse these stories. Even after Jordan has solved the crime, wrapped up all the facts, provided the answers, the fundamental mysteries linger, reminding us that not everything in life is knowable or solvable.

Four of the stories might seem like typical mysteries with ingenious and suspenseful plots that challenge Jordan's powers of deduction. Yet by the endings, we've glimpsed the larger mysteries at the center of the stories—mysteries that recede from our grasp like clouds drifting overhead. In "Bad Blood," an elementary teacher is found bludgeoned to death on the prison grounds. Jordan uncovers the facts and apprehends the killer, but the mystery of the infectious nature of evil and its power to spread into the most unlikely human hearts remains just that—a mystery.

"Blood Bought" and "Blood-Red-Rec-Yard-Ruse" brings Jordan face to face with the mystery of love and the way it exerts control over the human heart and will. And in the brilliantly plotted "A Taint in the Blood," Jordan struggles with the darkness in his own heart and with the possibility that his theory about "the great disconnect of prison"—the vast difference between how someone appears and what he may be capable of doing—may also apply to him.

Running through all of the stories is the mystery of divine grace and the way it can penetrate even the darkest places. The stories are religious in the best sense of the term—open to possibilities. Jordan is a chaplain with more questions than answers, yet he recognizes that grace—the sign of God's presence in the world—is capable of manifesting itself through the most unlikely people and in the most surprising situations. "Flesh and Blood" begins with the mystery of a pregnant nun who happens to be a virgin and concludes with the mystery of forgiveness and the way in which it can heal the human heart. In "A Fountain Filled with Blood," Jordan confronts the fundamental mystery that the truth may be something other than what is apparent when he is drawn into the case of a ten-year-old black girl who says she is Jesus returned to earth—and gives every indication that she just might be.

The remarkable story, "Image of Blood," weaves together the various strands that run through the anthology—mysteries of the human heart, of relationships and of God's presence in the world. At the request of his dying mother, Jordan sets out to determine whether the Shroud of Turin might be the actual cloth that had wrapped the body of Jesus following the crucifixion. His search through the scientific studies for what is real and authentic about the shroud becomes a metaphor for his relationship with his alcoholic mother. The facts he uncovers—the certainties—only lead to deeper questions. What is more important, fact or faith? Can something be at once real and unreal? Ironically, it is the mystery of the shroud rather than the facts that begins to heal the broken relationship. As Jordan says, the shroud "works its magic."

Indeed, mystery and magic fill these stories. They are in the richness of the language, such as the descriptions of the north Florida landscape with Spanish moss hanging from oak branches, forests so thick they block out the light, and the dark, greenish-black water of a slough filled with cypress trees. They are in the remarkable insights into men who are imprisoned—into what makes them want to live and want to die. They are in the deft details that reveal Jordan and the characters with whom he interacts. He can spot a murderer by instinct, he says, "by the pale green teardrop tattoos at the corners of his vacant eyes."

And mystery and magic are in the journey that we take with John Jordan into the unseen wonders permeating all of life, beyond the facts and the data and what we might imagine is the extent of reality. The idea that God's grace might illuminate even the darkest, most violent and disjointed places may be startling, even unsettling, but it is also comforting. That is what the best stories do: they startle and unsettle us and, in the process, expand our view of reality. Most of all, they touch us, perhaps with God's grace.

Margaret Coel
Boulder, Colorado
July 2006

Flesh and Blood

I was leaving Potter Correctional Institution following an unusual day when the call came. The day was unusual because it was good, and good days at PCI were about as rare as innocent men.

Anna Rodden, *the* one, and the one that got away, was next to me as we headed toward the parking lot on the other side of the chain link fence and razor wire, and though we would part ways when we reached our vehicles, I had no reason to believe that I wouldn't have as good a night as day.

"Chaplain Jordan," someone yelled.

I turned around.

It was a young female officer with toffee-colored skin, leaning over and yelling through the document tray on the back side of the control room.

I turned around.

I had been chaplain at PCI, the meanest prison in the Panhandle, since returning to North Florida from Atlanta following the breakup of my marriage and the general disintegration of my life. That had been a few years ago now, and I was beginning to settle into prison chaplaincy and the little life I was living among the least and the lowly.

Beside me, Anna stopped walking, as well.

We were inside the pedestrian sally port, having been buzzed through one gate into the holding area and now waiting to be buzzed through the next.

I walked over to the document tray, which was next to the

entrance door of the security building, as other employees continued toward the front gate. Anna followed.

It was a clear day in spring, the sun was still high in the western sky. The time had changed recently, and I was looking forward
to enjoying the extra light of the lengthening day after leaving the
institution.

"There's a call for you," the officer said. "I told her you
were leaving for the day, but she said it was urgent."

She was striking in spite of the correctional officer uniform
she wore, her dark, tumescent lips so full they looked nearly en-
gorged.

"Catch her name?" I asked.

"A, ah, Sister Abigail from St. Ann's."

St. Ann's Abbey was a retreat center near the coast, and Sister Abigail was a middle-aged psychologist, Catholic nun, and my
sometime counselor.

"I'll take it," I said.

She fed the telephone and its extra-long cord through the
document tray. The once white receiver was yellowish with grime
and held traces of makeup.

"Hello," I said.

"John," Sister Abigail said, "I'm so glad I caught you."

"What is it?"

"I've got a situation I need your help with," she said. "It's
extremely important and quite delicate and requires immediate attention."

"Name it," I said.

"How soon can you get here?"

"Less than an hour."

"Come as fast as you can," she said. "I've got a pregnant nun
who claims to be a virgin, medical evidence that confirms it, and
some hysterical zealots about to turn my retreat into a circus."

"I'm on my way," I said.

The serene, scenic drive to St. Ann's was made more so because, having nothing more interesting to do, Anna had decided to join me.

"Whatta you think she wants you to do?" Anna asked.

"Prove we're not about to have a virgin birth."

"Really? A nun?"

I nodded.

We were on a long, straight, empty stretch of rural highway in the midst of hundreds of thousands of acres of pine tree forests, my small truck the only vehicle as far as I could see in either direction.

"Why?"

"I don't think she believes in such things," I said.

"Does she believe in *God*?"

I shrugged. "I can't really speak for her, but if I had to guess I'd say she doesn't believe in a supernatural deity that breaks into nature to perform miracles. I think she sees God as more imminent—more a part *of* than *from* everything. But even if she didn't, and even if she believed that this nun was a pregnant virgin, she'd want me to disprove it if I could. It's like exorcism, exhausting everything else—all mental disorders and other explanations before even considering that it might be possession."

"But she's not exhausting all other explanations because she believes it really could be a miracle, is she?"

"She's a person of science as much as faith," I said.

"Not easy being a person of faith these days, is it?" she asked.

"Way *too* easy for some," I said.

She nodded. "True. I should have said it's not easy being a modern person fully engaged in the world of suffering, fully aware of science and existentialism, and still be a person of faith."

"But that would have taken too long," I said.

She smiled. "How do you do it?"

"Not well," I said. "Obviously."

"That's not true," she said.

"What about you?" I asked.

She shrugged. "I guess I really don't consider myself a person of faith—not like you, or a nun."

"But you are," I said.

Just ahead of us, a new bridge rose high into the air above the intercoastal waterway, its peak reaching the tops of the tall pines that spread out from it in all directions.

"I believe in you," she said. "And in what you believe in."

"Then you're in far worse shape than I thought," I said.

"Seriously," she said.

Why did all our conversations lead here, to an intense intimacy we couldn't move beyond—at least not without her husband's strenuous objections?

"How do I respond seriously to that?" I asked. "By saying 'thank you?' Thank you."

"Thank you is fine, but you don't have to do anything with it. It just is. It's true and it needed to be said."

We rode along in silence a few moments.

"Do you even believe in the virgin birth?" she asked.

I shrugged. "I did as a kid," I said. "Now, it just doesn't matter. It could have literally happened, or it could be a misunderstanding of an obscure verse in the Hebrew Bible, or it could have become part of the tradition because of competition with Greek and Roman sons of God who were said to have been born of virgins, or it could merely signify there was something extraordinary about the simple Jewish peasant of whom it was said."

As the highway ended abruptly at the edge of the Gulf, we took a left and drove along the beach for a few miles, each of us mesmerized by the bright orange afternoon sun pooling on the smooth blue-green surface of the Gulf.

"Tell me again why we don't live down here," she said.

I thought about all the recent development, all that was on

the way now that Florida's largest landowner had closed down its paper mill and had begun building resorts and golf courses, and all the "For Sale" signs of people who had lived here their entire lives cashing in as the beginning of the end had begun. Florida's final patch of pristine, unspoiled beauty was being sold to the highest bidder, and the only thing us locals who loved this area so much could do was stand by in our powerlessness and watch. In doing so, I felt like the Native American man in the commercial from the 1970s, standing on the side of the road, a single tear rolling down his creased face as he watched ugly European-Americans toss litter out of their large, gas-sucking cars.

"We can't afford it," I said. "At least I can't. You and Chris probably can."

We were having such a nice time. Why'd I have to mention her husband?

"If what they're dealing with is not a miracle, whatta you think's going on?" Anna asked.

I shrugged. "If she's not lying, it could be because she doesn't remember," I said.

"Date rape?"

"Technically," I said, "nuns don't date, but, yeah, something like that. I would've also thought about the possibility of a hysterical pregnancy or a tumor or some other medical condition, but Sister said she had medical evidence to confirm that she *is* pregnant *and* a virgin."

"What about artificial insemination?" Anna asked.

"I don't know," I said. "It's something we'll have to consider, but I'm not sure she could do it and still appear to be a virgin—and it's probably not something she could do herself, so there'd be evidence. Besides, Sister would have checked all these things out before calling me and saying she had a pregnant virgin confirmed by medical evidence."

Located near the coastal town of Bridgeport, on a tract of land that reveals just how beautiful north Florida can be, St. Ann's is situated on the site where once stood a Spanish mission.

Surrounding the small but ornate chapel at its center, St. Ann's consisted of two dormitories—one on either side—a handful of cabins down by the lake, a cafeteria, a gym, an education building, and a conference center with offices.

The natural beauty of St. Ann's was nurturing, and I found myself breathing more deeply as I tried to take it all in. The small lake was rimmed with cypress trees, Spanish moss draped from their jagged branches. Enormous, spreading oaks and tall, thick pines grew on the gently rising slope coming up from the lake, on the abbey grounds, and for acres and acres around it.

Dedicated to art, religion, and psychology, St. Ann's was operated by Sister Abigail, a wise and witty middle-aged nun who supervised the counseling center; Father Thomas Scott, an earnest, devout middle-aged priest, in charge of religious studies and spiritual growth; and the young Kathryn Kennedy, an acclaimed novelist responsible for artistic studies and conferences.

Sister Abigail, Father Thomas, and a diminutive, slightly feminine man in a Roman collar walked out to greet us when we arrived.

In her mid-fifties, Sister Abigail's pale skin, extra weight, and reddish-blond hair made her look older, but her wicked wit and the glimmer she often got in her eye made her seem much younger.

"John, you remember Father Thomas," Sister Abigail said. "This is Father Jerome. He's Sister Mary Elizabeth's pastor."

I assumed Mary Elizabeth was the pregnant nun, but wasn't sure, and didn't ask.

I hugged Sister Abigail and shook hands with the two priests.

Father Thomas Scott was a trim man with receding gray hair, neatly trimmed gray beard, and kind, brown eyes that shone with intelligence. His body, like his voice, was soft without being effeminate, and his black suit and Roman collar hung loosely on his narrow frame.

Father Jerome was small and pale with light blue eyes, and though his boyish face contradicted it, my guess was that he was as old as the other priest. He looked frail and sickly, and I could see enough of what was under his black felt fedora to know that it was covering hair loss—the result of chemotherapy, I suspected.

"This is Anna Rodden," I said.

Sister Abigail arched an eyebrow where only I could see it. She had heard all about Anna in our sessions.

"It's very nice to meet you, Anna," she said.

"I hope you don't mind me coming," Anna said. "We were leaving work when you called and a ride along the coast to this beautiful place sounded too good to pass up."

"I'm so glad you came," Sister said.

"I can walk around the lake or drive into Bridgeport while you all—"

"From what John's told me about you, we could use your help."

Anna looked at me, her eyebrows raised, an expression not unlike the one Sister had given me a few minutes before. "You've been talking about me in therapy?"

"In therapy, in my sleep, in AA, in chat rooms, to strangers," I said. "Women like you are the reason therapy was invented."

It was spring break and the abbey was largely empty, its dorm rooms and cottages temporarily vacant. Not only were the various attendees, counselees, artists in residence, and troubled teens away, but part of the staff was, too, which meant I wouldn't get the opportunity to meet Kathryn Kennedy, one of my favorite contemporary novelists.

St. Ann's was so empty, in fact, that it was jarring to see a late-teens/early-twenties surfer-looking guy with wavy bleached-blond hair step out of the chapel and head toward the dining hall.

"I was just checking on Sister Mary," he said to Sister Abigail.

It was obvious by the way he moved and spoke that he had both physical and mental impairments.

"Thank you, Tommy," Sister said, then lowering her voice, "I believe our young Tommy Boy has a bit of a crush on the lovely Sister Mary Elizabeth."

"We need to make sure he doesn't bother her too much," Father Thomas said.

"Come on," Sister Abigail said to us. "Let's talk in Thomas's office. It's big enough for us all to be comfortable."

Father Thomas's study was filled with scholarly texts and reference books, many on the more mystical side of his religion—miracles, exorcism, speaking in tongues. Beneath the musty smell of the dusty books and the mildew odor caused by Florida humidity, the sweet ripe-raisin aroma of pipe tobacco lingered in the still air.

Father Thomas was seated behind his desk, the rest of us on chairs scattered around him.

"I asked you here, John, to see if you can help us make sense of this before it gets official and the church gets involved," Sister Abigail said. "Father Thomas is satisfied that we're dealing with a miracle and believes we need to involve the church immediately."

"We've done everything else we can," he said.

"Father Jerome, Sister Mary Elizabeth's pastor, is not so sure," she said. "As you can imagine, *I* believe there must be an explanation other than a miraculous conception."

I nodded my understanding of everyone's position.

"Before coming here about six months ago, Father Jerome and Sister Mary Elizabeth worked in a parish in Pensacola," Father Thomas said. "Father Jerome took medical retirement and moved here. Sister Mary Elizabeth joined our staff shortly after."

"She doesn't want me dying alone," Father Jerome said. "I mean, without someone I'm close to. At least that's part of it. I think she genuinely likes it here, as well."

I looked at Sister Abigail. She knew what I wanted without me saying it.

"Here's what we know for sure," she said. "All based on medical examinations. Sister Mary Elizabeth *is* pregnant—about four months. She's also a virgin. The same doctor who verified she was pregnant said her hymen was intact and that she had never had intercourse. The only place she's been beside the abbey is the soup kitchen, so couldn't have had any medical procedures or anything like that. Not that I believe she would. Mary says she's never had sex, never even done anything sexual with a man, and that she has no idea how she got pregnant."

"And I believe her," Father Jerome said. "I've known her for many years now, as her pastor and co-worker. She's the purest, most precious person I've ever met. She's not capable of lying. She's a true innocent. And there's a sense of the divine about her, a presence of the spirit. I've never said this about anyone I've ever know, but I think it's possible that she is a saint."

"But you're not convinced there's a miraculous explanation for her pregnancy?"

He shrugged. "I'm open to any explanation—or none. I just don't want to see her become an object of scorn or devotion or media frenzy."

I nodded.

"If we didn't have medical evidence, we wouldn't be sitting here," Father Thomas said. "But we do. And we can't ignore it. I'm not saying this is a miracle, a sign from God at a time when humanity needs it most, but it might be, and we have a duty to report it to our superiors."

There are people in this world who seem not to belong to it. Sister Mary Elizabeth was one of them. Her simple beauty was radiant, with a palpable presence of otherness. Surprisingly, she wasn't wearing a habit, but a plain blue dress that matched her eyes. Her long, thick blond hair was in a ponytail, and her pale, porcelain-like complexion was without makeup or blemish.

Though Sister Abigail already had, I explained to her who I was and why I was here.

"So you're sort of like Father Brown?" she asked. "A spiritual Sherlock Holmes."

I smiled.

I had expected her to speak in one of those high, airy voices that so many pseudo-spiritual people and eccentrics use, but, like her words themselves, her voice was genuine and came from a woman whose soulfulness was obviously rooted in an earthy humility.

I liked her immediately.

"Unfortunately, not nearly as clever or successful as either of them," I said, "but yes a bit of a detective."

"Sister says you're very good."

"To keep from calling an esteemed nun a liar, I'll say she was being generous."

"Well, I hope you can find out what's going on with me," she said.

"You have no idea?"

"None," she said.

"Do you believe it's a miracle?"

She shrugged. "I find that very hard to believe," she said, "but I know there's no way I could be pregnant."

A touch of red appeared on her white cheeks as if being brushed on with fine bristles by a delicate hand.

"No *possible* way?" I asked. "Even if highly improbable?"

The red on her cheeks darkened and was joined by crimson splotches on her neck.

"I've never been with a man. I've never even shared a bathroom with one, so as improbable as an accident would be, I've never even been in a situation that would make it remotely possible."

We were silent for a moment.

The back doors opened loudly and we turned to see who it was.

"I just wanted to make sure you were all right, Sister Mary," Tommy said.

"I'm fine, Tommy, thank you," she said.

"Can I get you anything?" he asked. "Some tea or a snack?"

"I'm okay right now, but thank you very much," she said.

He studied me without expression for a moment, then stepped back out and closed the door.

"He's so sweet to me," she said.

I nodded, but didn't say anything.

"So do you believe me?" she asked.

"That Tommy Boy is sweet?"

"No," she said with a smile. "About all the other."

"I have no reason not to."

"But you're skeptical?"

"About everything," I said. "Don't take it personally."

"I don't," she said.

I thought about everything she'd said for a few moments.

"You work with a lot of law enforcement types, don't you?" she asked.

I shrugged. "A few."

"Do you know anyone who could give me a lie-detector test?"

I nodded.

"Would you be willing to set one up for me?" she asked. "It would mean a lot to me if everyone involved could know for certain that I was telling the truth."

When I stepped out of the chapel, the others were waiting for me. The lengthening days of spring meant that there was still light, and they were gathered, pacing like expectant parents, beneath an enormous oak tree.

Father Jerome was seated on a bench, the others standing

around him. He looked to be in pain, but he rose the moment he saw me, and walked over. The others following, Father Thomas tapping out a pipe on the bottom of his shoe.

"*Well?*" Father Jerome asked.

"You were right," I said. "She is a very special person."

"I told you, didn't I?" he said. "She's an angel, a holy handmaiden of the Lord."

"Any ideas on what's going on?" Sister Abigail asked.

"Need some more information first," I said.

I looked at Anna. "You okay?"

"I'm great," she said. "I've really enjoyed getting to know Sister Abigail."

"This is going to take a while," I said. "Do you want me to take you home?"

She shook her head. "I'm good, and if I need to go, I'll get a ride. Don't worry about me. Just do what you need to."

"I'll tell you what we *need* to do—and I mean all of us," Father Jerome said. "We need to protect that godly young woman in there." He nodded toward the chapel. "Regardless of how she got pregnant—a miracle, an accident, an indiscretion, or a violation—the last thing she needs is a media frenzy or some clueless cardinal deciding her fate. Let her stay here, have her baby in privacy, with dignity."

"We have an obligation to the church," Father Thomas said. "This could be the sign so many of us have been waiting for."

"And if it is," Jerome said, "you trust a bunch of old gay men and pedophiles to know what to do with it, with her? No. As her pastor, I won't allow it. I'm not going to let you make a spectacle out of her because you think we need a sign."

"It's not up to you," Father Thomas said. "We—"

"She's asked for a lie-detector test," I said.

They all whipped their heads around toward me.

"*What?*" Father Jerome asked. "*Why?*"

"Just to further corroborate that she's telling us the truth."

"But we know she is," he said. "The doctor has already confirmed that."

"She requested it," I said. "And I don't think it's a bad idea. I'm going to set it up. I think I can get a buddy of mine to do it tonight."

"So what do you *really* think?" Anna asked.

"Pretty much what I told them," I said. "There really *is* something remarkable about her—an effortless grace. She's quite extraordinary."

While waiting for Keith Coleman, a friend of mine from FDLE, to arrive to administer the lie-detector test, Anna and I had decided to drive back into Bridgeport and talk to the doctor who had examined Sister Mary Elizabeth.

"You thinking her pregnancy might be miraculous?"

I shrugged. "I'm not there yet," I said. "But I'm even more open now to all possibilities after having talked to her."

"Do you believe in saints?" she asked. "I mean people who have a closer connection with God?"

I nodded. "I think they're very rare. Lot of posers and pretenders, but some genuinely touched people, too—like Sister Mary Elizabeth."

"You know that already?"

I nodded.

We found Dr. Dee Norton throwing a Frisbee to her Australian Shepherd on the beach, backlit by the evening sun. She had agreed to talk with us as a personal favor for Sister Abigail.

Short, stocky, and slightly masculine, Dr. Norton had coarse, curly salt and pepper hair worn close to her head, glasses, and a plain, smooth face without a hint of makeup on it.

"What can I do for you?" she asked, following the introductions.

"I'm trying to help Sister Abigail figure out how Sister Mary Elizabeth got pregnant."

"So she says."

"You're the doctor who determined she was both pregnant and still a virgin?" I asked.

She nodded. "Let me just say for the record that the only reason I'm talking to you about this is that Sister Mary asked me to. Ordinarily, I'd never discuss a patient's private information with anybody but the patient."

"I understand," I said.

The empty beach around us was peaceful, the deepening green waters of the Gulf calm and serene with a glass-like quality. The warm glow of the setting sun seemed to permeate everything with beauty and tranquility, and a hush rested over sea and sand, muting all sounds as if in reverence.

"I did a very thorough exam," she said, "and I drew two conclusions to a medical certainty. Sister Mary is pregnant, and she is a virgin."

"When you say virgin . . . ," I said.

"She still has an intact hymen," she said.

"Is it possible to have intercourse without breaking the hymen?"

"The hymen is simply a ring of tissue near the vaginal opening," she said. "It's not a barrier."

"So it's possible?"

"Theoretically," she said. "But it's very rare. Some hymens are ruptured without intercourse at all."

Down by the water, Norton's Australian Shepherd was barking at the incoming tide, chasing it as it went out and backing up to avoid getting wet as it came in, all the while jumping and yelping playfully like a puppy, though he seemed too big to be one.

"It's highly improbable," Norton continued. "Any stretching of the hymen will usually tear it. Sometimes they heal in such a way that it is very difficult to determine if it has been broken or not, but that's not the case here."

I nodded, and thought about it.

"I've heard of a procedure that recreates the hymenal ring," Anna said. "It was very popular for a while. Could she have had that done?"

"That's the trouble with jumping from the general to the specific, isn't it?"

She paused to make a point and we waited.

"You asked if it were possible for a woman to have intercourse and still have a hymen," she said. "Yes, it's possible. And you asked if she could have had surgery to recreate the hymen. She could have, in theory, but reality is a different matter entirely."

"How's that?" I asked.

"After my examination, we're no longer in need of theory," she said. "We have fact. And that fact is, Sister Mary isn't just a virgin because she has an intact hymen—as we've said, you can have one of those and still have had sex—improbable, but not impossible. But Sister Mary isn't just a virgin because she has an intact hymen. She's a virgin because she's never had intercourse."

When Anna and I arrived back at St. Ann's, Keith was administering the polygraph to Sister Mary Elizabeth. They were inside one of the classrooms in the education center. Sister Abigail, Father Thomas, and Father Jerome were in the hallway outside the door seated in school desks—slid out here, no doubt, for that purpose because they were the only ones in the hall.

"I hope you don't mind, but he said he didn't have much time, so we gave him the background information, a list of questions, and let him get started," Sister Abigail said.

I shook my head. "That's fine."

"Did you have specific questions you wanted him to ask?"

"Yeah," I said, "but he knows what he's doing. It'll be fine."

"John, would you convince him it's better if we not involve the outside world in this?" Father Jerome asked me, nodding toward Father Thomas.

"It's not just me you have to convince," Father Thomas said. "Word of this has already spread through St. Ann's. It won't be long before somebody calls the bishop."

"What'd the doctor say?" Sister Abigail asked.

"That Sister Mary is a pregnant virgin," I said. "Something she's convinced of to a medical certainty."

"See," Father Thomas said. "There's no way we're keeping this quiet, and if it gets back to the bishop and doesn't come from us, we'll probably lose St. Ann's."

"I've never tested a more honest or transparent person," Keith Coleman said. "She even made the obviously embarrassing admission that she finds John here handsome."

"So she doesn't lie, but she's got a vision problem?" Anna offered.

Keith laughed.

"Bottom line," he said, growing serious again. "She's telling the truth. She has not had sex, she has not withheld any information, she doesn't have any idea how she got pregnant."

"I told you," Father Jerome said. "Now, can we please leave her alone? She's done nothing wrong. She doesn't deserve to be a sideshow attraction."

"The fact that she passed the test is all the more reason why we have to notify the church," Father Thomas said. "We might actually be dealing with a miracle. What if she and her baby have been sent from God, do you want to stand in the way of that?"

"Even if what you're saying is true," Father Jerome said, "and I just can't fathom that it is, why do you think it has to be a spectacle? Mary had Jesus in obscurity. Let Sister Mary Elizabeth have the same consideration."

Though a lot younger and in a different type of clerical garb, it occurred to me just how much I must look like I fit with these two men in my suit and clerical collar, but I doubted I could be any different and still be a minister in the same religion.

As the two Fathers continued to argue, Keith, Anna, and I stepped down the hallway for some privacy.

"You didn't just ask her about having sex with a man, but about doing anything that could have gotten her pregnant, right?"

He nodded. "I covered everything," he said. "Test-tube, artificial insemination, accidents. Everything."

I nodded as I thought about it some more.

"Thanks again for doing this, Keith," I said. "I owe you."

"You can pay me be telling me what the hell's going on here," he said. "Is this some spooky second coming shit?"

I laughed.

"Seriously, is she a pregnant virgin? That older nun told me they had medical evidence."

"For the moment it remains inexplicable," I said, "but we're not finished looking into it just yet."

"Well, hey, let me know if I need to start living right anytime soon," he said.

Sister Mary Elizabeth opened the door of the classroom and stepped out. Most everyone looked at her differently, nearly reverentially.

"Thanks again for coming to test me, Mr. Coleman," she said. "Especially on such short notice. I really appreciate it."

"Can we get you anything, dear?" Father Jerome asked.

She shook her head. "I'm fine. Chaplain Jordan, did you need to see me again? I thought I might take a walk down by the lake."

"If you don't mind some company, I'll join you," I said.

"So," she said, "if I'm not lying and I *am* a virgin, how can I be pregnant?"

I shrugged. "The work of the Holy Spirit,?" I offered.

She laughed.

It was a clear, cool night, and the nearly full moon shone brightly on the smooth surface of the lake. Though peaceful, it wasn't quiet. The nocturnal noises, the chirps and croaks and calls, were so loud they seemed amplified.

"Do you have any idea when this happened?" I asked. "I mean specifically."

She shook her head.

"Anything strange happen to you around the time of conception?" I asked. "Anything at all?"

She looked up, narrowing her eyes and pursing her lips. "That would've been a little over four months ago."

"Do you live alone?" I asked.

"I have my own room in the girls' dorm," she said. "It's close to Sister Abigail's."

"Anything strange, odd, or different happen?"

She shook her head and frowned. "Not that I can remember," she said.

"Anything at all?" I asked. "No matter how small."

"I really don't think so," she said. "I mean, thinking back now, it'd be easy to read something strange into ordinary occurrences that if I weren't inexplicably pregnant would otherwise not cross my mind."

"Such as?"

"I usually don't recall my dreams, but for a while there I would wake up in the morning with vivid memories of them," she said.

"Any recurring?"

She shook her head. "Not really."

"Nightmares?" I asked. "Any of them related to getting pregnant?"

She shook her head again.

"What else?"

"I passed out a couple of times," she said, "but I think that was after I was already pregnant. I'm just not sure."

"Where were you when it happened?"

"Different places," she said.

"The dining hall, the chapel, down here on the path, the porch of Father Jerome's cabin—I was delivering some medicine to him, he's very sick—and the soup kitchen in Bridgeport where I volunteer."

"Ever pass out before or since?"

"Not that I recall."

"What else?"

"I don't know," she said, frustration eating at the edge of her words. "Do you want me to say that I woke up a few mornings with my panties twisted and a funny feeling in my vagina? Maybe I did. I'm just not sure, but if I did, my panties get twisted up all the time when I sleep, I'm a tosser and turner. And as far as funny feelings in my private parts, well, that happens from time to time, too, and it's never resulted in pregnancy before."

I nodded, and we were silent a few moments.

She shivered as a breeze blew in through the trees, rustling their branches, raining down leaves, and rippling the otherwise smooth surface of the lake.

I took off my suit coat and draped it around her shoulders.

"Thanks," she said. "And I'm sorry I was snippy. I'm just so tired of all this. I know you're only trying to help and I'm being awful."

I shook my head. "No, you're not."

"I'm usually a nice person," she said.

"Still are," I said.

"You're very kind."

"You feel like going just a little longer?" I asked.

"Sure," she said.

"Can you think of anything else strange or odd?"

"I really don't want to go into detail," she said, "but late one night, while I was praying in the chapel by myself, I had an intense mystical experience. It was unlike anything I've ever known, and it meant a lot to me, but there were no angels announcing I would soon be with child."

"Maybe that's when it happened," I said. "Maybe it *is* a miracle."

"You don't believe that any more than I do," she said.

"I don't know," I said. "If it were going to happen, I couldn't think of a better modern Mary."

"That's very sweet, but I just don't believe it. I haven't even believed Mary was a virgin for a long time now either."

"How do you feel about the church getting involved?" I asked.

"I haven't told anyone this," she said, "but I'll leave first."

"Leave?"

"The church," she said. "My order. No longer be a nun. I just can't go through that, put my baby through that. I'll leave quietly and disappear"

By the time I returned from my walk with Mary, Father Thomas had retired to his room. Sister Abigail and Anna, sitting on a couch in the reception area of the education center, were whispering to one another, the feeble Father Jerome asleep in the chair beside them.

"Where's Mary?" Sister asked.

"I walked her to her room," I said. "She's exhausted."

"Please tell me you didn't enter the girls' dormitory," Sister said. "One scandal at a time is about all I can handle right now."

I smiled. "Could I interest you ladies in a cup of coffee?"

They nodded.

"Will he be okay here?" I asked, nodding toward Father Jerome.

"He'll be just fine," Sister said.

"You say that," Anna said, "but we could come back and find him pregnant."

I laughed.

"I like this girl," Sister said to me.

As we quietly exited the building, I looked back at Father Jerome.

"How bad is he?" I asked.

"He doesn't have much longer," she said. "He's basically come here to die. He's stopped all treatment, given up. What he said about sweet Mary is true. She came here to take care of him—which she's done, even in her condition. He's like her own personal ministry, but she does it in such a way that it seems like she's getting something out of it, too. They drink tea on his porch in the evenings and talk theology and church history, she playing the part of eager student to his sagely master. She looks at him the way Tommy Boy looks at her, though in her case it's an act of compassion."

"Well," Sister Abigail said, "what do you think?"

"I'm baffled," I said. "I really am."

"Could we have a miracle on our hands?" she asked.

I shrugged.

Anna said, "Medical and scientific evidence confirms that she's a virgin, that she has never had sex, has never even been near a man, she has no idea how she got pregnant. There's no way she can be pregnant, but she is."

"Have we exhausted every possibility?" I asked, more to myself than either of them.

"Sure seems like it," Sister said. "It just seems impossible."

The word 'impossible' made me think of the famous oft-quoted Sherlock Holmes line, and, as if reading my mind, Anna said it aloud.

"Remember what you're always saying to me," she said. "Eliminate the impossible and whatever remains, however improbable, must be the truth."

I nodded and smiled at her.

"What's left?" she asked.

I thought about it.

"Okay," I said. "Here's what we've eliminated. She couldn't have gotten pregnant by sexual intercourse—she hasn't had it, even while unconscious. The medical exam proves that. It wasn't the result of some procedure she underwent. The lie-detector test proves that. It wasn't caused by some sort of close-proximity accident. She's never so much as shared a bathroom with a man. So what's left? Is there anything left at all?"

"An act of God," Anna said. "Is there anything else?"

I thought about it some more. At first, I couldn't think of anything, but then something began to emerge from the fog of improbability. Turning it over and over, examining it from every angle, I thought I just might have an improbable solution where once there had only been impossible ones.

"Anything?" Sister asked.

"Maybe," I said. "I'll need Internet access, Anna's help, a list of everyone at St. Ann's and the soup kitchen in Bridgeport, and your permission to search every room in the abbey."

When I got back from my search of St. Ann's, I found Anna asleep in front of one of the computers in the lab inside the education center, her head resting on the list of names on the desktop beside the keyboard.

I gently touched her shoulder.

"Come on," I said. "I'll take you home."

"Huh?"

"I'm sorry," I said. "I've been so focused on trying to figure out what's going on with Mary that I forgot how late it is."

Since I didn't sleep much, I'd often had no concept of time—especially at night.

"John, if I wanted to be at home, I would be," she said. "I want to help."

She covered a yawn with her hands, then extended them out, stretching her arms and arching her back.

"Find anything?" I asked.

I had asked her to check for registered sex offenders among the names on the list Sister Abigail had made for us.

"Nothing," she said. "If there are any sexual predators here, they haven't been caught and convicted yet."

"Or it's sealed by the courts," I said.

"A juvenile?" she asked. "Like Tommy Boy?"

I nodded.

"It's possible," she said. "How about you? Come up with anything?"

I shook my head. "Not a thing," I said, "but I didn't really expect to, any more than I expected you to find a wolf among the lambs."

"Then why did we—"

"Eliminating the impossible," I said.

"And we've done that now?"

I nodded. "I can't think of anything else we can do," I said.

"And that leaves us with . . . ?"

"The highly improbable," I said.

"A miracle?" she asked. "Is that so much more improbable than any other highly improbable scenario?"

I shook my head. "No," I said, "I guess it's not."

The following morning, after a few hours sleep in a dorm room—Anna in the girls', I in the boys'—and a shower, we were gathered in Father Thomas's office.

Father Thomas was sitting behind his desk, Sister Abigail standing not far from him. Father Jerome was seated on the other side of the desk, Sister Mary in a chair beside him. Anna was sitting on a love seat, pulled over from the seating area on the other side of the room. I was standing in the corner leaning against a filing cabinet.

Tommy Boy was serving coffee to everyone while we waited for Dr. Norton's arrival.

"Does this gathering mean you've come up with a solution?" Father Thomas asked.

"I haven't come up with anything so much as excluded everything else," I said.

"But you're saying after you've excluded everything, there's still something left?" Sister Abigail asked.

"Yeah," I said, nodding, "a pregnant virgin."

"Do you mean . . .?" Father Thomas asked, his voice rising.

"My solution requires faith," I said.

Father Jerome sat up in his seat.

"Praise be to God," Father Thomas said. "It's exactly what the world needs right now—a sign of God's presence among us."

"Surely that's not what you're saying," Sister Abigail said.

"I'm saying that I've eliminated the impossible," I said. "Sister Mary says she hasn't had sex, hasn't even been near a man—which means no room for accidents—and she's telling the truth. A lie-detector test proves it. I'm saying that she is both a virgin and pregnant and medical evidence proves that."

"But that is impossible," Sister Abigail said.

"Maybe with men, but with God all things are possible," Father Thomas said. "We've got to call the bishop immediately."

"John?" Sister asked.

"Most cases I'm involved in have clues and evidence," I said.

"Tangibles that when fitted together the right way create a picture or tell a story. With this one, though, what we have is nothing."

"Nothing?" Father Jerome said. "You've lost me."

"We have no clues, no evidence, just a process of eliminating the impossible in hopes of finding an improbable."

"And have you?" Sister asked.

I nodded.

The door opened and Dr. Norton walked in.

"Sorry I'm late," she whispered.

"Someone here is in love with Sister Mary Elizabeth," I said.

Tommy Boy, who was replacing the carafe of coffee onto the tray, dropped it, and it clanged loudly, but only spilled a little since it was nearly empty.

"And the person wants Mary to have their child," I said. "Or, if not their child, at least a child who is part of them."

"But she hasn't had sex," Father Thomas said. "You said so yourself."

"That's right," I said. "But there are other ways to get impregnated. Aren't there doctor?"

She nodded.

"Could it be done without tearing the hymen?"

She nodded again.

"With?"

"Any number of instruments," she said. "From a syringe to a turkey baster."

Sister Mary cringed.

"Surely you didn't call me out here just to confirm that?" Dr. Norton said.

"No," I said.

"Then why?"

"We'll get to that in a minute," I said.

"So you're saying someone impregnated Sister Mary with an, ah, instrument?" Sister Abigail asked.

I nodded.

"But she'd remember that," Anna said. "And according to the lie-detector, she doesn't."

"And I'm a very light sleeper," Mary said. "No way someone could do that to me and me not know it."

"Unless," I said, "you were unconscious."

She frowned. "I haven't been unconscious," she said.

"Yes, you have," I said. "You called it passing out and you couldn't remember if it was before or after you got pregnant, but you were really being drugged."

"Drugged?"

I nodded. "Probably roofies, special K, or GHB."

"Date rape drugs," Anna said, the light of revelation sparkling in her eyes.

"Somebody drugged her and raped her?" Father Thomas said.

"Rape of a sort," I said. "They didn't have sex with her, but they did impregnate her. A violation like rape, just not as violent."

"Who?" Mary asked.

"Who gives you tea all the time?"

She turned and looked at Tommy Boy. Everyone in the room followed her gaze.

"Who's in love with you?" I said.

No one said anything, just continued to stare at Tommy Boy, who was now backing into the corner.

"Who's dying?" I asked.

Everyone looked away from Tommy Boy, back to me, then to Father Jerome.

"What?" Jerome asked, trying to sound outraged, but unable to pull it off. "Are you mad?"

"Improbable, yes," I said, "but it's possible—and all that's left after we've eliminated all the impossibles. You love her, worship her even. You're dying. I think you wanted to leave something of yourself in the world—something of your best self, which Mary brings out. She does that for everyone. Good people always do.

This wasn't about sex. That's why you didn't rape her. This was about mortality, about not wanting to die."

"Jerome," Father Thomas said.

"It's not true," he said. "I would never do anything to Mary." He turned to Mary. "You've got to believe me, Mary. I love you. I would never hurt you. This is all madness." He began to look around the room. "This is insane. Don't believe him. Don't do this to me. Ask him if he has any evidence."

"Do you?" Father Thomas asked.

"Is that why you searched the abbey?" Sister asked.

I nodded.

"What'd you find?

"Nothing," I said. "Whatever he used is long gone."

"See," Jerome said. "See. I told you. This is—"

"A matter of faith," I said. "I told you all that at the beginning of this discussion. It's not like other cases. There's no evidence. It's the process of elimination. What we're left with is the truth."

"John," Sister Abigail said. "We can't very well accuse a man of such an awful crime without evidence."

"So you're saying our faith needs science to back it up?" I said. "The way the lie-detector confirmed what we already knew— that Sister Mary doesn't lie?"

"Yes," she said.

"Okay." Turning to Dr. Norton, I said, "Is it possible to determine paternity during pregnancy?"

Her face lit up. "That's why I'm here," she said. "Yes. If we do an amniocentesis I can harvest fetal cells that can be used to compare DNA."

At that, Father Jerome dropped his bald head into his feeble hands and began to sob.

I returned to St. Ann's a few days later.

Spring break was ending, and the abbey was beginning to fill up again.

I found Father Jerome and Sister Mary Elizabeth sitting on the front porch of his cabin drinking tea. At first, I was surprised, but only for a moment. *She's forgiven him*, I thought.

"Would you like a cup of tea?" Mary asked, as I reached the porch.

"No, thank you," I said.

At first, Father Jerome wouldn't look at me, but after a few quick glances, he must have seen that I wasn't here to condemn him.

"I'm so sorry," he said to me, his eyes filling, "but I'm so glad you figured it out. I felt so guilty. I knew I should confess, let everyone know what an evil thing I had done, but I just couldn't. I was too weak, too self-centered."

Mary said, "You don't need to keep confessing to everyone you see," she said. "It's time to put it behind you."

"But John was involved," he said, "and I didn't really get to tell him how sorry I was and how much I appreciated what he did."

"Okay," she said, "but let that be the last one."

"Can you believe her?" he asked. "She forgave me."

His eyes filled again, and this time he broke down.

I nodded., looking over at Mary. "I'm not surprised at all."

She smiled up at me, and in that moment, I had to agree with Jerome. Sister Mary Elizabeth was a saint.

"How are you?" I asked.

I was leaving St. Ann's, and Sister Mary Elizabeth was walking me to my truck.

"I'm okay," she said. "I really am."

"What are you going to do?"

"Stay close to Father Jerome," she said. "I hope he can stay alive until our baby is born. Then I'm going to raise our child—

where I'm not sure—perhaps as a nun, but probably just as a teacher."

"If I can ever do anything," I said. "Anything at all, just let me know."

"Thank you," she said. "Don't be surprised when I call."

"You're an extraordinary person," I said. "I find you to be enormously inspiring."

Her big blue eyes glistened with moisture.

"I don't say this often," I said, "because I don't think it's true of very many people, but you are, in the very best and most profound sense of the word, a Christian."

"That's the nicest thing anyone has ever said to me," she said.

"Well, it's true," I said. "In fact, it may be the truest thing I've ever said. Father Thomas and some of the others thought this was a miracle, a sign from God to anyone willing to see it. Well, it is—*you* are. You are a grace. You make me believe in God, in goodness, in love, in compassion, and in a virgin birth."

Bad Blood

The body lay face down in the greening grass of late March, damp with dew, its limbs splayed out at odd angles. There were no signs of trauma, the brown correctional officer uniform, though wrinkled and ill-fitting, was neither torn nor blood-soaked.

I had a feeling things would change once the body was turned over.

I was standing near the back corner of the Potter Correctional Institution rec yard at a little after seven in the morning, having been met at the front gate by a new captain named Baker who escorted me past the chapel where I had been headed and through the closed compound to join the warden, the colonel, and the inspector.

Everyone looked more or less masculine in the brown CO uniforms—especially from the back—but the long, overly processed, white-blond hair let us know we were dealing with a woman. I could tell the fried hair had been straightened a few too many times, that its length, a little longer than her shoulders, was made possible by extensions.

Baker said, "She spends a lot of time and money on her appearance."

I nodded.

Baker was tall and thin with dark skin, a quick smile, and kind eyes.

"You can tell that from looking at her back, Sherlock?" the colonel said.

Colonel Patterson was a middle-aged white man with a sour disposition and an enormous southern-fried gut spilling out over his belt. He had bushy eyebrows dangerously close to meeting in the middle, and thick, perpetually sweaty hands.

"Look at her hair," Baker said.

"Can we turn her over, Inspector?" the warden, Edward Stone asked.

Stone, an aging black man with graying hair, was one of the most formal people I had ever known. He was the only person at the prison to call Pete, Inspector. He seemed stiff, but the movements of the thin body inside the three-piece suit, like everything he did, were more measured and careful than stilted.

"I'll catch hell from FDLE if we do, but I'm used to it," Pete said.

As if Stone's opposite, Pete Fortner, the institutional inspector, was pale, short, pudgy, and unkempt, his eyes blinking often behind glasses that perpetually slid down his nose—underneath which was an unruly bushy mustache.

The morning was cool, a bit of bite in the wind, the sun yet to penetrate the clouds and fog.

We waited a moment, but Pete didn't do anything.

"Well . . ." Stone said.

Pete nodded, but looking down at the body again, hesitated.

Before becoming the institutional inspector, Pete had been the local high school football coach. His cousin, a Potter County Commissioner, had gotten him the job, and though he had undergone countless hours of training and had been in the positions for a few years, he wasn't getting any better at it—and wouldn't. He just wasn't suited for his assignment.

"Hell, I'll do it," Baker said.

Without waiting, he leaned over, reached his long arms down and rolled the body over.

It was a woman all right, the large augmented breasts busting out of her uniform appeared glued on—not moving when the rest of her did. Beneath her badly beaten and bloody face, her white skin was pale, her lifeless eyes green. It was hard to tell for sure in her condition, but she appeared to be in her forties, which was why the braces mounted on her small teeth looked so out of place.

"Anyone recognize her?" Stone asked.

No one did.

With more than three hundred officers and new ones transferring in all the time, it was nearly impossible to know them all.

The only blood on her uniform was a small amount that had come from her face, but how she had been murdered appeared obvious. It was around her neck. Beneath the blood-smeared brown collar of the CO shirt, her pale neck was ringed with bruises apparently made by large, powerful hands as they chocked the life out of her.

"Is it because of the . . . ah, condition of her face?" he asked.

"She don't look even close to any of my people," Patterson said, then, turning to Baker added, "Does she?"

Baker shook his head. "We've got a lot of officers and I'm sure I haven't learned them all yet, but I don't recall anyone with blond hair like that and braces."

"Maybe the braces are new," Pete offered. "Or the hair."

"Definitely not her natural color," I said, not to be left out.

"What the hell she doin' out here?" Baker asked.

Less than ten feet from the perimeter fence, the salon blonde was about as far back as she could get.

"Meeting someone?" Pete said.

"When?" Stone asked. "How?"

The rec yard had been closed since two o'clock yesterday afternoon when a thunder storm rolled in.

"Body's not wet enough to have gone through the storm," I said.

"So she came after . . . .When? What time did it stop raining?" Stone asked.

"It was clear by four when we left for the day," Pete replied.

"So she was killed after four, but how'd she get out here and why wasn't she missed and how did her killer get out of here?"

The rec yard of PCI is surrounded by its own fence with two gates and a tower at its entrance. To enter or exit, the officer in Tower III needs to buzz the gates open. The gates are separated by a twenty-five-foot square holding area, and only one gate is opened at a time. The murdered woman had to have been buzzed into the rec yard at some point and her killer had to have been buzzed out.

"She could have been down here a while before she was killed," I said. "She also could have been killed earlier somewhere else and dumped out here later."

"We need to talk to the rec yard supervisor and the Tower III officers from yesterday," Stone said.

Though unusual, it was obvious that he was planning to run the investigation.

"I'm on it," Pete said. "They should be here in a few minutes."

"And we need to know who she is," Stone said. "See if the control room can tell us."

When following protocol, which wasn't always as consistent as it should be, the officers in the control room were supposed to visually identify everyone entering and exiting the institution by matching their employee photo ID with the person holding it. They were also in charge of logging and distributing institutional keys to staff.

"At some point we need to call FDLE and get a crime scene unit down here," Pete said.

"At some point we will," Stone said. "At the same point we give them two identities—this woman's and her killer's."

"You wait that long, you're gonna catch hell from them."

"No, Inspector, you are," Stone said. "I plan on blaming you. Now, all of you, find out who this woman is and who killed her, and find out fast."

The three towers of PCI provided one of the best views of the flat North Florida landscape. In addition to the entire prison complex, we could see the seemingly unending pine forest that surrounded it.

Stone and I had climbed up Tower III with the officer who had been on duty last night and were now standing with him and the duty officer inside the tower.

"Who saw the body first?" Stone asked.

I glanced down at the body. It was nearly two hundred yards away, but clearly visible. Colonel Patterson was standing next to it smoking a cigar.

"I did," Eric Taunton said.

In his early thirties, he was a thick-bodied white man with a thin mustache and freckles. His shift began at seven this morning.

Josh Weeks nodded.

"Josh was gathering his things when I first got in here," he continued. "I just took a quick look around and—bam, there she was."

"She?" I asked.

I looked down at the body again. It was difficult to tell from this distance that it was a woman.

"Yeah," he said, following my gaze. "I've got real good eyes. It's one of the reasons I got this post. It was easier to tell when she was on her stomach. I could see a lot of blond hair."

I nodded.

"She just jumped out at me," he said. "At first I didn't believe what I was seeing, thought my eyes were playing tricks on me, but when I looked back and saw she was still there I called Josh over and showed him."

"Why didn't you see it?" Stone asked. "There was at least an hour of daylight before Officer Taunton arrived."

"I just missed it," Weeks said. "I guess my eyes ain't as good as his."

His eyesight wasn't the only thing that made me question his assignment to this post.

Much larger than Taunton, Weeks was nearly six-and-a-half feet tall and over three hundred pounds. He had dirty blond hair that was too long and needed washing, and breasts that could have benefited from the support of a bra.

"How do you miss a dead body on the rec yard right under you?" Stone asked.

"Warden, I'm sorry, but I just missed it," he said.

"Did you even look in that direction once the sun came up?"

He started to nod, but stopped. "Honestly, I can't remember," he said. "Thing is, no one's on the rec yard 'til after the shift change, so I usually concentrate on the compound."

Stone nodded slightly, but his deep frown and posture communicated how displeased he was.

"What time'd you buzz her through?" Stone asked.

"I didn't," Weeks said.

"You sure?"

"Positive," he said. "Hair like that, I'd remember."

"She was in there before eleven last night when you started your shift?" Stone said. "That's a long—"

Weeks shook his head. "I worked a double yesterday," he said. "I was here from three yesterday afternoon 'til seven this morning. She didn't come through during that time."

Stone and I both looked over at Taunton.

He shook his head. "She didn't come through during my shift yesterday," he said. "I worked from seven until three and I'm positive I didn't buzz her in during that time."

"You realize what you men are saying?" Stone asked. "That she didn't enter the rec yard yesterday."

They both nodded.

"That seems far less likely to me than that one of you buzzed her in without realizing it."

"I'd remember," Taunton said. "No one gets in without me knowing it."

"Me, too," Weeks said, though a little less confidently.

Stone turned to me. "Anything else?"

"Either of you know who she is?" I asked.

They both shook their heads.

"Either she's new," Taunton said, "or we've never worked the same shift."

"Yeah," Weeks said. "Same here."

"So, you don't know her and didn't buzz her in," Stone said. "Yet there she is on the ground, murdered in a part of the institution you're responsible for."

When we stepped out of the tower, Pete and Baker were waiting for us near the gate.

"What've you got for me?" Stone asked.

He stepped up to the gate and the rest of us followed. We were buzzed into the holding area by Taunton, then once we closed the first gate and walked to the second one we were buzzed back into the rec yard.

"Nothing helpful," Baker said. "Everyone's accounted for."

Stone cupped the crooked fingers of his bony hand around his ear. "Retransmit."

"Everyone who entered this institution yesterday is accounted for," he said. "Logs look good. All the keys've been returned. I couldn't find any discrepancies."

"It just doesn't make sense," Stone said.

"But," I said, "it does fit with what Taunton and Weeks said."

Stone looked at me, his face a question. "You believe them?"

I shrugged. "Not necessarily," I said, "but the fact that it lines up with what the control room says gives it more credibility."

When we reached the body again, the colonel was puffing on his cigar. It was narrow and cheap and had a beige plastic filter tip on the end.

"Put that thing out," Stone ordered. "You're standing near a crime scene."

Stepping a few feet away, Patterson threw the cigar over the fences and in the direction of the small logging road peeking out of the woods beyond.

The perimeter fence is actually two, ten-foot high fences, both of which are topped with looping razor wire, with twenty feet between them and more rows of looping razor wire inside. The design makes it impossible to enter or exit the institution over the fence without getting tangled up in razor wire and having your flesh filleted.

"You trying to start a forest fire?" Stone asked.

"It landed in dirt," he said.

I looked over in the direction of the road. The cigar had landed on a patch of yellowish-brown grass between two square indentations about ten feet apart and close to the fence. At least if it started a fire, we'd see it.

"Did all the inmates eat breakfast before we closed the yard?" Stone asked.

Patterson nodded.

"How long can we keep it closed before we have to feed them lunch?"

Patterson looked at his watch. "I'd say we could go five or six hours."

Stone nodded, then turned to Pete. "How long before we need to call FDLE?"

"We should have already," he said. "Even when we do, it'll take them nearly two hours to get here."

As the small group of men continued to talk, I stepped over to the first fence and looked out. I knew the victim had not come through the fences—her body bore none of the scissored signs, but I wondered if her killer had escaped this way. It was highly unlikely. The fence sensors would have alerted the control room if he had attempted to climb the fence, and even if they had been malfunctioning, perhaps from the thunderstorm, he'd most likely be tangled up in the razor wire bleeding to death.

Still, it didn't hurt to check.

There was no flesh or blood on the gleaming blades of the razor wire. No one had been through the fence. I studied the narrow logging path. There were no tracks near the head of it and only some faint tire tracks, most likely belonging to an ATV further back.

"What the hell're you doin'?" Patterson asked. "No way he got out through there."

I nodded. "Just looking," I said, walking back over to join them.

"So we've only got a few hours," Stone said. "How do we proceed?"

"Has anyone talked to the rec yard supervisor?" I asked.

Stone raised his eyebrows, then looked over at Pete.

"I'm still tryin' to find 'im," he said. "He didn't show up for work today and he's not answerin' his phone."

Stone's eyebrows arched even higher.

"John, you think your dad would send a deputy by his house to see if he's home?"

I nodded. "I'll give him a call him in a minute."

"So how do we proceed?"

"We need to know who the hell she is," Patterson said.

"That's the other thing," Pete said. "No one seems to know. I described her to the control room officers, the admin lieutenant, the guy at the center gate. No one's ever seen her."

It was one thing for none of us to recognize her, but unless this was her first day, it seemed unlikely that no one in the control room or security building would. If it wasn't so unthinkable we might consider that she came in from outside, but it was as difficult to get in the prison as it was to get out.

"How can we identify the body?" Stone asked. "Think, people."

"What if that's a wig?" Pete asked.

I had already had the thought and looked closely. It was not.

"Try it and see?" Stone said.

Pete hesitated.

"Ah, hell," Baker said, and reached down and pulled on the hair. "It's hers—well, mostly. Feels like some weave in there."

"White girls call them extensions," I said.

He smiled. "Extensions, then."

"That's good thinking, though, Inspector," Stone said.

I knew what was coming next, one of the most well-worn phrases of business people and bureaucrats everywhere.

"That's what I need the rest of you to do," he continued. "Think outside the box."

I smiled.

"Something amusing, Chaplain?" Stone asked.

"No, sir," I said, "I just had an outside the box thought. May I borrow your phone?"

"What is it?"

"Let me check something first," I said.

He handed me his phone, and I stepped away from the group again and called Dad.

Jack Jordan, my dad and the Sheriff of Potter County, wasn't in his office, but at a crime scene, so I called his cell phone.

"Where are you?" I asked.

"Linton's," he said. "Some kids broke in here, the liquor store, and the co-op last night."

Linton's was one of the auto parts stores in town. Not a single bookstore, theater, or art gallery in Pottersville, but we had three auto parts stores.

"Stole some spray paint and painted the town," he said. "Cut some doughnuts behind the co-op and fucked up some of their equipment."

"How do you know it was kids?"

"Spelled whore H-O-R-E and damn D-A-M," he said.

"'Round here that doesn't necessarily mean kids," I said.

He laughed.

"Be careful," I said. "Sounds like you're dealing with some dangerous, hardened criminals."

"You know me," he said. "Always vigilant."

"I know you're busy with this big case and all," I said, "but can you spare a minute for a quick question?"

"Only because it's you."

"Has anyone reported a missing person?"

"I don't think so, but I can check," he said. "What's going on?"

I told him.

"Hold on a minute and let me see," he said.

I did.

In less than a minute he was back. "None so far."

"Okay," I said. "Thanks."

"Keep me posted," he said.

"I'll try," I said, "but I can't imagine you'll be able to break away from such a taxing case to even take my calls."

"Anything?" Stone asked when I got off the phone.

"Not yet," I said, "but I wanna try one more thing."

"What're you thinking?" he asked.

"That no one recognizes her," I said, "and we all say that if we'd ever seen her before, we wouldn't forget."

"Yeah?"

"What if she's not a CO?" I said. "Uniform doesn't really fit her and she's wearing tennis shoes."

"No way," Stone said. "Just can't happen."

"We've got to at least consider it's a possibility."

"Then who?" Stone asked.

"I'm about to check."

"No way a civilian got in here," Stone said.

"Control room just wouldn't allow it," Baker said.

"It's impossible."

"Almost, but not quite," I said. "It's improbable, but not quite impossible. It's a whole box and thinking thing."

He didn't smile.

"A uniform alone wouldn't do it," Baker said. "She'd have to have a photo ID and—"

"Check her pockets," Stone said.

Baker did. There was nothing in them.

"No way she got in without an ID," Patterson said.

"Maybe her killer took it," Pete said.

"Why would he do that?" Patterson asked.

"Conceal her identity," I said.

"If a civilian managed to get into my institution and get killed . . ." he said, but trailed off.

No one said anything.

"You thinking of someone in particular?" he asked.

I nodded. "Teacher at the elementary school," I said. "Been here a couple of years. Name's Wynn. I've heard her appearance has changed a lot lately. I think it's possible it could be her. "

"Make the call," he said.

I did.

First period was almost over and Melanie Wynn had yet to show up for work.

"How the hell'd she get in here?" Pete asked.

"Her husband's a sergeant in D dorm," Patterson said. "That's the one closest to the rec yard."

"Slow down," I said. "We don't know it's her yet."

"It can't be," Stone said. "It's just not possible."

"Joe Wynn worked last night," Pete said. "I saw his name on the log. You think he brought her in here to kill her—or have someone do it."

"Pete," I said, "you're getting way ahead of what we know. Let me call their home."

I punched in information, got the number for Joseph and Melanie Wynn, and was connected, but the sleepy voice that answered the phone was neither of them.

"This is John Jordan from Potter Correctional Institution," I said. "Who am I speaking with?"

"Kayla," she said.

She sounded about eight.

"Is your mom or dad home?"

"Hold on," she said.

She was gone a few moments, during which I heard her calling for her mom and dad.

"No one's here," she said, a slight alarm in her voice.

"Do you know where they could be?"

"No, sir," she said. "Mom was supposed to wake me up for school and Dad usually gets back from work before we leave."

"It's okay," I said, "I work with your dad at the prison. I'll find him for you. Do you have someone who can come and stay with you?"

"My Mema lives next door."

"Give me her name and number and I'll call her to come stay with you," I said.

After I got off the line with Kayla's grandmother, Stone said, "It's her, isn't it?"

"Could be," I said. "No way to know for sure yet."

Pete had stepped a few feet away and was talking on his cell phone.

"We're fucked," Patterson said.

"We've got to call FDLE," Stone said.

"You think Joe's on the run?" Baker asked.

"No," Pete said, snapping his phone shut and walking up to us. "He's in D dorm pulling a double."

With Pete waiting with the body until FDLE arrived, and Patterson and Baker returning to the security building to check in, Stone and I were headed to D dorm to talk to Joe Wynn.

"What the hell you think's going on?" Stone said.

"I have no idea," I said. "I really don't."

"You know more than you're saying," he said. "Always do."

I smiled. It was the closest thing to a compliment he had ever given me.

"Not this time," I said.

"You guessed the identity," he said.

"Only when I considered it might be someone from outside the institution," I said, "and we still don't know for sure it's her."

"It's her," he said. "And you know it as well as I do."

I nodded.

"You think the husband killed her?" he asked.

"We just don't know enough to even guess," I said, "but it'd be an anomaly if he doesn't have something to do with it."

He tapped on the glass of the D dorm door and gripped the large metal handle, waiting to be buzzed in by the officer in the wicker. "Thanks for helping with this," he said.

"You're welcome," I said, as the door was buzzed open and we walked inside.

The barrack-style dorm had an officer station or wicker in the center with glass on all sides for observation and two long wings spanning out from it, each with about seventy bunks in them. The bathroom and day room were next to the wicker.

The nearly one hundred and fifty inmates inside had been locked in since breakfast and were restless. They filled the day room watching TV and playing checkers, lay on their bunks and read or slept, sat on their bunks playing cards with the man in the bunk beside them. The dorm smelled of sleep, sweat, urine, and the burning twang of cheap tobacco—even though it was a non-smoking dorm.

Many of the men approached us, attempting to redress the warden, but he rebuffed them, telling them now was not the time.

We were buzzed into the officer's station, stepping up the few short steps into a cool, fresh, air-conditioned oasis in the center of the dorm.

"Warden," Wynn said, "Chaplain."

We both spoke.

The other officer, a short Hispanic man with salt-and-pepper hair said, "Warden, what's going on out there? Why are we on lock down?"

"Could you excuse us a moment," Stone said to him. "We need to talk to Sergeant Wynn alone."

"Sure," he said, and stepped down to the door.

Wynn buzzed him out, then looked at us, fear in his eyes. "What is it?"

Joe was soft and rotund with curly blond hair, a wide, full face, and glasses. His voice was wet and nasally, his mouth always full of saliva, his nose perpetually congested. Until recently, his wife, Melanie, had been large and shapeless, too, but following a hysterectomy, she had lost nearly all her excess weight—and with it her interest in Joe, or so the town talk had it. Town talk also had it that she was proud of her new boobs, tucked tummy, processed hair, and straight teeth—and showed them off to any man she could—even if she had to drug his drink and tie him up to do it.

"Do you know where your wife is, Sergeant?" Stone asked.

He shook his head. "In her classroom I guess," he said. "She teaches first grade at the elementary school. I'm pulling a double. Haven't spoken with her. Is something wrong?"

"She didn't show up for work," I said. "We called your home and your daughter answered. She had overslept and missed school and said your wife wasn't there."

"What?" he asked. "Kayla's home alone?"

"Not now," I said. "Your wife's mother is with her."

"Do you have any idea where she could be?" Stone asked.

He shook his head. "We're separated," he said. "Well, we still live together until I can find a place—I'm sleeping on the couch— but I'm about to move out."

"Do you mind if I ask why?" Stone said.

"Because," he said, "she cheated on me."

"I'm sorry," I said.

He shrugged. "It happens."

"How do you feel about her?" Stone asked.

"Sir?"

"Do you still care for her?" he asked. "Any chance for reconciliation?"

He shook his head.

"We've got to tell you something difficult to hear," Stone said.

"As long as Kayla's okay, it won't be too difficult," he said.

"Kayla's fine," I said.

"We've found a body on the rec yard," Stone said.

"Okay," Wynn said, but it sounded uncertain, almost like a question.

"We think it might be your wife."

He shook his head. "Can't be," he said. "She doesn't work here. Never been inside. I told you, she's a school teacher."

"We think it might be," Stone said. "Will you come look at it and let us know?"

"Sure," he said, "but it ain't her. It can't be."

When Joe saw the battered face of his wife, he started crying.

"How the hell . . .? What is she doing in here? Why is she wearing a CO uniform?"

"We were hoping you could tell us," Stone said.

"No," he said. "I have no idea. How . . .? I mean, there's no way she could . . . . It can't be her."

"But you're saying it is," Stone said. "Are you sure?"

He nodded. "It's Melanie."

"How'd she get in here?"

"I have no idea," Joe said. "I can't believe it. Why would she even want to?"

"Is that your uniform?" Stone asked.

Because there were no controls in place for tracking and accounting for CO uniforms, there was no way to know whose uniform Melanie was wearing. It could've been almost anyone's—except someone like Joe.

Joe looked down at his girth and then at the warden with an incredulous look. "Are you kidding? Look at me. . . . Look at her."

"She's changed a lot lately, hasn't she?" I asked.

He nodded. "She's like a whole different person since her surgeries."

"What happened?"

He was quiet for a long moment before responding. "I think she finally felt . . . you know, like she had options. I mean, look at her."

I did. Even without the battered face and blood, she wouldn't have been my type. She had that fake, plastic, Barbie Doll look. She appeared sad, even pathetic more than anything else—a middle-aged woman trying to pass for a pop princess.

Feeling guilty for my harsh assessment of Melanie and sorry for Joe, I nodded, and said, "She's very beautiful."

"Look at her now," he said. "Who could've done this to her?"

It was cruel to make him stand here staring at his dead and disfigured wife for so long, but he was our most likely suspect. Most forensic profilers say that when a victim's face has been beaten, their killer was someone close to them—or at least knew them. Most closers, cops who specialized in getting confessions from suspects say that having something of the victim's in the room breaks the killer down.

"What's she doing in here, Joe?" I asked. "Just tell us. We'll understand. I've been divorced. I know how hard it is to be married, how cruel beautiful women can be."

"She wasn't difficult," he said. "She was just a little lost, but she was trying to get better, seeing a counselor, trying to break things off with her boyfriends. I always thought we'd wind up together."

Just a few minutes before, he had indicated there was no chance of reconciliation.

"How did it happen?" I asked. "It was obviously an accident. You didn't mean to kill her. Everyone'll understand. This kind of thing happens all the time."

"You think I—*I* didn't kill her," he said. "I swear on my daughter's life. I'll take a lie detector test—whatever you want, but I didn't kill her." He looked up from the body, turning toward the rec yard gate. "I've got to go be with Kayla. She doesn't know, does she?"

"She's fine," I said. "She doesn't know."

"I've got to be with her," he said.

"You can in just a little while," I said.

He shook his head. "No," he said. "Now."

"Just help us understand how your wife got in here," I said, "and what happened to her."

"I didn't do this," he said. "There's nothing I can tell you. I swear to God on my daughter's life. I wouldn't say that if I had done this. I love Kayla more than anything in this world. I'm going to be with her. If you want to arrest me, then arrest me and get me a lawyer. If not, let me go check on my girl. I know my rights."

"Don't you want to help us figure out who did this to your wife?" Stone asked.

"Of course I do," he said, "but I'm not stupid. I know you think it's me. Hell, I've watched enough cop shows to know. Husband's always the number one suspect."

"Because he's usually the one who did it," Stone said.

"Well, not this time," he insisted. "I told you—give me a lie detector test."

"Tell you what," I said. "Just give us your clothes and the names of the men your wife was seeing and you can go be with your daughter."

Stone looked over at me, eyebrows raised, frown deepened. "More like boys," he said. "Some of them half her age."

"Any of them work here at the prison?" I asked.

He shrugged. "Probably, but I'm not sure. I wasn't her pimp. I didn't keep up with who she was sleeping with, but according to some busybodies it was half the town."

"We need names," I said.

"I don't have any," he said, but I knew he was lying. He had heard the same small-town gossip we all had. "You might want to talk to Brother and Sister Clark. She was going to them for help."

Roy Clark was the pastor of Eastside Baptist Church in Pottersville. He and his wife Gwendoline lived in the parsonage next to the church out on River Road.

Stone and I were heading toward it in his state-issued warden's car. He was driving.

FDLE had arrived and was processing the crime scene, the D dorm wicker, and Joe Wynn's uniform.

"Pete should be here, not me," I said.

"The inspector's happy to be dealing with FDLE," he said. "He knows he's not very good at this, and he doesn't seem to mind you helping. But even if he did, it doesn't matter. We can't worry about protocol or hurt feelings. We've just got to find out how a civilian got into our institution and got killed."

I nodded, and we rode along in silence for a while.

"You think he did it?" Stone asked.

I shrugged. "I don't know."

"Do you have a feeling either way?"

I shook my head. "Not really."

"What if he runs?"

"We'll know he did it," I said.

"But—"

"Pull in the co-op up here and I'll get Dad to put someone on him."

Forgotten Coast Electrical Cooperative consisted of a large redbrick office building in front and an acre filled with light poles, transformers, cable, trucks, a warehouse, and utility sheds in back—all surrounded by a tall chainlink fence.

Dad was on the side near the large gates where the vandals had broken in. Stone stayed in the car while I got out to talk to him. The two men, each king of his respective kingdom, had often been at odds over the role of the sheriff's department in criminal investigations inside the prison. They didn't care for each other, and didn't seem to care much that I was often the one caught in the middle of their conflict.

"Your warden doesn't want to get out and talk shop a while?"

"What's going on here?" I asked, attempting to change the subject.

"What happened to the good ol' days when kids' idea of joy-riding was taking their parents' car around the block?" Dad said.

I didn't say anything.

"They used bolt cutters they stole from Linton's to get in here and Whitehurst Timber Company," he said. "Drove some of the trucks around and defaced them with spray-painted stick figures and misspelled obscenities. Why they broke in up here instead of around on the other side, I'll never know."

The large, double front gates were well-lit and right off the main highway, but the small, single gate on the side was dark and hidden.

"Nothing scarier than a brilliant mind bent on crime," I said. He smiled.

"Get this," he said, "they wiped everything down, but left the Potter Elementary School gym shirt they used."

"Just make sure they have to take art and spelling at boot camp."

"Whatta you got?" he asked. "Why you slumming with the warden?"

I told him.

"You think Wynn's gonna run?" he asked.

I shrugged. "Can you put someone on him without him knowing?"

He nodded. "I'll call you if he runs."

"Thanks," I said.

"Sure," he said, "just tell the warden he owes me."

"Yeah," I said, "I'll be sure to do that."

I got back in the car, and we continued toward the Clarks'.

"What'd he say?" Stone asked.

"That since it was you, he'd do it," I said.

His perpetual frowned deepened again.

"He'll call us if Joe runs," I said.

"You think they can handle it?" he asked. "Looked like that vandalism was taxing them."

"Dad's a good sheriff," I said, "and he's got a decent department."

He didn't comment, and we rode the rest of the way without speaking.

Gwendoline Clark was a large woman with enormous breasts and a slightly masculine manner. She dressed in loose clothes meant to help conceal her bulk, but their formlessness gave her a shapeless appearance that had the opposite affect.

"Hey, Warden, Chaplain," she said when she opened the door. "Come on in."

She knew both of us from various prison events and the annual volunteer banquet.

Ushering us into a livingroom and offering us coffee, Gwen acted as if she were genuinely glad we had dropped in unannounced. This gift of hospitality made her popular among her husband's parishioners, who felt their preacher and his family were as much theirs as the home they lived in.

It's how most congregations feel, and one of the reasons I wasn't suited for pastoral ministry and why Susan had chafed at being a pastor's wife when we were together in Atlanta and serving a large church.

Of course, I was fairly certain the Clarks were happy to have the little parsonage. The church paid Roy so little that even without a mortgage, Gwen had to clean businesses in town at night to keep them just slightly north of the poverty line.

"Roy's over at the church," she said. "Let me give him a call. He can be right over."

"Thank you," Stone said.

She called Roy, then poured coffee for all of us, bringing it into the living room on a coffee-and-cream-ringed serving tray.

"Ma'am, we're here to talk to you and your husband about Melanie Wynn," Stone said when she sat down across from us in a faded recliner that bore the indentation of her generous backside.

We were on a soiled and stiff sofa.

"Poor girl," she said. "She's doing better, I think, but she's had a rough spell. Just sort of lost. Roy meets with her far more than I do, but I doubt there's much he can tell you—confidentiality and all."

In another moment, Roy arrived and we all stood to greet him.

Unlike his short, round wife, Roy Clark was tall and narrow, his stomach seeming concave beneath his flat chest. When they were standing beside each other, the physical oddness of their pairing was accentuated, and I wondered, as I always did with such unusual couples, what sex was like for them.

"They're here about Melanie Wynn," Gwen said when we were all seated.

"Is she okay?" he asked.

He was sitting in a high-back chair on the other side of the room from his wife's. The chair, which clashed both in style and pattern from the other furniture in the room, seemed overdressed and out of place.

"Is something wrong with Joe?" he asked. "Kent said he's been having a very difficult time."

Kent Clark, aka ManSuper, the Wynn's youngest and very much closeted gay son, was part of our K-9 unit and on the pistol team.

"We understand you've been counseling her," Stone said.

Roy nodded.

"We need to know who she's been seeing," Stone said. "We understand it might be quite a number of young men."

"I'm sorry, Warden," Roy said, "but I can't talk about anything Melanie's discussed with me—though I can assure you it hasn't been that."

"Confidentiality is not an issue," I said. "Melanie's been murdered."

"Murdered?" he said in shock.

"Oh, my dear sweet Jesus," Gwen said. "That poor girl. Any idea who did it?"

"That's what we're trying to find out," Stone said.

"I don't understand," Roy said.

"I know it's a shock."

"Yes, it is, but that's not what I meant," Roy said. "Why are you two here about it? I would think the only possible connection would be Joe. Is he a suspect? Are you trying to clear him?"

"It's complicated," Stone said, "but we *are* trying to help Joe. He's the one who sent us to you."

"That poor man," Gwen said. "He really loves Mel so much."

"Confidentiality's not an issue," I repeated, "Joe sent us to see you. Please tell us who she was involved with."

He hesitated, then nodded to himself slowly.

"The only person I know for sure was Judy Williams' son, Sean," he said.

I nodded. Sean Williams was a correctional officer. His mother, Judy, was one of Melanie's fellow teachers at PES. They had been close friends until recently, when suddenly they weren't, and no one seemed to know why. It was little wonder. Sean was barely twenty and Melanie was just a few years younger than Judy.

"That one nearly split our church in two," Gwen said. "Judy and her family stopped coming and took a lot of their friends with them after Roy preached a sermon on not judging one another and defended poor Melanie, who was working so hard to get her life back together."

"Judy just can't forgive Melanie," Roy said. "And now she hates me and our church."

"Roy just told her what the Bible says," Gwen said. "Warned her about the path of hate she was headed down."

"Surely *she* didn't do anything to Melanie," Roy said.

"She couldn't have," Gwen said. "She was angry, but she's no murderer."

I was surprised when Sean opened his door so quickly. I had assumed he'd be asleep. I was even more surprised when it wasn't Sean opening the door, but his mother, Judy. I had expected her to be at the school.

"John," she said. She quickly cut her eyes over toward Stone and then back to me. "Come in."

We did.

Sean and his mother lived in a large, two-story brick home with enormous white columns in the front and a swimming pool in the back. Inside, the immaculate house were tile floors, art-covered walls, and exquisite furniture—too nice for a single mom who made her daily bread as an underpaid Florida school teacher. It had come from life insurance money Judy had collected when her husband Tony drowned after capsizing his boat in the Chipola River. Sean had a trust coming his way, too, but not until he turned twenty-five.

If the abuse Sean took for still living at home with his mom bothered him, he didn't show it. His indulged life was too good, and he loved spending all the money he made on motorcycles, trucks, video games, boats, and beer. Though his mother was refined and sophisticated, Sean had succumbed to his surroundings and become a redneck.

"I'm surprised to find you home," I said.

"Just didn't feel like going in today," she said. "Tell you the truth, the older I get, the more I feel that way and the more I go with the feeling and just take a personal day."

"Good for you," I said, though I was thinking how suspicious it was given the circumstances.

"Mrs. Williams, this is our warden, Edward Stone," I said.

I couldn't call her by her first name, and it wasn't just that I was raised in the South, but the fact that she had been my teacher in elementary school.

They shook hands.

"It's nice to meet you," she said. "I've heard good things about you from Sean."

She led us into the kitchen.

"Would either of you like some coffee?"

Neither of us would and we told her so.

"Have a seat," she said, motioning to the stools next to the counter.

"I'd be worried when the warden and chaplain show up at my door if I didn't know Sean was safe and sound up in his room."

Judy Williams was trim for a middle-aged woman, except for her bottom, with white skin that appeared to be thin. Her shoulder length hair had a red tint to it, and even in casual clothes you could tell she had money.

"We need to talk to him," Stone said. "I'm going to have to ask you to wake him up."

"He just went to sleep," she said. "He hasn't been home from work more than a few hours. Can't this wait?"

"I'm afraid it can't," he said.

She sighed, hesitating. "Okay."

"Before you get him up," I said, "perhaps we could talk to you for a few minutes."

"Do I need my lawyer?"

"Why would you ask that?" I said.

"I was just kidding," she said. "Do I? You're starting to make me worry."

"We want to talk to you about Melanie Wynn," I said.

"Oh," she said.

"We understand you two had a falling out recently."

She laughed. "Something like that," she said. "But I really don't want to talk about it."

"We really need you to," I said.

"Why?"

"Melanie's been murdered."

She smiled.

"That pleases you?"

"I just wondered as recently as yesterday if what she's been doing would catch up with her."

"What's she been doing?" I asked.

"Poppin' pills and sleepin' with any and everything that moves," she said. "You can only do that for so long until someone gets so hurt or jealous or betrayed that they strike back."

"Any idea who might have gotten to that point?"

She shrugged. "Could be anybody in town," she said. "I'm serious. She was with somebody new every night. She went from this neurotic little overweight schoolteacher to trashy, indiscriminating nymphomaniac overnight. The transformation was stunning. I don't know that she had ever been in a bar before her surgery, but after, it was every night—sleeping with guys in their cars in the parking lot, going back in, drinking some more, picking up another guy, going to his car—over and over again."

"Is that what she did with Sean?" I asked.

She didn't smile this time. After hesitating, taking in a breath and letting it out, she nodded. "He thought they had a future, but after one time in the backseat of his car in the parking lot of the Sports Oasis, she wouldn't have anything to do with him. Wouldn't even talk to him, be with other guys in front of him. She gave him more than one STD. And Roy's gonna get up in his pulpit and defend her. I walked out and won't go back. I don't hate him. He means well, but I loath her. I'm sorry she's dead. I didn't kill her, and neither did Sean, but it shouldn't be surprising that somebody had enough of her shit and just snapped."

"I can understand that," I said, "somebody snapping like that. It'd be—"

"Don't try to work me, John," she said. "I didn't kill her and I don't know who did. I'm just being honest with you. Sean didn't do it and I didn't do it. It's why I'm willing to talk with you, but if I need to call my lawyer I can."

"No need for that," I said. "We're just trying to get some information. More background than anything else. If we can talk to Sean for a few minutes, we'll leave you alone."

"I'll go get him," she said.

When she was gone, Stone said, "What the hell are you doing? It's obvious they did it—her or her son—and you're treating them like innocent friends."

"We're asking questions because that's all we can do," I said. "We can't make an arrest. We have no authority. Unless someone confesses, a case has to be built, and it'll be a combination of interviews and witness statements, and most important of all, physical evidence."

He thought about it.

"Just for fun, though," I said, "tell me how she did it. Did she dress up in a CO uniform, too, sneak into the institution with her good buddy Melanie, somehow get into the rec yard, choke the life out of her, then somehow get out of the institution?"

"Well, maybe not her, but her son," he said. "Melanie sneaks in to have sex with him and he kills her—or she's there to meet someone else or a group, maybe even of inmates, he sees her, snaps, and kills her."

"She was killed inside the institution?" Sean asked.

We turned to see him standing behind us in the opposite door of the kitchen than the one his mom had exited by. He had most likely not been asleep, but listening to everything we said.

I nodded. "Any idea what she was doing there?"

"Probably what the warden said—meeting somebody or a bunch of somebodies," he said. "Fuckin' new people in a new and dangerous place. Sounds just like the twisted shit she would go for."

Sean had blond hair and green eyes. He was muscular and he held himself like he knew it—holding his abs in and his chest out, and his arms out a little from his sides.

"She ever done it before?" I asked.

He walked into the room and stood across the counter from us.

"She was always doin' shit like that," he said. "She fucked the president of the bank in his office when the bank was full of people. She fucked a couple of the high school students in the locker room after school. Hell, she used to blow men in the bathroom at church with their wives and children just a few rooms away in Sunday School. You've never seen a more sick, twisted bitch."

"And you didn't kill her?" I said. "Didn't have anything to do with it?"

Like too many of the young men around here, Sean's seeming toughness was actually a mother-enabled self-centeredness that led to emotional stuntedness. Unfortunately, what was actually weakness was presented as strength, a don't-give-a-damn-about-anything attitude that made too many of the gullible young women believe they were men-of-few-words, cowboy types.

"I didn't care enough to kill her," he said. "I took a turn fuckin' her like everybody else in town, but I didn't love her. Hell, once was enough for me. She couldn't fuck for shit no way. And if I was gonna kill her, I wouldn't do it where I work. I'd do it as far away from where I live and work as I could."

"Unless you didn't mean to kill her," Stone said. "If this was just an accident . . . ."

"It could've been," he said. "I don't know. I didn't do it. And I don't know who did."

Judy, who had stayed out of the kitchen until now, no doubt to avoid the embarrassment of having us witness her hearing the way her son talked, came back in now.

"Chaplain, Warden, we've tried to be helpful, but we just don't know anything," she said. "Given that, for you to continue to interrogate us would border on harassment."

"And we wouldn't want to do that," I said, standing.

"Seems to me you need to be talking to Joe anyway," she said. "I always wondered how much he could endure before he finally wrung her faithless little neck."

As we were leaving the Williams' house, Dad called.

"Don't tell me Joe's on the move already," I said.

"No," he said. "Where are you?"

"Near Potter Landing," I said. "We're just leaving Sean Williams'. We talked —"

"Now isn't that interesting?" he said.

"Why's that?"

"We just found Melanie Wynn's car," he said. "Less than a mile from Sean's house."

I told Stone.

"Where is it?" he asked.

Dad must have heard him because he told me before I could ask.

"We'll be right there," I said.

In under a minute, we were pulling down a small dirt road off the county highway, and parking behind a highway patrol car— the last of a handful of emergency vehicles, all of which had their lights flashing.

Walking past the vehicles and the small group of uniformed men, we proceeded another ten feet or so down the landing to the slough. Dad and one of his detectives, wearing latex gloves, were carefully going over the car.

Both doors were open. Dad was squatting down near the passenger side, leaning and looking through the glove box. The detective, Wayne Mitchell, in plain clothes like Dad, was squatting next to the driver's side watching.

The car, a late model Toyota sedan, didn't appear to be damaged, and a large pink handbag sat on the front seat beside a small pile of clothes. The keys were still in the ignition. The car was immaculate inside and out.

Dad looked up. "FDLE crime scene techs are on their way," he said, "but nothing appears out of place." He looked at me as he spoke, not even acknowledging Stone. "It's her purse on the front seat. Wallet, jewelry, cell phone, cash, and credit cards still inside. I guess it's her clothes, too."

I looked down at the car, the doors, the seats, the steering wheel, her things.

"Were the doors open?"

He shook his head.

"Anybody moved the seats?"

"No," he said, shaking his head again. "Why?"

"They're all the way back," I said.

Stone and Mitchell listened without saying anything.

"How tall would you say she was?" he asked.

"Five-three?" I said. "Maybe."

Above us, the midday sun shone down through the Spanish moss hanging from long oak branches, and dappled the loose sand of the road beneath us. The forest around us was thick for spring because of a mild winter, blocking out all artificial sights and sounds, giving the illusion that we were miles away from civilization. The water of the slough, like the rivers and lakes that fed it, was a dark greenish-black and filled with cypress trees, its surface wind-rippled and shimmery.

"You check the trunk yet?" I asked.

"Just got here," he said.

Without being prompted, Mitchell reached in with his gloved hand and pressed the trunk release on the keyless entry remote. The trunk popped open, and all four of us stepped around to the back of the car. As we did, the small group standing a few feet away, an EMT, a deputy, and a highway patrol officer joined us.

The trunk was as spotless as the rest of the car.

"Clean car," Mitchell said. "Think it got that way before or after she was murdered?"

No one answered at first, then Dad shrugged, and said, "No way to tell. Hopefully FDLE can help with that."

The animosity between Dad and Stone was palpable, and the others seemed to sense it, their hesitant, awkward manner and furtive glances uncharacteristic and otherwise inexplicable.

"Think this is where she and the Williams boy would meet?" Mitchell asked.

I shrugged.

"Here's how I see it happening," he said. "They meet here, she changes into one of his uniforms, then he takes her to work, sneaks her in, and she gets killed—maybe he does it, maybe someone else."

"Why not come back this morning and move the car?" Dad asked.

"We found it too soon," Stone said. "He thought he'd have more time. We were there talking to him while you were finding it."

"He'd have to know it'd be found soon," Dad said. "It's not even hidden. None of this adds up."

"We'll get to the bottom of it," Stone said.

"Actually, you won't," Dad said. "FDLE is in charge now and my office will be assisting them."

"But—"

"The regional director and IG are waiting for you at the institution," he continued. "They're hoping you can tell them how a civilian got into your institution and got murdered."

After being shut out of countless investigations inside the prison, Dad was finally able to let Stone know how it felt, and he was enjoying himself. He had waited patiently for Stone to say something so he could deliver his blow. I understood his frustration, had tried to help by keeping him in the loop of the investigations I was involved in, but the way he was acting now was childish and petty.

Without saying another word, Stone turned and headed toward the car.

"Sorry, John," Dad said.

"No you're not," I said.

"Not for that arrogant bastard, no," he said, "but for you. I'd like to have you in on this one. Maybe we—"

"That's okay," I said. "I'll be busy trying to help the warden keep his job."

He shook his head, lowered his voice, and leaned in so that his mouth was at my ear. "Don't let your white guilt get the best of you, boy."

Possessing a racial sensitivity my Dad did not share, often put us at odds, my identification with the small minority of African-Americans in our community more than my own race, though never overtly expressed, was viewed as a betrayal.

Where had my appreciation of and concern for the disenfranchised come from? Why did I feel so much more at home in prison than behind the pulpit of an all-white, middle-class congregation? I didn't know, exactly. I knew it had to do with Jesus, his fringe movement and radical compassion, and there was something in me that responded to it when I first heard it. Where it came from was as mysterious as temperament, personality, or palate.

I thought about these things as we rode back to the institution in silence, while also imagining Edward Stone in the seat next to me contemplating the end of his correctional career.

"Your dad's not a bad sheriff, is he?"

I shook my head.

"Think they'll get to the bottom of this?"

I shrugged. "FDLE is good," I said, "but there's just not a lot to go on. Coming up with a theory of what happened is one thing. Making a case is something else."

"Do you have a theory?" he asked.

"I've got one forming," I said, "but it's very nebulous."

"Would you be willing to keep working on it for a little longer?" he asked. "Unofficially."

I nodded.

"Thank you," he said. "Obviously, I'd like to keep my job, but I also really want to know how it happened and who did it."

"There wasn't a woman down here at all yesterday," Patty Aaron said. "'Sides me."

"You're sure?" I asked.

"Positive," she said. "Nowhere she could've been I didn't check."

It was later in the day. I was back on the rec yard talking to one of the officers assigned there—a large white woman with long blond hair. Broad shoulders and flat-chested, she looked as if the attractive, if plain, head of a woman had been placed on the body of a man.

The crime scene processed, FDLE was gone, only flapping yellow crime scene tape left behind. Lunch had been served, count cleared, the compound opened, but the rec yard remained closed.

"Let me show you," she said.

We were standing beneath the pavilion on the backside of her office—the only structure on the rec yard. Stepping around the

Ping-Pong table, she walked over to the chainlink fence-enclosed weight pile. I followed.

"Every time the yard closes and the inmates leave, I do a walk through," she said. "I start here with the weights."

The much maligned weight pile consisted of several benches, bars, and free weights. There was nowhere for anyone to hide.

"After I close and lock the gate," she said, "I walk over to the storage closet and check it."

She crossed the open area again, between the Ping-Pong tables, and over to the small closet from which all equipment was distributed. She opened the half door with the counter on top and walked inside, with me right behind her.

The closet was narrow and held horseshoes, basketballs, bats, softballs, volleyballs, and the ping-pong paddles and balls. There was nothing for anyone to hide behind.

Stepping out of the closet, she paused and waited for me, then closed and locked the doors.

"After I check and lock the bathroom, I go into my office, and that's it," she said. "Nowhere else anyone could hide."

Just down from the closet door was the office door for the rec yard supervisor. Through its steel-mesh plate glass window I could see that the small office of a desk, filing cabinet, and three chairs was empty. The inmate bathroom was on the outside of the building, but there was no need for us to look at it. She was obviously very thorough.

"It's the same every day," she said. "Check every area and lock up."

"You were working yesterday?" I asked.

She nodded. "And the day before and the day before that. And there ain't been no woman down here."

"Where's Jeff?"

Jeff Bruen was the new rec yard supervisor.

"He's off this week," she said. "He's in Key Biscayne for his daughter's wedding."

"He hasn't been here at all this week?"

She shook her head. "That's two people you can check off your list," she said.

"Two?"

"Yeah," she said. "Him and me. 'Cause I didn't kill the bitch and he couldn't've."

"I hear Stone's out," Pete said.

He had been standing near the center gate and fell in step beside me when I entered the upper compound.

"Don't count him out just yet," I said.

"You actually trying to help him?" he asked. "He hasn't exactly been your biggest fan over the past few years."

"How long before you'll have the prelim?" I asked.

"Should be soon," he said. "They've made this thing a priority."

"Would you mind letting me know when you know?"

"Sure thing," he said.

As we passed by the medical building, a small African-American female officer opened the door and called out to us.

"Phone for you, Chaplain," she said. "You can take it in here if you want."

I veered off toward her as Pete continued on to the front gate.

"I'll holler at you when I get the prelim," he said.

I walked inside the waiting room for medical, psychology, and classification, the cool air greeting me, and picked up the phone.

"John, it's Gwen Clark."

"Hey, Gwen," I said.

"Sorry to call like this," she said, "but something's been bothering me."

"That's okay," I said. "What is it?"

"There's more you should know about Melanie," she said.

"Roy was just too embarrassed—especially in front of the warden. We really don't know him well, and Roy gets embarrassed so easy anyway, but I think you need to know. Could just the two of us meet? I'd be happy to come out there. I know you're in the middle of this thing."

"Sure," I said.

"It's no big deal," she said, "and I doubt it'll help you find out who killed her, but it might—and it certainly will give you insight into her and her struggles."

"That'd be very helpful," I said. "Thanks."

"During our sessions, she shared so much with us," she said. "Intimate, detailed things."

"Such as?"

"Her fantasies," she said. "At least some of them. The one that keeps swirling around in my head is . . . well, she said she always wanted to be raped by a gang of inmates."

When I got back to the chapel, I called Mr. Smith, my inmate orderly, into my office and closed the door.

"You know what's going on?" I asked.

"Heard a female officer got killed on the rec yard," he said.

Mr. Smith was an old black man of indeterminate age with graying hair, dark skin, tapered fingers, and a slow, cautious manner.

"Anybody braggin' about doing it yet?" I asked.

He shook his head. "No, but there will be. Just a matter of time."

"What about a gang bang?"

"With her?"

I nodded. "Any of the guys braggin' about that?"

"Not that I've heard so far," he said, "but if it happened, there'll be talk."

"Could you go back down on the compound and see what you can find out for me?"

He nodded. "I'll find out what's bein' said."

"The sooner the better," I said.

He nodded again and didn't waste any time leaving the chapel.

Locking my office door and turning off the light, I sat in the quiet, cool, dark room and thought about everything I had seen and heard the past several hours, allowing my mind to go where it would. I thought about the crime scene, how difficult it would have been for Melanie to get to it. I wondered where she had hidden if she had been in for as long as the Tower III officers said she had, or if they had lied about buzzing her into the rec yard that night. Were they a part of this? Had they participated or benefitted in some way? I thought about Joe and their marriage, and the transformation that had occurred in Melanie. Was he really as patient and understanding as he seemed? Did seeing her inside the prison cause him to lose it and become violent? I thought about Judy Williams and Sean. Judy was certainly bitter. Had she killed Melanie to protect her son? Had Sean brought Melanie in to have sex in a dangerous setting, caught her with inmates instead, and killed her himself?

When Mr. Smith returned to the chapel, he was shaking his head.

"What is it?"

"Nobody sayin' nothin'," he said.

"Not exactly what I had expected," I said.

"Me neither," he said. "Convict do somethin' he gonna brag about it to somebody."

"Nobody braggin' about having sex with her?"

He shook his head. "Not a word."

"And ideas?" I asked.

He shrugged. "Maybe . . . nah, I got no ideas. Never seen nothin' like this before."

"Maybe there just hasn't been enough time yet," I said. "Yard was closed all morning. Maybe enough of them don't know enough about it to say anything."

"Maybe," he said, "but that ain't ever stopped 'em before."

As I was leaving the chapel, Pete was coming in. Gwen Clark had arrived and, unable to come on the compound, was waiting for me in the admin building, and I was on my way to see her.

"Got the prelim results," he said.

"You mind walking up to admin with me?"

He shook his head. "No problem."

He took a few steps back and waited while I locked the chapel doors.

"Before I forget," he said. "Sean Williams and Joe Wynn are on their way in. IG's gonna interview them officially."

I nodded.

"I doubt I can get you in," he said, "but I can probably mic the room so you could hear it."

"Thanks," I said.

"Regional director's still in Stone's office," he said. "Today is Stone's last day. They haven't said who the new warden will be, but the rumor is there's an assistant warden at Calhoun CI that'll get it."

I didn't care about any of that, but I nodded, paused for a moment, then asked, "How'd she die?"

"Asphyxiation caused by strangulation," he said. "Somebody choked her to death."

I thought about it. No surprises there.

We were buzzed into the holding area next to the control room, walked to the front gate, and waited.

"She was pretty kinky, wasn't she?" Pete asked. "What if she was doin' that thing where the guy chokes her while she comes and it went too far? Could've been an accident, right?"

I shrugged. "Maybe," I said. "Had she had sex?"

"They think right before she died, but they don't think she was raped," he said. "No sign of trauma. But get this. Whoever it was wore a condom, and she had been douched afterward—they found traces of latex and vinegar inside her."

I thought about that.

The front gate was buzzed open, and we walked through, and closed it behind us. As we did, I waved to the two female officers inside the control room.

Things were beginning to emerge from the nebula of my mind, starting to take shape.

"Did she have any other injuries?" I asked.

He nodded. "Weirdest of all," he said. "She had several broken bones—all postmortem."

I nodded, as everything fell into place. "That's it," I said. "Thanks, Pete. I really appreciate it. Now I just need one more favor."

On my way to Pete's office to meet with Gwen, I stopped by the warden's office.

Sean Williams and Joe Wynn were seated next to each other in Stone's outer office across from his secretary, neither man speaking to the other. Their fear and awkwardness filled the room with a tension obvious to everyone. To the extent they acknowledged one another, it was with suspicious, furtive glances.

As I stepped to Stone's open door, it was obvious the new regional director and the IG had taken over. The regional director, Daryl McDonald, a young, white guy with a crewcut and glasses, and high on power, was sitting behind Stone's desk. Tom Daniels, the state inspector and my ex-father-in-law was seated across from him. Stone was packing his personal belongings into a small cardboard box.

"We're real busy right now, Chaplain," McDonald said. "You'll have to say goodbye to the warden another time."

"This won't take but a second," I said.

"I'm sure he's come to reveal all," Daniels said. "That's his thing. He's a—What are you? I mean, besides an unmitigated bastard?"

"An ecclesiastical sleuth," I said.

"A . . . ?"

"A clerical detective," I said. "A hound of heaven."

"I wasn't kidding when I said we're busy," McDonald said.

He seemed to me to be the type of obnoxious prig who was constantly picked on in high school and now he was getting back at the world one cruel act at a time.

"You a bettin' man, Daryl?" I asked.

He didn't like that. He looked up at me angrily. How dare I speak to him so casually?

"What?"

"If I can prove there was no way Warden Stone could have prevented the victim from entering the institution, can he have his job back?"

"Can you?"

"Can he?"

He hesitated. "Sure," he said. "This should be good. Let's have it."

"I'll be right back with it," I said. "Don't go anywhere. I've just got to get a little more information. In the meantime, can you get Weeks and Taunton up here?"

"Who's that?"

"Tower III officers," I said.

He nodded. "Sure," he said, "I'm nothing if not accommodating."

"Thanks," I said.

He looked at his watch. "You've got fifty minutes," he said.
"I only need about half that."

"We told you that she was into extramarital sexual activity," Gwen
said. "We just didn't tell you how perverted it was."

I nodded.

We were seated in Pete's office, each of us in the chairs on
the front side of his desk. We had turned the chairs so that they were
facing each other and were sitting close together.

"Part of the reason was Roy's embarrassment," she said.
"And not wanting to talk ill of the dead, but I got to thinking that it
might be the very thing that helps you find out who killed her."

I nodded again. "I appreciate you being willing to talk to
me," I said.

"Are y'all close to finding out who did it?"

"I think so," I said, "but I'm sure your information will help."

"I just keep wondering if there's anything we could've done
to have prevented this from happening," she said.

"You can drive yourself crazy with those kind of thoughts,"
I said. "I've done it before."

Though the same size she had been earlier in the morning,
she seemed slightly smaller somehow not juxtaposed with her tall,
skinny husband.

"She was just so lost, so perverted," she said. "It was as if
she had just given herself over to defilement, and she was infecting
everyone in her life. . . . Poor men—most of 'em didn't know what
hit 'em."

I didn't say anything, just listened.

"Men are bad enough, but boys," she said. "Boys are a different matter. I told you about her inmate fantasy, well, I thought
you should know what she said about that poor boy."

"Which one?"

"Sean Williams," she said. "She told us she could get him to do anything she wanted him to—anything, and if you could've heard the things she told us she got him to do, you'd know she meant anything. I'm not sure why she even came to counseling—not for help, that's for sure. I think she just liked a place to talk about all the things she was doing."

"You're probably right," I said.

"Do you think she talked Sean into bringing her here, and it got her killed?" she asked. "Should we have done something to stop her?"

"What could you have done?" I asked.

She shrugged. "I'm not sure," she said. "I thought we tried everything, but . . . now I just don't know."

I nodded.

"I can't imagine it'd help," she said, "but I can give you more details about Mel's fantasies and activities."

I shook my head. "I wouldn't put you through that," I said. "Just tell me one thing."

"What's that?"

"Did she ever mention any dangerous or violent activities she'd engaged in?"

"A lot of her fantasies were dark and violent," she said, "and all of her activities were dangerous, but there was one thing she used to do . . . . She'd get guys to choke her during sex. Said it made the, ah, experience more intense."

We were quiet for a moment as I thought about what she had just said.

"How do you think you'll find him?" she asked. "I mean her killer."

"A lot of little things all working together," I said. "Witnesses, histories, activities, breaking down alibis, catching suspects in lies, and information like you've given me, but most of all in a case like this, physical evidence."

"Whatta you mean?"

"Once we find our prime suspect—which is what you've helped us with—we can match trace evidence found on the victim."

"Trace evidence?"

"Hairs and fibers and such transferred from the killer to the victim," I said. "Her murderer obviously moved the body, so there was a lot of contact. Melanie lost an earring, and I'm betting it's on the guy or in his car, but best of all we have his uniform. We'll be able to confirm it's him by matching the laundry soap he uses with what was used on this uniform."

"Wow," she said.

"I'm about to go interview Sean again," I said. "It won't take long. Would you mind waiting around until after I do—just in case there's something else I need."

"Sure," she said. "I don't mind."

"Thanks," I said. "Just make yourself at home. I won't be long."

I walked out of Pete's office, and closed door behind me.

"Did either of you ever choke Melanie during sex?" I asked.

Sean and Joe looked up at me in shock.

They were seated in Stone's office across from McDonald, who was still behind the big desk. Daniels was beside him, Stone continuing to pack his things.

"What the hell're you doin'?" McDonald said.

I kept my gaze on the two suspects. "I know it's insensitive to ask, but we're trying to find out who killed her, and since you both cared for her, I figured you wouldn't mind helping—no matter how difficult the questions."

Sean shook his head.

Joe just continued to stare at me, eyes glassy, skin pale, expression confused.

"Well?"

"No," he said. "We never . . . . We hadn't even *had* sex in over a year."

"Chaplain," McDonald said. "What's this all about? Do you know who killed Melanie or not?"

"I think I do," I said.

"Think?"

Pete walked in, caught my eye, and nodded.

"I know," I said.

"Who?" he asked.

"First things first," I said. "Warden Stone's job."

"Okay," McDonald said. "How is he not responsible?"

"Melanie didn't come in through the front gate," I said. "The uniform made us think so—that was a nice touch—but nobody snuck her in and no officer mistakenly buzzed her in—not the control room, not the internal gate, not the rec yard gate. The rec yard officer, who does a very thorough job of inspecting her area once the inmates have returned to the dorms for count, didn't miss her because she wasn't there."

"Then where was she?" Daniels asked.

"Not even dead yet," I said. "Eliminate all the other possibilities and what's left?"

"Come again," McDonald said. "How did the victim get into the institution?"

"You know those square indentations on the outside of the fence?" I asked. "Where the colonel tossed his cigarette."

Stone and Pete nodded.

"That's how she got in."

"Huh?"

"Those are the impressions left by out-riggers—the hydraulic stabilizers of one of the co-op's bucket trucks," I said. "They come down to keep the truck from tipping over when the bucket is raised. Melanie's murderer broke into the hardware store, stole bolt cutters and spray paint, then broke into the co-op and stole one of their bucket trucks. That's why the supposed vandals broke into the big well-lighted double gate instead of the small single gate in the back—they had to get a truck out. To make it appear to be kids, they spray painted misspelled profanity on some of the equipment and made it look like they just drove the trucks around inside the fence, but they took one out, drove it out here, down the logging road, and used it to dump the body over the fence in the rec yard. They covered the tracks close to the fence, but you could see them further down the road. It's why the body was so close to the fence and why so many of her bones were broken postmortem."

"Son of a bitch," McDonald said.

Stone smiled.

Joe began to cry.

Stepping over to the regional director, Stone said, "I think you're in my chair."

McDonald got up and relinquished the chair, continuing to look at me, not Stone. "So who killed her?" he asked.

"Inspector," I said.

Pete stepped over and sat a small digital recording device on the front edge of Stone's desk and pressed a button.

"Roy," Gwen said. "Roy, are you there? Pick up."

"I'm here," he said. "What is it?"

"One of Melanie's earrings is missing," Gwen said. "You've got to find it. Fast. And take all the laundry detergent and fabric softener and get it out of the house. Dump it in a trash can somewhere. Quick. Hurry if you don't want to get caught."

Pete stopped the recording.

"She wasn't missing an earring," McDonald said. "And laundry detergent. You can't—"

"What the hell is that?" Daniels asked.

I smiled. "That," I said, "is the lie that reveals the truth. Inspector."

Pete pressed a few more buttons and the device played what I had said to Gwen before leaving Pete's office.

"Who the hell is that?" McDonald said.

"It's her goddam preacher and his wife," Joe said.

I nodded.

To the extent that Sean showed any emotion at all, he looked relieved.

"Roy was having an affair with Melanie," I said. "I'm not sure if he killed her or Gwen did, but, as you can tell from the phone call, they're certainly in it together. I began to suspect him when Judy Williams told us that Melanie was into sleeping with men in power— like the bank president—and that she was also having sex in the men's restroom at church. Roy was willing to let his church split over her. He preached a sermon defending Melanie, which everyone thought had to do with what she was doing with Sean here, but it was with him. After she was dead, they came up with this scheme because Joe and Sean worked here at the prison, put her in one of their sons's CO uniforms, and dumped her body on the rec yard. Gwen had access to the co-op truck's key because she cleans the building at night. Roy drove Melanie's car down to the landing close to Sean's house. We know it was Roy and not Gwen because he forgot to move the seat back up. And from the moment we spoke with them, they've been pointing us toward Sean. The reason Gwen's out here now is to further implicate Sean and to find out how much we know."

"We don't know shit," McDonald said, "but you know everything. You want to go back and get her confession?"

I shook my head, weary of all of it. "Inspectors Fortner and Daniels are better suited," I said. "I've got chaplaincy duties to attend to, but can I make a couple suggestions?"

"Of course," he said.

"I'd have the Potter County Sheriff go ahead and pick up Roy Clark," I said. "And go at Gwen with understanding and sympathy—after all, an evil Jezebel tried to destroy her holy union and her husband's ministry and all she was doing was defending them."

A Fountain Filled With Blood

I was depressed.

Regarding myself like a stranger in the small mirror, I cupped water from the tap with my hands and brought it to my waking face. Was this how it was for everyone—birth, childhood, college, black hole?

A tinge of guilt shot through my mid-section like a hunger pang, as it almost always did when I had such thoughts. There was so much in my life to be thankful for that even the mildest existential angst seemed self-indulgent, but this was something that only vaguely registered, an intellectual raindrop in an emotional storm. The nothingness I found myself in wasn't something I could talk myself out of.

It was as if the tropical depression that gave birth to Katrina had come ashore when she did, its life-draining force still present in the oppressive pressure I felt in my chest.

Hurricane Katrina had been the deadliest storm to hit the Gulf Coast since 1928, its 175-mile-an-hour winds not just ripping through the coastal structures of Florida, Mississippi, Alabama, and Louisiana, but the fragile stitches of the fabric of our society, the rent garment revealing our great hypocrisy beneath.

But I couldn't count my despair among Katrina's collateral damage, for it didn't arrive in her aftermath, but on the early autumnal winds that brought with it the hint of change, even as everything in my meager little existence remained the same. Still alone, still addicted, still living among the least and lowest. Still . . . .

And then the phone, its piercing ring jolting in the early-morning silence.

Stepping out of the small bathroom and stumbling down the narrow hallway of the tight, tiny, and dilapidated mobile home, I looked at the clock beside my messy unmade bed as I lifted the phone.

I had to be at the prison at seven. That was a little more than an hour away. Whatever this was, it wasn't good news.

My voice was dry, unused, my depression bleeding through its edges. I didn't recognize it.

"John? Is that you?"

A male voice, distantly familiar, but unidentifiable.

I cleared my throat.

"Yes."

"I'm so glad I caught you," he said.

"Call before six in the morning and there's a better than average chance you will," I said.

"Sorry it's so early," he said, "but it's an emergency. I need your help."

"Who is this?" I asked, too down to care about being tactful.

"Charles," he said. "Charles Simms."

Charles and I had been in seminary in Atlanta together, but had never been friends—especially not call-at-five-something-in-the-morning friends. In addition to having different interests and being very different people, we were on nearly opposite ends of the theological spectrum. Charles was an evangelical fundamentalist. I wasn't sure exactly what I was, but it wasn't that.

"How are things at the retreat?" I asked.

Charles was the director of a retreat center on Panama City Beach. I had only seen him a couple of times since seminary. He only called when he needed help. Not long ago I had helped his sister out of a jam.

"We've taken in about four hundred victims of Katrina," he continued. "Mostly from New Orleans, but some from Mississippi and Alabama."

"That's great," I said. "That's a really good thing to do."

And it really was, though I suspected those receiving his shelter would also have to endure his impassioned Puritanical preaching.

"Yeah," he agreed. "The Lord's really blessing us to be a blessing to a lot of lost people—and I don't just mean because their homes have been destroyed."

I knew what he meant. In his world, everyone could fit neatly into one of two categories—the lost and the saved.

My condition was causing me to be less patient than usual. I was already weary of him.

"What can I do for you, Charles?" I asked.

"What do you think about the Second Coming?" he asked.

"Charles, I really don't want to—"

"Just answer the question," he said.

"I guess I'm more or less in favor of it," I said.

"Well, it's happening," he said. "Right here. Right now."

"On Panama City Beach?" I asked.

"Can you believe it?" he asked, his voice filled with excitement.

"No," I said. "I can't."

My head began to ache—not the sharp shooting pains of stress or exertion, but the constant dull pressure of sleep deprivation, stagnation, and depression.

"Jesus is at my humble little retreat center," he said.

"I thought he was spending all his time in prison these days," I said. "You sure it's not just some Hispanic guy?"

"Don't blaspheme, John," he said. "Please just get out here as fast as you can."

"For what?" I asked.

"Before I realized who she was, I contacted Children and Families Services about her," he said.

"Her?" I asked, far more interested now, and it showed in my voice.

In Charles's religion, women were subservient, meant to submit to men. His faith also ignored the feminine aspects of God found in sacred literature, history, and nature, and held a literal view of everything—including Jesus' return in the clouds.

"Yeah," he said. "A little black girl."

"And you think she's the Second Coming of Christ?" I asked.

"It's a real mystery, man," he said.

"Don't a lot of homeless people think they're Jesus?" I asked.

"This one's different," he said. "She might actually be."

"Run that shit by me again," Merrill said.

I did.

We were in my truck in Panama City, heading west on Highway 98 toward the beach. My truck was old and small, and Merrill's massive bulk seemed stuffed into the passenger side. Today was his day off, so instead of his correctional officer uniform, he was wearing jeans, a long, untucked black shirt, and stylish black leather shoes.

"I been tellin' you Jesus was black," he said when I had finished.

"You never mentioned he was a little girl," I said.

"Didn't know that shit myself," he said, his lips twitching in something that had there been more of it would have been a smile. "But I ain't surprised none."

Merrill Monroe was a large, muscular man with very dark skin, very white eyes and teeth, and a nearly perpetual look of amusement on his face—as if we were all actors in a Shakespearean comedy, but he was the only one who knew it. He was my best friend, one of the best and smartest men I knew.

"Still don't explain why we takin' a day off to go see her," he said.

"We're the wise men," I said.

He laughed. "We light one."

"You count as two," I said.

He smiled.

Merrill and I both worked at Potter Correctional Institution, the meanest prison in the Panhandle, he as a CO sergeant, I as a chaplain.

"And didn't you already have the day off?" I said.

"Didn't mean I didn't have shit to do," he said.

The morning traffic on 98 was heavy, but moved well considering. It was cool for an August morning in Florida—even the north end—and the sun was just beginning to do something about it.

"Let me tell you a little something about Charles Simms," I said.

"Who the hell is Charles Simms?"

"The guy who called me," I said.

"Oh, right. Okay, tell me something about ol' Chuck."

The cars on the dealership lots on either side of 98 were wet with condensation, which glistened in the increasing sunlight, the pavement around each vehicle looking as if it had just rained.

"He's a Fundamentalist," I said.

"A what?"

"Jerry Falwell."

"Oh shit," he said. "What the hell you got me into?"

It was the end of the semester, and the parking lot of Gulf Coast Community College was largely empty, but across the street, Berg Pipe and the Port of Panama City were busy.

"Not only is he superstitious and a literalist, but he's sexist and racist—"

"So if he says a little black girl is Jesus . . ."

"Then it's something I've got to see."

"Still don't explain what my black ass is doin' here," he said.

Panama City Beach Christian Retreat was in an old converted hotel on the north side of Highway 98, across the street from the Gulf. It was painted bright pastel colors and catered to the religious teenage spring break crowd, especially church youth groups. It was not what I pictured when I thought of a spiritual retreat center, and was nothing like St. Ann's Abbey down the coast near Bridgeport—which was where I went when I needed retreat and renewal.

The converted hotel was three stories with external walkways lined with room doors. The L-shaped structure surrounded a medium rectangular swimming pool and had very little parking.

Clothes and sheets were draped over the balcony railings, doors were open, and people, mostly African-Americans, were everywhere. Though far better off than those still trapped in the Superdome, the people crowded into the Panama City Beach Retreat resembled them—both in their impoverished condition and in their boredom.

"That's a lot of Negroes," Merrill said.

I laughed.

"Not used to seeing that many at the beach," he said.

I pulled off 98 and parked near the little office out front, and before Merrill and I could get out of the truck, Charles Simms was at my door.

"Little thing, ain't he?" Merrill said.

I nodded. "Anxious too," I said.

"Probably all the aforementioned Negroes," he said.

"That'd be my guess," I said. "Though, he could just be excited that Jesus chose his humble little retreat center for his Second Coming."

"We don't have much time," Simms said.

This came without preamble and after he opened my door.

"Why's that?" Merrill asked.

We climbed out of the truck.

"Who's he?" Simms said.

"Ask him."

"I'm sorry," he said. "It's just that I'm . . . I mean things are .
. . . Here's the situation. Before I realized what was going on, whom
we were dealing with, I contacted the authorities. They'll be here to
get her soon. I want you to talk to her before they get here and help
me figure out what to do."

"It's cool," Merrill said, and introduced himself.

"Come on this way," he said, leading us toward a one-story
building in the back left corner beside the hotel. "Meet her first.
Then we'll go over everything."

To our left, behind the office, a pickup truck of supplies was
being unloaded by a couple of teenage boys in baggy clothes and
do-rags, while two buttoned-up white men watched. To our right,
on the hotel balconies, grown men sat on the cement floor playing
cards, checkers, and chess, as nearby women held babies and kids
ran around engaged in improvised games. Nearly all of them had a
weary, resigned expression, their eyes without light or joy.

"What can you tell me about her?" I asked.

The moist morning air was thick with the pungent, greasy
smell of a southern breakfast cooked commercially in cafeteria style.
It reminded me of a school lunchroom or the chow hall at the prison.

"Not much," he said. "We don't know anything about her
before she arrived here."

"That 'cause she was in heaven," Merrill said with a straight
face.

Ignoring him, Simms continued. "She has no ID, no known
relations, no—"

"I know, I know," I said, "no beginning and no end."

Merrill laughed.

"You laugh," he said, "but no one here knows her. We have
no idea how she even got here. She has no parents."

"Sure she does," Merrill said. "All you got to do is call the Temple of the Black Madonna."

"You're Jesus?" I asked when I stepped into the small cell-like room and saw the beautiful pre-teen girl with the big black eyes.

Somewhere around ten years-old, she was long and lean with corn rows that extended down nearly to her shoulders and held colorful beads at their ends. She wore faded blue jeans, brown sandals, and a fitted white t-shirt.

"I said I'd return," she said, the hint of a wry smile dancing on her dark full lips.

That was a quick come back, but perhaps she had prepared it ahead of time.

The small, mostly empty room was used for counseling. Two folding chairs facing each other were in the center on the cheap linoleum floor. She was in one. I sat in the other. Merrill had remained outside with Charles. It was just the two of us.

"Is it so hard to believe?" she asked.

"I just didn't recognize you."

"I get that a lot," she said.

I smiled at her.

She smiled back.

There was something about her, and it wasn't just that she was breathtaking, her dark skin flawless, her kind, intelligent, slightly sad eyes penetrating. It was her presence. There seemed to be something of the divine about her, as if she were a spirit-person, not really meant for this world. What she didn't seem was mentally ill, which, didn't mean she wasn't.

"Weren't there supposed to be trumpet blasts or something?" I asked.

"Who says there weren't?"

"Oh, well, it's just . . . I didn't hear any," I said.

"It's a very noisy world," she said.

Wow. She's good, I thought, deciding to play along for a while longer to see how well she held up.

"That must be it," I said. "So, I guess what we'd all like to know is . . . well—why'd you take so long to come back?"

"I come back all the time," she said. "Haven't you seen me— hungry, sick, poor, in prison?"

"You're good," I said.

"You don't see me at Potter CI every day?" she asked.

I started to say something, but stopped. Charles must have mentioned I was a prison chaplain at PCI.

"I try to," I said, "but it's not easy."

She didn't say anything, but her face revealed she knew what I meant.

"Where are your parents?" I asked.

"Who are my mother and father?"

"Don't you think they're out there somewhere looking for you?"

"My mother and father and brothers and sisters aren't out there looking for me, but here with me looking for God."

She obviously knows Scripture, I thought, *but so do a lot of kids.* She could have been raised in an extremely religious home where Bible verse memorization was part of the compulsive behavior. *But she doesn't seem obsessive. She doesn't seem unbalanced or deranged.*

"So whatta you here for?" I asked.

"Same as before," she said. "The Mother has sent me to reveal her love."

"The *Mother?*" I asked.

"Or Father. Lover. Friend. Other. I just happen to know you're very comfortable with the mother metaphor."

How could she know that? Not even Charles would know that, would he? Had Sister Abigail said something to him? She must have. That had to be it. There was no other explanation . . . except—there was no other explanation. Still, it was disconcerting.

She's remarkable, I thought. Her clarity and wisdom are amazing. Her IQ must be astronomical.

"What does the *Mother* want from us?"

"To love her back. To love each other."

"That's it?" I asked, hearing in her simple words the distinct echo of "You should love the Lord your God with all your heart and with all your soul and with all you strength and your neighbor as yourself."

"Pretty much, yeah."

I had to remind myself I was talking to a ten year-old. There was something ageless about her, and it wasn't just her wit and wisdom, but her presence and bearing.

We fell silent a moment. I searched for a way I might trip her up, break down her defenses, penetrate her delusion. And yet it didn't seem like delusion at all—of course I knew it was, but she seemed so sane, so centered, so full of . . . of what? Life? Soul? God? How else could I explain the presence in the room? I recognized in her the same spirit that had been in other saints and spirit people I had known.

"You think I'm crazy, don't you?" she asked.

"No," I said, shaking my head. "A little confused, maybe."

"The first time I was here, my family thought I was mad," she said. "They were going to lock me up at one point, but I got away. Several people said I was possessed. Not much has changed since then."

"Could you do a miracle for me?" I asked. "Just a little one."

"It's a wicked and adulterous generation that looks for a sign."

I smiled. She had an answer for everything. She may not be the only begotten daughter of the *Mother*, but it was obvious she was very special.

"I know what you're thinking," she said, "but blessed are those who haven't seen and still believe."

"That's very convenient for you," I said.

"Perhaps," she said, "but that doesn't make it any less true, does it, John?"

She was so quick. I was having a hard time keeping up. And she didn't seem to be calculating or straining to come up with something clever to say, but just conversing naturally, nearly effortlessly.

"How do you know my name?"

"I heard Charles say it," she said, "but I know a lot of things about you. Things no one else knows."

My eyebrows shot up as I cocked my head. "Like what?"

"I know you're depressed," she said.

I didn't say anything. For a moment, I couldn't. I hadn't told anyone how I'd been feeling. Not even Merrill. Whatever her condition, she had uncanny abilities. Perhaps I was in the presence of a genuine child psychic. That would explain—

"You're lonely," she said. "You wonder if you're making a difference, or if you're just wasting your time working in a prison, and, of course, you wonder if you and Anna will ever be together."

Mouth dry, pulse pounding, I was speechless. She was reading my mind. I felt awkward, vulnerable, naked. I knew there had to be an explanation for how she was able to do what she was doing—whatever it was—but none seemed adequate at the moment.

"I know you're afraid you're going to wind up like your mom," she said. "Drink yourself to death. Die alone with nothing."

The hair on the back of my neck stood up as goose bumps popped out on my arms.   "Do you believe me now?" she asked.

I hesitated a moment, searching for something to say. "I believe *you* believe it."

"Could you be just a little more patronizing?" she asked. "You almost set a record. A little more and you'll have it."

"Sorry," I said. "I think you're a remarkable young woman."

"Just not God incarnate?"

"Of course not."

"Is it so unbelievable?"

"Well . . . yeah, it is," I said slowly. "I mean, think about it—about what you're asking me to . . . If there *is* a God, which is a big if in itself, and he—or *she*—wanted to become human for some reason, why a little girl? I mean, who's gonna listen to you?"

"Someone might."

"*Might?*" I asked. "Someone *might?*"

"Sometimes that's all there is," she said.

"What all did you tell her about me?" I asked.

"Nothing," Charles said.

"You must have said something," I said. "And she must have overheard you talking about me, too."

"I told you, didn't I?" he said, a huge smile on his face. "She knew things, didn't she?"

He had been waiting—anxiously, from the look of it—and approached me the moment I stepped outside the education/recreation building.

Merrill wasn't with him.

"I want to know exactly what you said to her or what she might have overheard," I said.

"John," he said, "I swear. I didn't tell her anything but your name. And she couldn't have overheard anything because I called you from home this morning and haven't talked to anyone else here about you or her or any of this."

I shook my head slowly, thinking about what I had just experienced.

"Whatta you think?" he asked.

"There's something about her," I said.

Glancing over toward the converted hotel, I saw Merrill standing on the second story balcony talking to a group of people. Even among so many black faces, he stood out, and it wasn't just his physique. Like the little girl I had just spoken with, there was something about Merrill—a power, a presence, a gift.

"Told you. So will you help me?"

"How exactly?" I asked. "I don't know anything I can do."

"I want to find out what's going on," he said. "No matter what it is. If she's some sort of incarnation of God—I mean, that is possible, isn't it?—or if she has some special ability to know things about people, or if she's mentally ill."

"I just don't think I can help with any of that."

"We've got to move fast," he said. "When Children and Families, come they'll take her away, and there won't be anything we can do. They'll be here any minute now."

"Is there any way you can stop them from coming?" I asked.

"If we found her parents," he said, "but that's not very likely. Maybe there's something legal we could do. I'm just not sure."

I nodded as I thought about it, still a little dazed.

"Please, John," he said. "We don't have long. Just see what you can do in the little time we have."

"What the hell's goin' on?" Merrill asked.

I was standing near the front of the retreat center, not far from the highway, cell phone out, wishing I could see the Gulf instead of the enormous concrete hotels and tacky t-shirt shops.

"I'm calling in reinforcements."

He studied me for a long moment.

We could hear the waves rolling in and pounding what little shore there was after this year's hurricane season, but we couldn't see them.

"You sayin' you think she's—"

"I'm sayin' I don't know what to think," I said. "She's a mystery. I'd like to help her if I can."

He nodded. "I found a kid you need to talk to about her when you get a chance."

I looked up at him from my phone. He jerked his head back toward the retreat rooms and the people crowding the balconies. I saw one little white face looking back at us.

"Thanks," I said. "I will."

"You callin' Anna?" he asked.

"How'd you know?"

"Knew it was just a matter of time," he said. "Anyone else?"

"DeLisa Lopez," I said.

"Two extremely beautiful women," he said.

"Who can help," I said. "One with legal questions, the other with a psychological evaluation."

"Sure," he said. "And look damn good while they doin' it."

"That never hurts," I said.

"No, it don't," he said. "No, it sure as hell don't."

Merrill's bulk made the notebook computer in his lap look like a child's toy, and his large fingers were too big for the keyboard. We were in the retreat center's front office, I on a desktop, Merrill on a laptop, each of us searching missing children and Katrina sites in an attempt to locate the little girl's parents.

We weren't having any luck.

I hadn't figured we would, but it was something to do while we awaited the arrival of DeLisa Lopez. I hadn't been able to get through to Anna, but Lisa was on her way.

The small office was in a room behind the reception area and the paneling-covered check-in counter.

A small TV atop a filing cabinet was tuned to CNN's coverage of the Katrina-ravaged Gulf Coast, in particular the submerged New Orleans. Conditions at the Superdome had deteriorated, lawlessness was escalating, and evacuation efforts were being frustrated.

Amidst the flooding and fires, there was looting, shooting, and anarchy. The disconnect between what was actually happening and what the politicians were saying during their press conferences went beyond irony into tragedy.

"You know this shit is like this all the time," Merrill said, nodding toward the TV. "We just don't usually have reality juxtaposed with it."

I nodded. He was too angry, and rightly so, for me to kid him about using "juxtaposed."

"We're on our own," he said.

I knew who the "we" was, and it didn't include me. He was talking about the people, who after all this time, were still strangers in a strange land—a land that forced them to come in chains and now treated them like refugees.

When my phone rang, I knew it was Anna.

"Where are you?" I asked.

"Bed," she said. "I'm sick. Sorry I missed your call."

She sounded weak and nasally.

"I'm sorry you're sick," I said.

"It's not bad," she said. "I just didn't feel up to facing the day. I'm a little blue."

I smiled. Even our depressions were in sync.

The office was painted pastel pink with green trim, its matching carpet worn and gritty from all the sand that had been tracked in from outside. Even with the air conditioner running, it was humid, and just beneath the industrial orange scent was the faint hint of mildew.

"You feel up to answering a few legal questions?" I asked.

In addition to being a classification officer at Potter Correctional Institution where we worked together, and being all-around brilliant, Anna was in law school.

"Sure," she said. "What's up?"

I told her.

"You're life's never dull, is it?" she said.

"The thing is, Charles has already called Children and Families," I said, "and I'm wondering what I can do to stop them from taking her."

"Why?"

"That's complicated," I said.

"You're not thinking—"

"That she's who she thinks she is?" I said. "No. But there is something about her."

"And no one knows anything about her?" she asked. "No idea where her parents might be or—"

"Nothing," I said.

"You could go to dependency court and ask a judge to grant you temporary custody," she said, "but without being a foster parent or having any connection to her, I'm not sure you could get it. And once it's known that she has psychological problems, the judge is going to want her to get treatment."

"What happens if they show up and she's not here?"

"John," she said.

"We could go for a ride or something and lose track of time."

"It's called kidnapping," she said.

We were silent a moment.

"Any friends at Children and Families?"

"Chris might," she said.

She rarely said her husband's name to me. It was as if when we were together, he ceased to exist. Of course he didn't. He was always with us, between us.

"Anybody else?"

She laughed.

"Let me make a few calls and see what I can figure out."

While DeLisa Lopez met with the little girl to, among other things, perform an informal psych evaluation, I crossed over 98 and walked through the sand down to the water. The Gulf was never more beautiful than following a storm, its green waters sparkling in the midday sun.

The beach was mostly empty, the sunburned tourist it produced long since fled in search of higher ground, returning from whence they had come. Above me, gulls glided on the wind. In front of me, they ran from the incoming tide, leaving tiny prints in the wet sand. Behind me, the empty buildings, monuments to selfishness and shortsightedness, rose out of the sand like remnants of a primitive civilization.

Few places were as inspiriting to me as the Gulf. I always felt more connected, more centered, more myself—or the me I wanted to be. Ordinarily, the warmth of the sun, the sound of the sea, the softness of the sand, the breezy airiness would all conspire to make me pause and somehow take in something I needed, something that was often missing or in short supply.

But today was different.

Even in the midst of all this beauty, that for me had so often been an almost direct conduit to the divine, I still felt depressed, which meant I wasn't feeling much of anything. It was as if an unseen barrier prevented the warmth, sights, and sounds from penetrating my senses. I felt more like a distant observer than someone having a direct experience.

After a while, because he knew I needed some time to think and do whatever else I was doing, Merrill appeared through the diminishing dunes. He was joined by a pre-teen boy with too-long blond hair and very pale skin.

We walked toward each other, meeting in the middle.

"Junior here got somethin' to say," Merrill said.

The boy looked uncomfortable, avoiding eye contact with either of us.

"Tell him what you told me," Merrill said.

The boy hesitated.

"What's your name?" I asked.

"Drew," he said.

"What's up?"

"I seen somethin' he said I should tell you," he said.

"What's that?"

"You helpin' that little colored girl?"

I looked at Merrill. He smiled and shook his head.

"You know who she is?" I asked.

He shook his head. "Don't know nothin' 'bout her," he said. "But I seen her do somethin' I ain't likely to ever forget."

I waited. Eventually, he continued.

"I don't know where she come from," he said, "but a group of us was walking through Elysian Fields and she was with us. I never seen her before. Not sure when she joined the group, but she wasn't with anybody."

He paused, but neither Merrill or I said anything.

"There was water everywhere," he said. "We had just passed this little food store. There was nothing in it. It had been gutted clean, and we was wading in about two to three feet of water up under this interstate overpass and they was this big colored man floating face down in the water. He was like all bloated. They was this yellowish brownish rubber-looking shit all over him, and people was sayin' it was his skin since he had been rottin' in the water so long. Must'a been days. The whole group walked around him. It wasn't the first body we seen. We's almost gettin' used to it. When we got good and past him, I looked back and I seen her—the little colored girl everybody's whisperin' about—she was back there wit him. She leaned over, put one hand on his back, and took him by the hand with her other. I was thinkin' 'what the hell's she doin'?' And then I seen it. I think I was the only one what did, but she said somethin' I couldn't hear and that dead man got up, lookin' alive as you and me. I couldn't believe it. I blinked and shook my head and looked back and I seen the same damn thing. There he was standing up beside the little girl, his big hand completely hiding hers. No more yellow brownish shit on him. He joined our group. He's up there in a room in the retreat center, just like he never died."

"Whatta you think about that?" Merrill asked.

We were walking back toward the retreat. Drew had run ahead of us after we crossed 98 to retrieve the man he had told us about.

"I don't know what to think," I said. "I really don't."

"Mental illness might explain some of this," he said. "But it can't explain raising the damn dead."

I nodded.

"Do you think she could be . . . you know, who she says she is?"

"There's certainly some evidence," I said. "I haven't even been allowing for the possibility, but maybe I need to."

"Don't a whole lot of people believe a lot stranger shit?"

I nodded.

"I mean, why not?" he said. "She look a lot more like Jesus looked than most of the paintings, holy cards, and statues in the world."

"True that," I said.

By the time we made it back to the retreat center, Drew was walking toward us with a very large black man, and just behind them, DeLisa Lopez was headed our way.

"Is it true?" Merrill asked.

"She told me not to tell anyone," he said.

"We tryin' to help her," Merrill said.

"Still . . ."

"Just nod your head or something," Merrill said. "Were you dead?"

The man nodded.

"Are you sure?"

He nodded again, this time more vigorously, his eyes filling with tears.

"You think she's—"

"All I know," he said, "is I was dead, and now I'm alive again."

Merrill nodded. I did, too. I think we were both speechless.

When Drew led the big man away, Lisa stepped up.

DeLisa Lopez had tea stain-colored skin and tarnished copper-colored hair. Her green, gold-flecked eyes were as stunning as they were intense.

"Did I just hear what I thought I heard?" she asked. "She raised someone from the dead?"

"It looks that way," I said.

She nodded as if that confirmed something for her.

"What can you tell us?"

"Before going in there, just based on what you told me, I figured she was delusional, had an extremely overactive imagination, was suffering from post traumatic stress disorder, or some form of schizophrenia, but after talking with her . . . well, I'm at a loss."

"You saying you don't think she's any of those things?" I asked.

"She's not schizophrenic," she said. "I didn't think she would be—even signs of early onset schizophrenia don't usually occur until late teens, early twenties. Obviously, it's not just imagination—the things she's saying, not to mention what she's doing—are way beyond her years."

"Is there anything that can explain . . . ?"

"I've only done a very preliminary evaluation, but I can't find anything wrong with her," she said. "Certainly nothing that would explain what she's saying or what she believes."

I nodded as I thought about it.

"John, what the hell's going on here?" she asked. "I'm a good Catholic girl. I can't buy that I just talked to my God face to face in that little room."

"Then explain it to me," I said.

"Obviously, she's delusional, but she doesn't seem deluded— I mean she doesn't act the way a deluded person normally acts. In fact—"

"What about trauma?"

"I would think trauma," she said. "From Katrina or losing her family. But she doesn't seem to be traumatized. If we could locate her parents, they might bring her back to reality."

"We're trying to find them now," I said, "but . . ."

"Of course, what she's telling us could be reality," she said. "I mean, she seems so calm and integrated, so much more healthy than most people. And if that's the case, if she is well-adjusted and completely in touch with reality, what in the world do we do?"

"Would you mind if I took your fingerprints?" I asked.

The little girl shook her head. "But why would you want to?"

"To figure out who you are."

"I told you who I am," she said.

"I know you have," I said. "But who were you before you became him?"

"Is that relevant?" she asked. "Who were you before you became the man you are today?"

I thought about that for a moment. "Someone in the process of becoming who I am now, just as who I am now, is the person in the process of becoming who I will be tomorrow."

"But when tomorrow comes, will it matter who you were today?"

We were quiet a moment, her question lingering in the air as I thought about it.

"I think so," I said. "Can't become one without the other."

"And if my fingerprints say I'm Jakira Carter, does that mean that's who I am?"

It was a good question, one I didn't have an answer for.

"Who decides who we are?" she asked. "Is it up to us? Is it for others to decide?"

More great questions. Who determines who we are? Do we? Do others? Is it some sort of combination of the two? Is it for me to say who she is? Who is this person?

"Who do you say that I am?" she asked.

I didn't respond at first, just let her question, and the ancient one it echoed, hang in the air between us. Eventually, I said, "That's what I'm trying to find out."

"But you're going about it the wrong way," she said. "Fingerprints and files can't tell you who a person is, not really. We are what we say and what we do. We are our hearts and minds, not our fingertips. Go ahead, take my fingerprints, but don't expect them to tell you who I am—even if they do."

"You okay?" Merrill asked.

I shook my head.

We were sitting in the empty dining hall, having just eaten a very late lunch of leftovers. Well, Merrill had. I had mostly stirred my food around while trying to figure out what to do next.

"Noonday demon?" he asked, using a phrase I often did. I had gotten it from a book I read.

I nodded.

He knew I occasionally felt the Saturnine oppression of an inexplicable depression, which in itself was amazing, but to have the awareness and sensitivity to know when it was present, even in such a mild state, was truly remarkable.

He nodded to himself, and we were quiet a few moments.

I was grateful he was here. He didn't offer any trite words of pseudo comfort or attempt to fix it or talk me out of it. He just sat there, his understanding and powerful presence in themselves healing.

"Is the way you feelin' affecting the way you lookin' into this thing with the little girl?" he asked.

I thought about it. "I'm sure it is," I said. "But how do you mean?"

He smiled. "I just ask the probing and penetrating questions," he said. "You gots to come up with the answers."

"Sure, Doc, I understand that," I said, "but you had something in mind. How do *you* think what I'm experiencing is affecting the way I'm handling this investigation?"

He shrugged. "Not sure," he said. "It just seems like you're goin' through the motions."

I nodded. "That's the way it feels."

"You don't seem as open to all possibilities as you usually are."

"You think she's Jesus?"

"That's your thing, not mine," he said, "but theys a lot of evidence that she's something extraordinary and you seem to just be looking for ordinary explanations."

He was right. Had I been feeling better, I'm not sure I would have done anything differently. I'd still try to exhaust all possible explanations, beginning with the most logical, but I'd probably be more open, more amazed, more in wonder at the wonder of what we were witnessing—whatever it was.

"I'm just lost," I said. "I feel so out of it, so . . . I honestly don't know what to do."

"Why don't you ask her?" he said. "God knows you've done crazier shit."

In the late afternoon, I led Jakira, (I had to think of her as something other than Little Girl or Jesus) out of the room that had become like a prison cell, across the street to the Gulf. We walked along the shore as the sun began its descent into the sea.

"Could you walk out there on the water?" I asked.

"Sure," she said, "and so could you."

I was again amazed at her quick wit and esoteric insight. Why couldn't she be a reincarnation of Christ? Why wasn't I even allowing for the possibility? Maybe the reason I wasn't had far more to do with me than with her. And maybe I had spent so much time investigating temporary mysteries that I was no longer equipped for transcendent ones.

"Do you hear voices?" I asked.

"Doesn't everyone?"

"Who do you hear?"

"In my head?" she asked. "Most are my own thoughts—parental programming, social and cultural training. Some are lines from movies I've seen and books I've read."

"Does God speak to you?"

"Sure," she said. "Just like she speaks to everyone. Some listen, others . . . not so much."

"What is she trying to say to me?" I asked.

"Only you can truly know," she said.

"I can't hear anything," I said.

"It's because of how you feel," she said, "but it will pass."

She then took my hand, and it did. From the moment her coffee-colored skin touched the pinkishness of my palm, a warmth began to work its way up my arm, into my chest, up into my head, down my other arm and torso, until it reached my toes.

Any depression I had been feeling was gone.

Suddenly, the Gulf was a garden again, a place where God could come down in the cool of the evening and walk along the sandy shore with us. The setting sun emanated warmth that was far more than merely physical, the green waters were a mysterious domain again, the womb of life on earth, God's womb, my home.

"I can see," I said. "I can . . . thank you."

"Don't thank me," she said. "Thank God."

"I am."

Though still not sure what to do with Jakira, I returned to the retreat, her hand still in mine, much better equipped to figure it out.

"My appetite's back," I said. "You hungry?"

She nodded.

"There's not much left," I said. "If I can find some bread and fish, can you do something with them?"

She laughed.

It was a spectacular laugh, one that infused her entire face with joy, lighting up her dark eyes and causing the large white teeth she had yet to grow into, to sparkle.

As we neared the dining hall, I heard someone calling me. I turned to see Charles running up behind us.

"Children and Families is here," he said. "She's in the front office. Whatta I do?"

I looked over his shoulder to see an overworked social worker standing in his office talking on a cell phone.

"Tell her it was all a misunderstanding," I said.

"What?"

"That she had just gotten separated from her parents, but they were here after all and found each other."

"You want me to lie?"

"Yeah."

"I can't do that."

"Charles, you're being ridiculous," I said. "Just—"

"Why don't you want them to have her?" he asked. "Do you believe she's—"

"They won't know what to do with her," I said.

"And you do?"

"No, but they work with dull, blunt instruments," I said. "They'll stick her in some foster home or psychiatric unit somewhere and—"

"It's okay," she said.

I turned to see that her face was set toward the front office and the fate that awaited her there.

"I'll go with her," she said.

"Just come with me," I said. "We'll go somewhere else and—"

"No need to run, John," she said. "Don't you realize I could call a legion of angels down right now if I wanted to? I must do this. My powerlessness is the point."

"Is this her?" the social worker asked, as she walked up to us. "Honey, do you have any idea where your parents might be?"

"My mother's in heaven," she said.

"Your mom died? When?"

"No, she's very much alive," she said. "In all things. Can't you feel her? She's the dancing strings of the cosmos. She's the wind and she blows where she will."

"Oh dear," she said.

"I'd like her to stay here with us," I said.

"Who are you?"

"John Jordan," I said. "I'm a chaplain and I've been spending some time with her today. We're really making some headway. I think to snatch her out of here now would be traumatic. She's feeling better. She's talked to a counselor, she's making friends. She's loved and cared for here."

"I can't—"

"Just for a little while longer," I said. "We're searching for her parents. They could turn up at any moment."

"I'm sorry," she said. "I just can't."

"Please," I said. "Please. It's what's best for her."

She studied me for a moment. "It might actually be," she said, "but I don't have the authority. You'll have to petition the judge. Sometimes in cases like these, if there's no family around, a judge will grant temporary custody to someone who is already helping the child. That's the best I can offer you. She'll have a shelter hearing before a judge in dependency court in the morning. That's just a few hours. Overnight. It'll be okay."

When I walked into the courtroom, I knew something was wrong. It was something I felt more than observed, and I wasn't sure exactly what it was, but I knew it. Jakira, wearing new clothes, was seated at a table between the social worker and her guardian ad litem. Her back was to me, so I couldn't see her face or read her expressions, but I could tell even in the slumped manner in which she was sitting that something wasn't quite right.

There were very few people in the courtroom. Because this was a closed, confidential hearing, Charles, Merrill, Lisa, and Anna weren't allowed to attend, and I was only permitted because of my petition. Everyone in the room was there for a reason, including the bailiff and court reporter, and all of them were dressed professionally. I was wearing my best navy blue suit and a sky blue clerical collar.

A tall, young man in a blue suit of his own was sitting at a table across from Jakira's, a leather satchel on the table in front of him. Based on what Anna had told me, I guessed he was Children and Families' attorney.

Much of the previous night, as Children and Families conducted an intake investigation on Jakira, Anna had educated me on dependency court and the process, helped me secure an attorney and file a petition.

At a shelter hearing like this one, the judge typically determines if a child is a dependent of the state or can continue to live with his or her parents or guardian. However, in this situation, with no family present, Jakira is already, at least temporarily, a dependent of the state. The question was what would the judge do with her? He wasn't deciding between a parental or non-parental home, but which non-parental home. I had petitioned the court for it to be mine.

Depending on what happened here today, and if the judge would even hear my petition at this time, there could be another hearing in about a month or a fact-finding trial within three months—neither of which seemed likely, since this didn't appear to be a case of neglect or abandonment but the result of a natural disaster.

My attorney, David Clyde Rish, was seated on the front row. He was a well-respected, semi-retired local man who had served in the Florida legislature for several terms. He had a farm in Potter County, where my dad was sheriff, and was doing a family favor. I couldn't have afforded him otherwise. I sat down beside him.

As Judge Jerry Atkins went through the preliminaries, I began to relax a little. He was a kind, soft-spoken man in his sixties, who ran a very informal courtroom.

As he listened to the facts and circumstances surrounding Jakira, he seemed genuinely concerned for her and saddened by her situation.

During the entire hearing, Jakira never looked in my direction. In fact, she never looked any direction but forward, and before the preliminaries were concluded, I knew why.

As part of the intake investigation, she had undergone a psych evaluation and was deemed to be in need of treatment. Though it wasn't mentioned in the proceedings, it was obvious that she was on medication.

"Mr. Rish," the judge said, "I understand your client wishes to be granted temporary custody?"

"Yes, Your Honor," Rish said, standing, adjusting his suit, and stepping between the two counsel tables.

"What's his connection to the child?"

"He's been providing care for her since she arrived at the retreat center," he said, which he knew wasn't exactly true. "He has developed a rapport with the child and feels it would be in the child's best interest to have continuity of care."

"Your Honor," the young attorney said, rising to his feet. "Not only is Mr. Jordan a single man who lives alone, but he's had no foster care training and—"

"He's a highly educated minister who's conducted endless hours of pastoral counseling," Rish said, "and he's—"

"Your Honor," the young man said again. "With all due respect, I don't know anyone who would put a child in the home of a priest these days, and it's not pastoral counseling, but professional treatment the child needs—the court's own psychologist has said so."

"He's right," the judge said. "While I wouldn't wish to be as indelicate as Mr. Peavy, I would find it difficult to place a young female dependent in the home of a single man with no foster care training even under the best of circumstances, but when the dependent is in need of psychiatric treatment, it'd be negligent to do so."

Before I realized what I was doing, I was on my feet. "Your Honor, please," I said. "Please reconsider. She needs—"

"Mr. Jordan," the judge said, "I run an informal courtroom, but not that informal. I'm not even going to ask you why you want custody of a child you met just days ago, but—"

"Actually, Your Honor," Peavy said, "it was just yesterday."

"I'll tell you why," I said. "There's something very special about her. She's—"

"Still—" the judge began.

"You've heard of child prodigies," I said. "She's like a spiritual child prodigy, and my concern is that she's being treated by people who are at best insensitive to that and who may even see it as something that needs to be medicated."

"Your Honor—" Peavy began.

"Look at her," I said to the judge. "This isn't her. They've already got her so drugged, she can hardly hold her head up."

The judge looked at Jakira. "Young lady," he said.

She lifted her head slightly and gazed at him.

"How do you feel?"

"Fine," she said. "How are you?"

"I'm just fine, too," he said. "I'm just trying to figure out what's best for you. Do you know where your parents are?"

The court-appointed psychiatrist, who was seated in the front row opposite us, stood up.

"Your Honor," she said, "she doesn't even know her own name. She's been through an undoubtedly horrific experience and is now experiencing post-traumatic stress syndrome."

"Do you know who you are?" the judge asked Jakira.

"I am . . ." she said, but trailed off.

"You are . . . ," the judge said.

"I am," she said, but didn't say anything else.

"How do you feel?" I asked

She slowly turned from the TV mounted high in the corner to cast her unfocused gaze in my general direction.

It was the next day, and we were in the TV room of Riverdale Charter, the inpatient treatment center that was now Jakira's home.

The judge, more as a personal favor to David Clyde Rish than anything else, had graciously granted me visitation privileges, though stressed how easily they could be revoked if I abused them in any way.

I waited, but she didn't say anything.

"It's so hard to see you this way," I said.

I had failed. I had not solved the mystery. I had not saved the day. I had not been able to keep her out of this place.

She didn't say anything, but continued to look in my general direction.

"Do you know who I am?" I asked.

"Do you?" she managed.

An involuntary burst of something resembling laughter shot out of my mouth.

"I'm sorry I couldn't do more for you," I said. "But I haven't stopped trying. We're going to try other legal measures and we're trying to get you assigned to a different doctor."

She slowly reached over and patted my hand with the tips of her small, cold fingers.

"Does that mean not to do anything?" I asked.

She didn't respond.

"I've been trying to figure out what all this means," I said.

I had had all the obvious thoughts—that the Second Coming, whatever it was, was a personal appearance of Christ to each of us at some point in our lives, maybe many. It was one of the first things she had said to me—"I come back all the time. In the sick, the hungry, the imprisoned." Or maybe it was meant to remind us that the Christ nature, the potential to be our best selves, to be like him, like God, is in all of us, in all things. Maybe enlightenment or the Buddha nature or myriad other named and unnamed things in hundreds of traditions the world over were ways of expressing the same thing.

"But I can't," I added. "I can't come up with anything that satisfies. I just don't understand."

Perhaps this was just one of those true mysteries of life, not a vague unknown, but a specific unknowable, insoluble, unsolvable. No amount of investigating or deducting could help. It was beyond the limits of logic, beyond reason, beyond my understanding.

We were silent a few moments, continuing to look at each other. Eventually, the black orderly in white appeared at the door to let me know it was the end of our time together.

I stood and hugged her.

"I'll keep coming to see you as often as they'll let me," I whispered in her ear. "And it's not because I'm expecting anything or wanting you to be anything. I just want to be with you."

"When you've done it for the least of these . . . ," she said, then trailed off.

I pulled back from her, searching her eyes for some of the earlier light and life, but it wasn't there.

"What'd you say?"

She didn't respond, and eventually I started walking across the room toward the waiting orderly.

"I said . . ."

I turned.

". . . you're not depressed anymore, are you?"

I smiled. "No, I'm not," I said. "Confused, shaken, humbled, questioning my sanity, but not depressed."

"That's something," she said. "And sometimes, something is all there is."

I nodded and continued walking.

When I reached the door, I turned again and waved.

She lifted her small hand, but didn't really wave. "Keep your eyes open, John," she said. "You'll be seeing me again."

Blood Bought

"Something's wrong with Keli," I said.

"How can you tell?" Merrill asked. "She look just the same to me."

He was right. It wasn't obvious, but I could tell something was wrong from the moment I saw her across the large parking lot. There was nothing overt, but it was there. It was as if she were walking around with the knowledge that the red dot of a high-powered scope was on the back of her head.

"I'm observant," I said.

We were in the staff parking lot of Potter Correctional Institution. Merrill had given me a ride to work this morning, when my truck wouldn't start. It was early, the February air still damp, the ground still wet with dew.

"You something," he said with a smile. "And it may even start with an O."

"Optimistic?"

He laughed, his bright white teeth contrasting his dark skin. "Obsessive," he said. "Try that on, see how it fit. How long it been since you had a puzzle to worry your mind with?"

I smiled. "A little while."

"Aha," he said, as if a detective hearing an important admission.

I laughed.

Situated on a cleared plot of nearly a hundred acres and surrounded on all sides by planted pine forests, PCI included a main unit, an annex, training facilities, an obstacle course, a firing range, a warehouse, gardens, and an on-site staff housing trailer park—nearly all of which were visible from where we stood.

Merrill wasn't the only one who didn't seem to notice Keli's odd behavior, but in addition to being an amateur noticer, I knew Keli well enough to know when something was wrong.

Keli Linton and I had gone to high school together. A kind, quiet girl with the insecurities that come with having an abusive alcoholic father, a larger than culturally-approved body, and the embarrassment of living in poverty. We had been friends. Many mornings in the school cafeteria, at a table that smelled of a dirty dish rag, I copied her homework while she told me the details of her life.

After graduation, we lost touch. She went into the military, got married, had a baby girl, got divorced, got out of the military, and eventually moved back to Pottersville.

In a small panhandle town like Pottersville, there's not a lot of jobs that enable a single mom who doesn't receive regular child support to provide for her family—especially if she only has a high school diploma. The obvious choice, particularly for a woman who's done time in the armed forces, is the growing field of corrections.

When Keli became a correctional officer at PCI, where I served as chaplain, she came into my life again. Working days put her at the prison during the administrative shift when I was there, which meant we saw a good bit of each other.

Getting out of her car, Anna joined us as we all headed in the general direction of the front gate.

"What 'O' word he remind you of?" Merrill asked her.

Anna looked at me, her brilliant brown eyes big and playful. "Orgasmic?"

"Yeah," I said, "I'm an orgasmic optimist."

"I've got to hear the part of this conversation that took place before I walked up," she said.

Merrill told her. As he talked, she looked across the parking lot at Keli.

I followed her gaze.

Keli's posture and movements were that of another person. It was as if she were wearing clothes that were too small, so stilted and strained were her movements.

She had parked on the far side of the lot, in the front row of the section reserved for employees who were having their cars washed. There wasn't anything very odd in that (though I had never seen her get her old banged up Honda washed before), except that she parked in the very last space on the end, passing several open spaces and nearly guaranteeing hers would be the last car washed.

"I'm with Merrill," she said. "I don't see it."

"He obsessing 'cause he ain't had a case lately," Merrill said.

"Obsessing's better than a seventh percent solution," she said.

I smiled.

"I thought it was a fifth of something that was eighty proof," Merrill said with a smile.

I laughed. "Too true, that," I said.

We reached the front gate and the security check that awaited us in the visiting park of the security building at the same time Keli did. Instead of speaking in her normal, friendly, loud, try-a-little-too-hard voice, she didn't speak, and when *I* spoke, her reply was the barely audible grunt of a distracted person.

"Are you okay?" I asked.

She gave me a quick nod. "I'm fine."

"Told you," Merrill whispered to Anna.

Keli had said it in such a way as to discourage further discussion, but I didn't let that stop me.

"You sure?" I asked. "You seem—"

"I'm fine."

"How about Kayla?"

Kayla was the thirteen-year-old daughter she was raising by herself.

"She's fine," she said. "Everything's fine."

Because of the steady flow of contraband into the institution, we started each workday with a pat-down. Herded like cattle into the sally port, through the security building, and into the visiting park, we placed our belongings on long folding tables, behind which were correctional officers who went through them. We were then taken into the restrooms—the men into theirs, where male officers waited, the women into theirs, where female officers waited—took off our shoes, our bodies then traced with a metal detector wand and an officer's hands.

You'd think all of this would prevent contraband from being introduced into the prison, but it didn't even slow it down. Part of the problem was how inconsistently and casually the searches were performed. Three shifts a day entered and exited the institution. These types of security measures would only work if applied to every shift, every day. They weren't, and most volunteers and contractors were never searched. The other problematic part of the equation was that the searches were performed by friends and coworkers, who already felt awkward and ambivalent about what they were doing.

After being searched, Keli hurried out of the visiting park without speaking to everyone she passed as she normally did.

Adjusting his uniform, Merrill walked up beside me. "No better way to start the day than gettin' felt up by a cracker ass redneck motherfucker," he said.

In another moment, Anna rejoined us and we began walking down the compound.

"How is she?" Anna asked.

"Fine," I said. "Everything's fine."

"Told you," Merrill said.

"Something's wrong," I said. "How about you two help me keep an eye on her?"

"Sho," Merrill said. "Gots nothin' else to do 'round here, boss."

"If we do, won't we be enabling your obsession?" Anna asked.

"Look at it as keeping me from drinking," I said.

My morning went as it usually did, filled mostly with the crisis counseling of inmates, their families via phone, and a few staff members. I had even managed a little time to reflect on what Merrill and Anna had said about me obsessing, because I was bored. I knew there was truth in what they said, but I also knew that awareness and observation, being mindful and meditative, were the keys to enlightenment—in life as well as detection. And since I didn't want to obsess about obsessing, I didn't do it for long.

I had wanted to check on Keli, but it was nearly time for lunch and I had yet to have the opportunity.

As the last of the inmates were leaving the chapel to return to the compound for count, followed by chow, the phone on my desk rang. I picked it up.

"Good morning, Chaplain Jordan," I said.

"What're you doing for lunch?" Anna asked.

"I'm open to suggestions," I said.

She laughed again. "How's Rudy's sound?"

"Not very good, but about our only option," I said.

"Oh, I asked around a little about Keli," she said.

"And?"

"Girl's just as much a saint here as everywhere else," she said. "Patient with the inmates, even kind."

"I knew that."

"Until today."

"Told you."

"So she's having a bad day," she said. "She's probably on her period."

"I realize I'm a guy," I said, "but—"

"And a celibate," she added.

"Not by choice," I said, "and it's a temporary condition."

"Okay, okay," she said. "Do you remember what you were saying or is your sexual frustration finally getting the best of you?"

"I know enough to know that she probably has a period about every twenty-eight days—and probably has since she was fourteen. Why is it just now turning her into Mrs. Hyde?"

"You know, if you put as much obsessive energy into dealing with your forced celibacy as you do little things like this, you might actually be able to renounce this vow you say you haven't taken."

"Is that what you really want?"

"Like I was saying, something is obviously very wrong with Keli, and you need to spend every waking moment trying to figure out what it is. How can I help?"

"Where is she posted right now?" I asked.

"She's over outside grounds," she said.

"Thanks."

"So how about lunch?"

"Sure," I said. "I'll see if Keli can join us."

"You go from celibate straight to threesome."

"I'm freaky like that," I said. "It's part of my addictive personality."

As Anna and I were hanging up, Merrill walked in and took a seat in one of the two chairs in front of my desk.

"Word on the pound is Keli's catching for the other side."

"Lesbian?"

He shook his head. "Only two sides in here," he said. Brown and blue."

I nodded, and thought about it. If Keli were involved with an inmate, it would explain a lot.

"Say she hooked up with Josh Miles."

"Inmate who washes cars?"

"Four-one-one is her car ain't the only thing he hosin'."

I smiled.

The number of female officers who get involved with inmates is staggering, especially since they are warned from day one of training and orientation of how smooth and persuasive so many of them can be. After all, they don't call them cons for nothing. It's an epidemic, but one to be expected with the sheer number of hours they spend together in this cauldron of desperation. No one is immune, but vulnerable, lonely women are especially easy prey for the predators that have spent a lifetime perfecting the hunt.

"He assigned to outside grounds?" I asked.

He nodded. "And the control room. Why?"

"She works outside grounds."

"So there may be somethin' to it," he said.

"Or not," I said. "You know how reliable the vine on the pound is."

"Say it is," he said. "She upset because of the guilt or because he broke it off or he whitemailing her?"

"Let's go ask him."

"What you mean *we*, white boy?" he said. "Some of us gots jobs and shit to do."

Working in the exciting and expanding field of corrections doesn't just provide a member of a rural community job security with great benefits and state retirement, but also the opportunity to have an inmate wash their car, as well. For just six bucks (or nine with a wax job), an employee of PCI can purchase a ticket at the canteen and have his or her car washed while they work.

Small wooden stakes holding square white boards with CW and the numbers 1 through 9 carved into them stood in the ground before nine spaces in the front right corner of the employee parking lot. Keli's car was in CW9, and I found Josh Miles buffing the last of the wax off it.

Keli's old champagne-colored Honda, dented and scratched though it was, actually looked a lot better than it had this morning.

"You work miracles," I said.

"Hey, Chaplain," he said.

The inside of Keli's cluttered car looked even worse than usual now that the outside was gleaming in the midday sun. In among all the half-consumed Sprite and Dr Pepper bottles, old newspapers, fast food bags, and wrinkled clothes, I saw Kayla's schoolbooks and gym bag, and Keli's Bible and Sunday school book.

"I may have to let you do that to my truck," I said. "I always thought it wouldn't do any good, but after seeing what you did with this one."

He looked up and across the lot.

Josh Miles was thick and square with blond hair and blue eyes. If I had to guess, I'd say he had German ancestry. He was soft-spoken and serene, hard working.

"It's not here today," I said. "It wouldn't start this morning."

"Is it that old white Chevy S-10 I've seen you in?"

I nodded.

"I'm good," he said, "but not that good."

"Really?"

"Man's got to know his limitations," he said with a smile.

"I respect that," I said. "Still, you did an amazing job with Sergeant Linton's."

He nodded as he walked over to the cart that held the brown plastic crates filled with his cleaning supplies.

"Looks like it took some time," I said.

Pulling out various crates, he returned his sponges, rags, soap, and wax to their containers. "I can usually do three to four cars before lunch," he said. "Today, this one took the entire time."

"Sounds like she owes you a big tip," I said.

"No, sir," he said. "'Course not."

"What did she do to earn such special treatment?" I asked.

"Nothing," he said. "I just wanted to do it for her. She's so nice. One of the few kind officers around here. Plus, she's my boss."

"There's a rumor going around that she's more than that," I said.

He shook his head. "It's not true," he said. "I swear. I'm married. Got kids. I'm about to get out. I would never—I swear. It's just talk. There's nothing to it."

If he were lying, he was good at it.

"How long you got?"

"Little less than a year if I get all my gain time."

I nodded.

Something caught his eye, and I turned to see Keli walking toward us. Average height and heavy, Keli carried most of her excess weight in the lower half of her body. Whatever was wrong with her accentuated her bulk because of the labored way it made her move.

"Miles, you ready?" she asked. "It's time for lunch."

"Yes, ma'am," he said, and looked over at her car.

She followed his gaze and her face fell. "What did you do?"

"Detailed it for you," he said. "It turned out—"

"I told you to do it last," she said.

"I know, but—"

"I even parked in the last spot," she said. "Look at all these other trucks and cars."

Most of the spaces were filled.

"Why didn't you do them in order?"

"I just wanted to do yours first so I'd know how much time I had left for all the rest."

"You're gonna have to do my again," she said.

I looked over at her in shock.

"This afternoon," she said. "Last one of the day, just like I told you."

"Yes, ma'am," he said.

"Okay," she said. "Report to the center gate. It's time for lunch."

She started to walk away after he left, but I stopped her.

"You okay?" I asked.

"I'm fine," she said.

"What was all that about?"

"Sometimes because I'm nice, an inmate won't do what I tell him to," she said. "I'm sick of it. He'll think before he disobeys me again."

"I'm worried about you," I said. "Let's go get something to eat and talk."

"Can't," she said. "But I told you, I'm fine."

"Is Miles doing anything to bother you?"

She shook her head.

"No manipulation?" I asked. "No blackmail?"

She had been avoiding my gaze, but now she looked at me directly, anger and the hint of tears in her eyes. "What would he have to blackmail me with, John?" she asked. "You think I'm involved with him?"

"Are you?"

"No," she said. "I'm not."

We were silent a moment.

"John, you know that place where well-intentioned concern becomes unwelcome meddling?"

I smiled. "We there yet?"

She shook her head. "We flew past it several miles back."

I laughed.

She almost smiled.

"Why don't I have him reassigned?" I said. "Or transferred. He could be gone by the time you got back from lunch."

"Did you not hear what I just said?"

"Yeah, but—"

"Whatever you do, don't do that. Not today. Okay? Promise me."

"But—"

"I don't care what you do tomorrow."

I didn't say anything, just wondered what was so urgent about today.

"Have I ever asked you for anything, John?" she said. "Anything? Please promise me you'll do this one thing for me."

"Okay," I said.

"Promise?"

"I promise."

"Why do you think she didn't want him transferred today in particular?" Anna asked.

We were in her car, but I was driving, headed toward Rudy's Diner for lunch. Unlike my vehicle, Anna's was spotless and smelled like floral air freshener and her perfume. It was also new and handled much better than mine, and I was driving a little faster than I should.

"I'm trying not to think about it," I said.

"Because it means she's up to something," she said.

I nodded.

"And whatever it is, she's gonna do it today."

"Most obvious would be an escape," she said.

I nodded again. "But to be working outside the fence, means he's short. Why run if you don't have much time left?"

"Why do they do half the shit they do?" she asked.

"Why do any of us?" I said, "But he seems very smart and committed to his family."

"You think she's involved with him?"

As I drove, I stole glances at Anna. She was never more beautiful to me than when she was concentrating and questioning, and the force of her intelligence shone through her bottomless brown eyes.

"It'd make the most sense, but I don't think so."

When we got into town, instead of staying straight, I took at left on River Road.

"Where are we going?"

"I need to swing by the middle school," I said.

"Oh, throw you in the briar patch," she said.

Pottersville Middle School was generally acknowledged to have the sexiest school secretary in the state.

"Why exactly you doin' a drive-by of PMS?" she asked. "As if I don't know."

"Thought I'd ask Kayla why her mom's acting so strangely today."

"A, they're not going to let you talk to her," she said. "And B, I thought you promised Keli you wouldn't do anything today."

I pulled up in front of the school office, placed the car in park, and left it running.

"I promised her I wouldn't have Josh Miles transferred today," I said. "I didn't say I wouldn't do anything."

"You think that's the way she understood it?"

I jumped out of the car without answering her question, walked into the office, and within just a few moments, walked right back out again.

When I got into the car, Anna said, "Told you they wouldn't let you talk to her."

"Clearly you underestimate my way with sexy school secretaries," I said.

"So they did let you talk to her?"

"They would have if she had come to school today," I said.

"So that explains it," she said.

"My way with sexy school secretaries?"

"Keli's just a stressed out single mom with a sick kid," she said.

"That's not exactly how I interpreted it," I said.

"Somehow I knew it wouldn't be."

Because of my little detour, Anna and I were late eating and late getting back to the prison. Count had already cleared, the yard was open, inmates back at work. Josh Miles was busy washing the small truck in the CW1 space.

When we got out of Anna's car, she quickly headed for the main gate, but I started in Josh's direction.

"You really gotta get a girlfriend," she said.

"Until then, let me find diversion where I can," I said.

"Have at it," she said. "Call me if you need backup, and thanks again for lunch."

I stood and watched Anna walk away for a moment, enjoying the confident and unconsciously sexy way she moved. A volleyball player in high school and college, Anna's natural athleticism was aging well. Eventually, I walked over and joined Josh near the truck he was washing.

"You gonna be able to finish all these before you have to return to the compound?" I asked.

"It's not gonna be my best work, but I can do it."

I glanced down at Keli's car, which was still spotless, its polished surface gleaming in the early afternoon sun. It had been a mild winter, even by North Florida standards, and the sun was bright, the warm day more like spring or early summer than February.

"What're you gonna do to Sergeant Linton's car?"

"Do it again," he said. "Do whatever my supervisor tells me."

"You didn't this morning," I said.

"I didn't realize doing hers last was so important."

I walked down past the other cars to get a better look at Keli's, thinking maybe she had gotten it dirty on the other side, but the far side was just as spotless as the side that had been visible to me.

I started to walk away when something inside the car caught my eye. It hadn't been there just a few hours earlier, and it made my heart start racing. There, in the backseat amidst all the clutter, was a CO uniform.

I walked quickly back over to Josh who had just started on the second car.

"Stop what you're doing and come with me," I said.

"But—"

"Now."

"Yes, sir," he said.

He dropped his soapy sponge into the bucket of suds and followed me.

The moment we entered the chapel, I put Josh in a chair in the hallway so I could see him through the narrow strip of glass in my door, then went inside my office and called Anna.

"Would you pull Josh Mile's file for me?" I asked.

"It's sitting on my desk," she said. "I think that makes me an enabler."

"What's he in for?"

"Not a whole lot," she said. "You in your office?"

"Yeah," I said.

"I'll be right there."

A few minutes later, I heard the chapel doors open and close, then Anna appeared at my door, an inmate file in her hand. When she came in, she looked back at Josh.

"What the hell's he doing here?"

"He's here for some spiritual counseling," I said.

"By choice?"

"Anything strange in his file?" I asked.

She sat down in one of the chairs across from my desk, and I shifted slightly so I could still see Josh over her shoulder.

"This is not normal behavior," she said.

"I know," I said. "It's obsessive. I need a girlfriend. Is there anything strange in his file?"

"No," she said. "If there were, he wouldn't be working out-side the gate."

"So why'd you come down here?" I asked.

"To try to keep you from doing something stupid," she said, "but obviously, I'm too late."

"I haven't done much yet," I said. "Why'd you bring his file?"

She handed it to me. "So you could see for yourself."

I flipped through the relatively thin file. Josh was certainly not a recidivist. I quickly scanned the face card, which had his picture and emergency contact info, the commitment of custody, the contact log, and the various other documents that told the story of a model inmate. There were no disciplinary reports. There were no inmate requests. Josh Miles didn't get into trouble and he didn't ask for anything.

He was in on a possession charge, a little less than half of his two-year sentence remaining, followed by another few years of pro-bation.

"Satisfied?" Anna asked.

"Almost never," I said.

She nodded. "Isn't that what all this is really about?"

"What the hell are you doing?" Keli asked.

She had walked into my office without knocking, even though I was on the phone. I quickly hung up and looked up at her. I had never heard her talk that way before. Her face was red, she was sweating, and her eyes were narrowed into angry dots.

"Trying to help you," I said.

"You're not helping," she said. "You're making things worse."

"What things?"

"You promised you wouldn't do anything today," she said.

"I promised you I wouldn't have him transferred," I said.

"Why are you doing this?" she asked.

"Because I care about you," I said. "I don't want to see you ruin your life."

"Ruin my life—John, what are you talking about?"

"If you help Miles escape, you're going to ruin your life."

She opened her mouth but couldn't get anything to come out.

I waited.

It took her a while, but she finally managed a soft, "What makes you think—"

"Why does he have to wash your car last?" I asked. "Even after he's already done it today. Why do you have an extra uniform in your backseat? Why isn't Kayla at school today? The three of you leaving town together?"

"If I give you the uniform, will you let Josh return to work?"

"Why is it so imperative for him to work this afternoon?" I asked. "Those vehicles can wait until tomorrow to be washed."

I then realized why she was willing to give me the uniform in her car and why earlier in the day, I had the thought that she was moving like her clothes were too small.

"You'll give me the uniform in your backseat?" I asked.

She nodded. "Yes."

"What about the one under the uniform you're wearing?"

She shook her head. "You have no idea what you're doing," she said.

She then turned, and, without saying another word, stormed out of my office.

"What's going on, Chaplain?" Josh asked.

I had called him into my office when Keli left.

"You tell me."

"Whatta you mean?"

I didn't say anything.

"Sergeant Linton looked upset," he said. "Is she okay?"

I remained silent.

"I know how things work around here," he said, "but I want you to know that I haven't done anything wrong. Not one thing. Not so much as taking an extra roll when it's offered to me in the chow line. So, if any of this has anything to do with me, it's a misunderstanding. I swear."

"What were you mixed up in when you got arrested?" I asked.

"Why?"

"I'm a curious guy."

"I know how this is going to sound," he said, "but it's true and I can't help how it sounds. I was holding some stuff for some guys I know and I got caught with some of it."

I laughed.

"It's true."

"I wasn't talking about what you were arrested for," I said. "I've got your file. I can read that. I'm talking about what you were mixed up in."

"That was it."

"How many guys you know in the life get busted for everything they're doing?"

"None," he said, "but I wasn't in the life. I was just—"

My phone rang and I answered it.

"Chaplain, it's Patricia."

Patricia was the Admin Lieutenant.

"Do you have an inmate Miles over there?"

"Uh huh."

"Will you tell him to report back to work," she said.

"Actually, we're in the middle of—"

"The Colonel says he's got to go the chapel on his own time."

"But—"

"Sorry," she said, "but he said to tell you he's not asking, to send him right now no matter what."

I spent the afternoon in meetings and counseling sessions but was distracted and ineffective, and as it got close to the end of the admin shift, I was no good for anything. Clearing the chapel and sending the inmates back to the yard a little early, I made my way through the gate and back out to where Josh Miles was pretending to re-wash Keli's car.

"I'm back," I said.

"You don't quit, do you?"

"Not known for it, no," I said.

"You afraid I'm gonna try to escape?"

"It's crossed my mind," I said.

"Why not just turn me over to security?"

I didn't say anything.

"'Cause," Merrill said, as he walked up, "ain't enough to stop crime, we got to save somebody, too."

"Me?"

"No, fool," Merrill said, laughing. "Kel—Sergeant Linton."

"We're here for you, too," I said.

"Well, you're wasting your time," Josh said. "I'm not going anywhere for about eleven months."

"He got a point," Merrill said me. "Why he gonna run when he's so short?"

"I'm not sure," I said. "Josh?"

"I swear I'm not—"

"Why don't you walk him back to the gate?" I said. "I'll wait here for Keli."

"Let's go," Merrill said.

"What about my cart?"

"I'll take care of it," I said.

"Okay."

Merrill started walking toward the gate, and Josh joined him without hesitation. They disappeared around the corner of the admin building and I began to place the remaining supplies into the crates on the cart as I waited for Keli.

It was about a quarter 'til four, fifteen minutes until the admin shift ended, and the parking lot was still empty. I hoped Keli would show up soon so I could talk to her without anyone else around.

I had finished putting all the carwash supplies away, and was standing near Keli's car waiting for her, when I saw Josh and Merrill walking back in my direction.

"Change of plans," Merrill said.

"Why's that?" I asked.

To my shock, Keli stepped out from behind them with a gun.

I couldn't have been more surprised by anything. Sure, Keli had been in the military, and, as a correctional officer, she had had training in firearms, but in spite of all this, she wasn't a gun carrying person. She was as opposite from femme fatal as you could get.

"What the hell are you doing?" I asked.

"What I have to," she said, glancing over her shoulder, and looking around nervously.

"Keli—"

"John, just don't," she said, then turning to Josh, "climb into the backseat of my car and put on the uniform."

"But—"

"Now."

With her free hand, she unlocked the car and Josh got into the backseat. We waited while he got dressed.

"I'm sorry about this, guys," she said. "I wish you would've stayed out of it."

"It's not too late to stop this," I said. "Only we know so far and we won't tell anyone. Think about what you're doing, the effects it'll have on your life."

As I spoke, I could see Merrill turning slightly, judging the distance between them, but Keli was smart. She wasn't right behind him, the mistake most novices make. She had left enough room so that he couldn't reach her.

In another moment, Josh Miles stepped out of Keli's car looking like a correctional officer.

"Cuff him," she said, nodding toward Merrill.

She handed Josh a pair of disposable strap cuffs, and he quickly placed them on Merrill. She then popped the trunk of the Ford Taurus next to hers and told Merrill to get in.

"How'd you—"

"I lied," she said. "Told him I needed to move it."

No one around here would question Keli or think twice about giving her their keys.

When Merrill was in the trunk, she slammed it closed.

"Get in my backseat and put on his uniform," she said to me.

"Keli, what are you—"

"Now," she said. "Hurry. I don't want to shoot you, but believe me, I will."

Looking into her desperate face, her crazed eyes, I knew she would.

I got in, changed quickly, and got out again, my dress shoes looking funny poking out from the pants legs of the prison blues.

Standing in front of Keli, I could see over her shoulder that Merrill had managed to push the seat forward and get free from the trunk, and was now in the backseat directly behind her. He had managed to cut through one side of the strap as well, the empty cuff dangling from the wrist of his other hand.

"Why're you doing this?" I asked.

"I'll explain it to you one day," she said.

As Merrill moved around in preparation to pounce, Josh, standing not far from me, saw him, and I waited to see what he'd do. To my surprise, he didn't do anything. Was he not a willing participant in his own escape?

Time was running out and Keli knew it. At a few minutes after four, the parking lot would begin filling with other COs and staff members. She had to act quickly.

When she glanced at her watch again, Merrill came flying out of the back door of the car behind her, tackling her to the ground, grabbing her gun hand, and smashing it into the asphalt, the gun coming loose and landing at Josh's feet.

He didn't even try to pick it up.

"Get out of that uniform," I said to him as I reached down and picked up the gun, "and get this one back on."

As Merrill helped Keli, who was crying now, to her feet, I unbuttoned the inmate shirt I was wearing.

"John," Keli said, "please don't. Please don't do this. Help me, please."

"I am," I said. "I'm—"

"You don't understand," she said. "They have my daughter."

"What?" I asked in shock. "Who?"

"If I don't have him at my house in ten minutes, they're going to kill Kayla."

"Are you sure this is going to work?" Keli asked.

"Absolutely," I said, as if I were.

We were in her car, racing toward the old farmhouse she and Kayla rented, the rural highway we were on was empty, the forests and pastures beside it silent.

I was still wearing Josh's uniform, in the pocket of which was the small revolver Keli had been pointing at us just a few minutes ago.

As we had pulled out of the institution, Merrill was walking Josh, in just his underwear, to the front gate. After coming up with a lie about what happened to Josh's uniform believable enough to convince the control room, and getting Josh securely back inside, Merrill would be providing backup, approaching the farmhouse through the woods that bordered its north side. Hopefully this would be all over by then, Kayla safely back with Keli, and whoever was holding her hostage in the back of a Potter County Sheriff's Deputy patrol car. I had called Dad for delayed backup, as well. We didn't need loud sirens and a lot of excitable small-county deputies right now, but if we failed, they'd be close by.

"Who's doing this?" I asked. "How many are there?"

"Two guys," she said. "Young. I haven't heard them use names yet."

"What do they want with Josh?"

"Not sure exactly," she said, "but I gather FDLE reached out to him in connection with some open cases that could really hurt these guys. Possession was the least of what Josh was into, but it's all he got caught for."

I thought about how nice and respectful Miles seemed, how dedicated to his family. That was the great disconnect of prison— the vast difference between how inmates appeared and what they were capable of doing. I had hoped Miles was different, but didn't find it surprising that he wasn't.

"Must be huge for them to do this," I said.

"They seem desperate."

When we neared the house, Keli stopped the car long enough for me to put on an inmate cap, the pair of strap cuffs that Merrill had had on, and climb into the back seat and lay face down.

"Okay," I said.

"John."

"Yeah."

"Two things," she said. "If it comes down to it, save Kayla, don't worry about me, and thanks for paying attention and being so observant."

"Actually I'm told it's obsessive," I said, "but you're welcome."

Most of what happened next I only heard. I was face down in the backseat, my hands in front of me. Keli pulled into her front yard at an angle, got out, walked around, and opened the back door, so the bottom part of my body could be seen from the house. If she did what we had discussed, she parked far enough away so the two guys couldn't get a good look at me without coming out into the yard.

"I'M BACK," Keli yelled from beside the car. "I brought him to you just like you told me to. Come get him and bring me my daughter."

I didn't hear anything at first, then a squeaky screen door opening.

The old wooden house had a wrap-a-round porch that held rocking chairs and a swing, and a screen door on a spring that slammed shut loudly unless you held it.

"I did like you said. Just give me my daughter and go."

One of the men must have said something, but I couldn't make it out. All I could hear was mumbled words.

"I had to knock him out," she said. "I gave him a shot. He's out cold."

There was another pause. This time I heard a few words, which meant at least one of the men was coming closer.

"Yes," she said. "I wouldn't risk my daughter's life."

The gun was in my hands beneath me. I thumbed back the hammer, hoping not to accidentally shoot myself and get us all killed.

"*You* roll him over," Keli was saying. "But I want my daughter first."

There was a longer pause this time, then the squeaking of the screen door again.

"Get that gun away from her head," Keli said.

She had said it for my benefit, giving me as much information as she could without being suspicious. I would have to aim for the guy with Kayla on the porch, not the guy closest to me. Keli would have to take care of him. I had no idea how far away the porch was or if I could even get a clean shot off, and he could easily kill her before I could fire a single round. It would all depend on if he hesitated or not.

I found myself wishing Merrill were here or that I had asked Dad to do more than be backup, but whatever was going to happen was imminent, and would be over long before any of them arrived.

I felt large, strong hands grab my ankles and yank. I came flying out of the backseat and onto the ground face first, my head striking the car and the ground. I was disoriented and in pain, but as soon as I hit the ground I started rolling.

I could hear movement behind me, and I knew Keli was jumping the guy who had pulled me out.

"GET DOWN," Keli yelled to Kayla.

She did, pushing away from the young white man who had her.

Not sure whether to shoot her or me, the man hesitated, and that fraction of time was all I needed.

I squeezed off a round.

It missed completely.

Another.

The second one found flesh.

I had been aiming for his right arm, the one holding the gun, but had missed and hit him in his right pectoral. He dropped the gun as crimson saturated his white Panama City Beach t-shirt.

Kayla scampered away from him on all fours.

Behind me, Keli and the other guy were rolling around on the ground.

As I turned toward them, his gun went off.

By the time I was facing them, the man was standing, Keli, bleeding into her light brown CO shirt, remained on the ground.

I was close to the man, close enough to hit whatever I aimed for, which was his gun hand. I put a round between his wrist and hand and he dropped the gun, yelling out in pain.

He fell to the ground as I jumped up.

A few steps and I was close enough to kick him in the face,

which I did. I wasn't sure if it knocked him out or not, but it was hard enough to encourage him to remain on the ground a little longer. I then kicked the gun away from him, glanced back at the man on the porch who was still down, and knelt beside Keli, Kayla coming up behind me as sirens sounded in the distance.

"What'd I miss?" Merrill said.

He and Anna walked up as two EMTs were loading Keli onto a gurney, while a few others were evaluating the two men under the watchful eye of Dad's deputies.

"A little gunplay," I said.

"You must not've played fair," he said. "You the only one didn't get shot."

"Kayla remained unleaded as well," I said.

Merrill laughed.

"Laugh it up," Keli said, her voice soft and strained. "It's all fun and games until someone gets shot."

"You find out what they wanted with Miles?" Merrill asked.

I shook my head. "They're not making much sense."

"Well, hell," Merrill said, "you shot one, kicked the shit out the other."

"How'd you get so violent?" Anna asked.

"Cartoons and video games," I said. "Misspent youth."

"Guys," Keli said, "can we get back to the fact that I was SHOT?"

"In a minute," Merrill said. "Right now I want to know how John knew."

"Knew what?" I said.

"That Keli was about to commit several felonies and didn't just have PMS."

"I didn't," I said.

"And if it had been PMS?" he said.

"Things wouldn't have gone so smoothly," Anna said.

"Or," Keli added, her voice even weaker now, "turned out so well."

The Blood-Red Rec Yard Ruse

I used to be a cop. Of course, that's like saying I used to be an alcoholic, and though I wasn't active at either for very long, both are more about who you are than what you do, so I guess you could say I'm a cop in recovery.

The title on my business card these days reads: Prison Chaplain, but in my heart—some part of my heart anyway—I'll always be a cop, which is why my Florida Department of Corrections co-workers often call on me for services that are other than clerical.

Like today, while I was in the middle of a counseling session with Todd Robbins, a racist inmate whose religion, after being processed through the dark filters of his head and heart, was transformed into a dangerous self-righteous hatred.

"Preacher, you know what the good book says, 'Do not love the world nor the things in the world.' Now how you gonna argue with that?"

Todd Robbins not only looked like an inmate—heavy from the starchy diet, muscular from the weight-pile, with short, badly cut hair—he also had the look of a killer. The two pale-green, teardrop tattoos at the corners of his vacant eyes testified to the fact even if his life sentence hadn't.

"I'm not arguing anything," I said. "You brought it up. All I'm saying is that the passage you quoted is about oppressive systems—political, economic, religious—not individual people or the planet, both of which God said were good when she created them."

"SHE?" he yelled, the sharp smell of tobacco burning my

nose as his breath shot across my desk. The cheap tobacco sold in the Potter Correctional Institution canteens had stained his tongue and the tips of his fingers so badly they looked jaundiced. "You mean HE, don't you?"

"That's just as appropriate," I said.

"Well, which is it?" he asked.

"Both," I said. "Or neither, but—"

He shook his head and let out a small, mean laugh. "Now God's a woman?"

"No," I said. "That's not what I'm saying," my sense of futility registering in my voice.

"That's what you said."

"No. God is no more a woman than a man. What I'm saying is that God is both masculine *and* feminine. If not, we wouldn't be in God's image."

When I moved back home to northwest Florida after being a cop and a cleric in Atlanta, I never would've imagined I'd become a prison chaplain. But God works in mysterious ways, and when I fell from grace in Atlanta, this is the grace I fell into.

Of course, most people wouldn't call leaving a wife, a good job, and a nice home in north Atlanta to live alone in a dingy trailer in northwest Florida grace.

"Adam was created in the image of God," he said. "Not Eve. Eve was created from Adam. . . . Like a copy of a copy, it's not as good as the original. That's why God gave men authority over women."

His brand of benighted religion was prevalent in prison and I was weary of it, and though it was pointless to do so, I couldn't resist the temptation to get into it with him.

"Oh?" I said. "I didn't know she had," then added with a smile, "and I don't think they do either."

"Damn," he said as he stood. "You're so full of shit. . . . Now look what you've made me do. I'm talking like the heathen I *used* to be."

I smiled. Like dryrot seeping through a fresh coat of paint, his true self had once again bled through his carefully constructed facade of religiosity.

"It's amazing how often that happens, isn't it?" I said. "If you're ever interested in figuring out why, there's a twelve steps group that—"

"That shit's of the devil—diggin' around in the past. My past is under the blood of Jesus Christ. It's as if I never done nothin'."

I wanted to ask if he thought the same were true for victims and their families, but instead said, "But your past is obviously affecting your present. It's why you have so much anger in general and toward women in particular."

He looked at his watch. "Fuck you," he said, jumping up. "I can't take any more of this." He was opening the door to leave when the phone on my desk rang. He stopped.

"Chaplain Jordan," I said into the receiver.

"Some white boy done gone and gotten hisself killed on the rec yard," Merrill Monroe said, an underlying amusement in his voice. "Ain't that some shit? How 'bout gettin' your crime-solving cracker ass down here 'fore Pete and his fellow fuckups do?"

I stood to leave immediately. I trusted Merrill with my life. He had, in fact, saved my life on more than one occasion. He was the biggest, blackest boy in our class at Pottersville Elementary School, and our friendship, which began then, had continued through the two decades that had followed.

"I've got to go," I said to Todd as I stood and walked around my desk.

He closed the door. "'Fraid I can't let you do that," he said.

He smiled as he pulled the small metal object from his pocket. The shank, a screwdriver filed down to resemble an ice pick with bad intentions, gleamed even in the dull greenish light of the fluorescent tubes.

"What're you going to do to me?" I said, trying to make my voice sound tight and frightened.

"Just relax," he said, "and say a little prayer for that big nigger you hang around with. For yourself, too, if you don't do what I tell you."

I cringed, as I did every time, at the use of the N-word. After living in the South my whole life, a small deep-South town most of it, I still always found it shocking. In addition to making me late, he was also making me mad.

"Oh, God. Oh, no. What're you gonna do to me? Please don't hurt me," I said frantically, attempting to sound hysterical as I continued edging slowly toward him.

"Settle down. I ain't gonna hurt ya. We're just gonna set here about twenty minutes and it'll all be over. Then I'm gonna leave. And you're gonna forget I's ever here."

"Sure," I said. "I've forgotten already. You're right, I do need to pray."

When I was within reaching distance of him, I said, "In the name of the Father," beginning to cross myself, up then down. "The Son." And then to the left, "And the Holy . . ." Coming from left to right at the same time I said, "Spirit," I snapped out a hard left jab that connected with his chin. His head jerked back, striking the door, then bounced back. When it did, I hit him again—this time with a hard straight right that hurt my hand. His head repeated the previous motion and he dropped the shank, which hit the thin carpet with a muffled thud a moment before he did.

In less than a minute, I was rushing out of the chapel with Todd Robbins draped over my shoulder, his shank in my pocket. I paused only long enough to lock the door and glance at my watch. It was 2:45 P.M.—nearly time for shift change, evidenced by the correctional officers entering and exiting the institution, many of whom gave me quizzical glances as I rushed passed them carrying Robbins on my way to the rec yard.

"Chaplain, what is it?" a new officer named Dale Johnson asked. "Can I help?"

"Yeah," I said as I handed him Robbins. "Would you please take him to medical? Tell them I'll be back in a few minutes to fill out a report. Tell them to watch him. He's dangerous."

"Sure, okay," he said. His face was a small round puzzle and his back bent under the weight of Robbins. "He's heavier than you made him look."

Walking as fast as I could, it would take me at least five minutes to reach the rec yard. I picked up my pace, and was soon approaching the center gate.

Every gate in a prison is actually two gates with a holding area in between called a sally port. The gates are controlled electronically by an officer in a tower or control room.

The moment I was buzzed through the two center gates, I sensed it. It permeated the air like a foul odor. The smell was the unmistakable aroma of death, and the vultures had begun to swarm. Energy was in the air. Excitement. And the taste for blood.

The gate leading to the rec yard and the adjacent fence was lined with inmates, all trying to get a glimpse of the body on the softball field. It took a minute for the officers in tower three to see me and buzz me through, and when they finally did, the inmates standing next to it tried to press through. I discouraged them, and ran through quickly before they figured out that I couldn't stop them if they insisted.

The rec yard was nearly empty, which on a beautiful, sunny day like today meant that the inmates had known there was going to be trouble. I ran over to the softball field, jumping the fence rather than running around to the gate. Inside the fence, on the grassy part of the outfield just beyond the shortstop position, were ten inmates and two officers, which didn't seem fair to the officers, but one of them was Merrill Monroe—still the biggest, blackest man around—which didn't seem fair to the inmates. The other officer was a woman named Chappel who worked with George Reed, the recreational supervisor. She was as pale as if her body had been drained of its blood, her eyes were glazed over and unfocussed, and her brown correctional officer uniform trembled on her small shaking frame. Still, she looked better than the bloody body lying at her feet.

The ten inmates were on their knees in a straight line facing away from the body, their hands clasped behind their heads. I recognized most of them. They were all members of the white supremacy gang, Rebel Nation, the very same gang to which Todd Robbins belonged. I had never known them to be violent—ignorance was their specialty.

Only Merrill could get ten racist inmates to kneel in submission without a weapon. The surprisingly compliant inmates were not only all white, but were also all lifers. My guess was they weren't putting up a fight because they couldn't possibly escape, they had nothing to gain and nothing to lose. They had only one life to give.

When my eyes met with Merrill's, he nodded toward the body. "Welcome back," he said with a smile. "How was chaplain training?"

I moved in for a closer look.

"They didn't cover this," I said.

He laughed.

"Where is everybody?" I asked. "I can't believe there aren't a hundred officers down here already."

"Will be any minute," he said. "Called you first."

The body, for that's all it was anymore, had been badly beaten, presumably with a baseball bat, and the blue inmate uniform covering it glistened wetly in the afternoon sun. The face was unrecognizable. The blood-covered bat still lay just a few feet away from the body, next to it a pair of the black brogan boots the inmates wore.

"Why are his shoes off?" I asked.

"They beat 'em off?" Merrill said with a shrug. "Or maybe he got hit by lightning. I hear that happen sometime when people get struck." His face remained expressionless, but there was sarcasm in his voice.

As I looked up at him, I was again reminded of how palpable his physical presence was. His upper body was a perfect V, broad shoulders tapering down into narrow hips, the light brown shirt of his uniform stretching tightly over the muscles in his shoulders, chest, and arms, especially the large round biceps which appeared perpetually flexed.

"Hell," he said with another elaborate shrug, "I don't know. You the fuckin' Father Brown around here."

Returning my attention to the body, I said, "Something's not right."

"You mean 'sides the fact he dead?"

"Yeah."

"He *is* dead, ain't he?"

"I'm pretty sure," I said, then glancing over at the Rebels, added, "Whatta they say?"

"They say he dead, too."

Looking back up at Merrill, I gave him an expression that let him know I was ready for a real answer.

"Say they just found him like this, but they the only ones on the rec yard. Ain't that a coincidence?"

Returning my gaze to the inmates again, I asked, "So how'd they get that blood on their uniforms?"

"Say they tried CPR and shit to save his life. Say they loved him, he was one of their homies and that they wouldn't hurt him for anything."

"Who is he?"

"What'd you say this con's name is?" Merrill asked the leader of the gang.

"Billy Ray Dickens."

"Oh, no." I said, beginning to shake my head.

"You know him?" Merrill asked.

"I know all of them," I said. "They don't miss Tuesday night Bible study, and . . . ."

"That's right," the leader said. "Chaplain's all right, he helps us out when we need it. Like ole Billy Ray, here." He nodded his head back toward the body of Billy Ray.

Merrill cut his eyes over toward me. "So what'd you do for ole Billy Ray, here?" he asked as he nodded down toward the bloody mass of flesh at his feet.

Standing again, I said, "His nine-year-old daughter was raped this past weekend by the man living with his ex-wife. They called me in Saturday night to try to help him deal with it."

"You did a good job, too, Chap." the inmate said again. "You straight up in our book."

"You sure about that?" Merrill asked. "You know he's part black, don't you?"

I glanced over at Chappel, who seemed oblivious to everything that was going on. She stared vacantly in the direction of the body. I walked over and patted her on the back, then led her a few steps away and sat her down on the ground facing away from the body.

"WHAT?" the inmate yelled. "He's as white as I am."

"He look white, but he way too cool not to have *some* black blood flowing through his narrow white ass," Merrill said.

"Right on, bro," I said in my best uptight white guy voice. Looking over at the inmates, I added, "Of course we've all got African blood flowing through our veins."

Merrill smiled broadly, pure pleasure registering on his face.

"WHAT?" the inmate yelled again. "How the hell you figure that?"

I motioned for Merrill to field his question.

"Two ways," Merrill said, ticking the points off on his massive fingers. "Your racist great granddaddys fucked their little slave girls and they became your great grandmothers. But more to the point, you dumb son of a bitch, human life originated in Africa."

The inmates began their protestations, but stopped as they heard the gate buzz open.

"Here comes the cavalry," Merrill said.

I turned to see thirty light brown shirts pouring through the first gate and into the rec yard sally port. The moment they were all inside, the first gate would be closed, the gate on this side would open, and they would be here.

"They'll be here any minute," Merrill said. "Whatta you think? Which one of them did it? Or did they all do it?"

"I really don't understand," I said kneeling down beside the body again. "They really *were* close. I can't see any of them killing one of their own."

"Unless he did somethin' they didn't like," Merrill said. "Maybe this how they let you out the gang."

I only vaguely heard him as I concentrated on the body before me. Cigarette papers and a small bag of tobacco protruded from his shirt pocket, above which was the patch that bore his name: Billy Ray Dickens DC# E13334. I had to look closely to see because it was covered with blood.

Starting to get up again, I noticed his hair.

In life, Billy Ray had light brown hair, roughly the color of my own. In death, his hair was nearly black. This was, of course, due to all the blood that covered it. However, when I started to stand, I saw a small piece of hair at the base of his neck that was dark brown—nearly black even, and it lacked the glossy, wet look of the other blood-soaked hair. I lifted his head slightly and pushed back the matted hair to find the strands that had caught my eye. They were dark brown, and they were dry. I moved in closer to smell his hair. It smelled of the artificial fruit flavor found in cheap shampoo.

My mind started racing as I sat up and began examining his hands. They were clean—nails trimmed, fingertips white. I smelled his hands and then his uniform. It was all starting to add up.

"What the hell you doin'?" Merrill asked.

"Here, smell this," I said pointing to the least bloody spot on the inmate's blue uniform.

Reluctantly, he smelled it. "Smell like that cheap ass shit they smoke to me."

"Now this," I said as I held the inmate's hand up.

He shook his head as he stood up. "I don't smell nothin'. And I ain't smellin' nothin' else, so don't ask."

Beginning to feel the uniform, I was pulling and tugging at it when the officers arrived. They immediately began to handcuff the inmates, each of them straining to see the victim as they did.

"What the hell's he doing?" Lieutenant Walker, the highest ranking officer on the scene, said.

"He's giving him Last Rites," Merrill said. "He's looking for the con's rosary."

I smiled. I didn't know Merrill knew what a rosary was.

"It must be in his shoe," I said as I crawled down to his feet. I grabbed one of the shoes, comparing it to his foot size. It was as least three sizes too small. I stood, looked over at Merrill, and said, "Come on. Let's go."

"What about Last Rites?" the Lieutenant asked.

"No rosary," I said. "I was wrong. He's must not be Catholic after all."

When I stood and began to walk away, Merrill joined me without asking why we were leaving or where we were going.

"*That's* all we were waiting for?" the lieutenant asked. "Where the hell are you two going?"

"I'm going to be sick," I lied. Alcohol and law enforcement weren't all I was in recovery from. "I'm going to the infirmary and I don't know if I can make it."

"I'll help him down there," Merrill said. "Then I'll be right back. She can tell you everything," he added, pointing to Officer Chappel who had yet to utter a syllable.

When we had been buzzed through both gates and were back on the compound, Merrill asked, "So which one of them killed Billy Ray?"

"None of them," I said. I looked around as we moved through the empty compound. All inmates had been sent back to their dorms and the yard had been closed due to the incident on the softball field.

"What?"

"Billy Ray's not dead."

"That white boy's way past dead."

"Sure," I said. "But that's not Billy Ray."

"Who then?" Merrill asked.

"My guess is George Reed," I said, glancing down at my watch to see that it was 2:55. "And we have five minutes to stop Billy Ray from escaping."

I began jogging toward the center gate, Merrill matching my pace.

"I'm listening," he said.

"That's not Billy Ray Dickens in that blue DC uniform. You saw it, it's too small. Billy Ray has light brown hair and that man has dark brown. The shoes were too small for his feet, which means Billy Ray can wear the officer's shoes, but not the other way around. And, Billy Ray's a smoker. The tobacco they sell in the canteen is the cheapest kind made. You said so yourself. It stains the fingertips dark yellow, and it makes the person reek of it. The uniform smelled of it, but the body and the hair didn't."

"Damn, damn, *damn*," he said, shaking his head. "You the real deal, dog. So Billy Ray killed an officer, traded uniforms, and vacatin' the premises on his way to kill the man who raped his daughter."

"That's my guess," I said.

"He probably ain't spent five days with her in his whole worthless life," he said. "Wasn't there to protect her, but now he gonna kill the punk who raped her."

"Exactly," I said.

Jogging through the center gate, Merrill said, "So how's he gonna get out?"

We were now two hundred yards from the front gate where the officers were gathering.

"He's just going to walk out the front gate with all the other officers at three," I said. "That's why they did it now. It's time for shift change. Fortunately for us, they can't leave the institution before three, even if they've been relieved from their post. So, he's up there in the sally port waiting with the rest of those brown shirts, biding his time until he becomes a free man."

"'Cept that ain't gonna happen," Merrill said.

Merrill sounded so certain, but Billy Ray had nothing to lose and we were without weapons.

I slowed my pace to a brisk walk. Merrill matched it and then asked, "Why we slowin' down?"

"Because we're leaving work for the day just like everybody else. We don't want him to know we're coming after him."

"How we gonna know it's him?"

"I'll recognize him," I said. "When we go into the sally port, you go over to the control room window and tell them not to open the outer gate. I'll try to find Billy Ray."

As we entered the sally port, Merrill turned left and disappeared into the security building and I vanished into the crowd of officers, my cursory glances of the crowd turning up nothing. No one stood out as I surveyed the nearly twenty correctional officers in the small holding area. Some stood quietly, most stood talking, and a few of them stood next to the ashtray, smoking. They held lunch boxes and small ice chests, and they all looked eager to go home.

Never once had I stopped and waited with the group of officers at the end of the day—I was on a different shift and didn't get off for another hour. However, Billy Ray wouldn't know that. I milled around the crowd looking at the officers trying not to seem as though I was looking at them. I took a deep breath and slowed down a bit. I knew I needn't rush now—I could trust Merrill to keep the gate closed.

I studied them one by one, checking first the ones standing by themselves. There was a middle-aged white woman with short black hair, an older man with almost no hair at all, a tall black man with huge hands, a young white man with a DC cap on who turned slightly so I couldn't see his face.

Searching a small group of officers standing near the entrance to the security building, I could see that three were women, two were in their fifties, and two were black. Another group standing close to them was comprised of all young white men, any of whom could have been Billy Ray. I walked over to them. They were sharing the exciting news: an inmate had been killed on the rec yard.

I stepped into their circle and asked what had happened and then looked at each of them carefully and slowly, which was difficult because of the adrenaline coursing through my veins. So strong was its effect, in fact, that I had begun to shake.

They told me what they knew and why they were here and not down where the action was, but Billy Ray was not among them. It made sense that he wouldn't be in a group, but he probably wouldn't stand completely alone either.

I spotted another small group, and, though they stood together, they weren't talking. I approached them, and as I did, one of them moved forward slightly. This put him closer to the outer gate . . . and freedom. When he moved, his shoes slid back and fourth on his feet the way his uniform did on his body. There was also an unmistakable light prison-green tattoo on his left arm.

When I turned to locate Merrill, I saw him coming out of the security building with a nine millimeter at his side. He was always a dangerous man—now he was deadly. And then, I felt it—an arm around my throat, a blade pressing into the flesh at my jugular.

It was a stupid mistake. I felt ashamed and embarrassed, and knew that however this ended—in my death or his—I would be partly to blame.

Merrill brought the nine up and aimed it straight at me. "Hands down, motherfucker," he said to Billy Ray. "No way outta here. 'Cept in a bag."

"I'll kill the preacher," Billy Ray yelled as the other officers in the sally port began to scatter. His mouth was at my right ear, which rang when he finished yelling, "Back off." His blade cut into my neck slightly and my skin burned with a small, but sharp pain.

"He die—you die," Merrill said. His tone was low, somehow soothing and threatening at the same time.

"I'm dead already," he said.

"Billy, listen to me," I said, barely above a whisper because of the pressure on my throat. "They can't let you out of here—even if you kill me. You could have Warden Stone and it wouldn't matter. I know you're hurting, but this will only make things worse. Stop this now and I can help you. I know an organization that will bring your little girl and her mother to see you. That's why I called you to my office this morning."

"Really?" he asked, his voice softening.

"Why didn't you come?" I asked, coughing from his grip on my throat.

"'Ts busy," he said, the edge back in his voice. "'Sides, I didn't want no more bad news."

"It's good news, Billy," I said as upbeat as I could.

Remembering the shank in my pocket, I tried reaching for it, but there was no way I could get it without getting my throat cut in the process.

"I don't want to see her," he said. "I wouldn't know what to say. I just want to kill the son of a bitch who did it."

"That won't help her," I said.

"It'll fuckin' help me," he said, spit flying from his mouth.

I nodded my head slightly. "I understand, but they're not going to let you out of here. They're going to kill you right here and now unless you surrender."

"I don't care, preacher," he said sounding on the verge of tears. "I don't care anymore."

"Do it for Jessica," I said. "She needs her daddy . . . now more than ever."

"I killed a cop today," he said. "They not gonna let me see her. I'm as good as dead anyway. I let you go and all these brown shirts gonna kick the shit outta me."

"I won't let that happen," I said.

He laughed.

"Times up," Merrill said. "What's it gonna be?"

"Death!" he shouted, releasing his hold on me and putting the knife to his own throat. I turned and looked at him. I could tell he was praying and I knew what was coming next.

I dropped to the ground and yelled, "Shoot!"

Merrill closed one eye, took a breath, dropped the hammer . . . and saved Billy Ray Dickens' life—what there was left of it anyway.

Billy Ray was on the ground now, the shank lying beside him. Blood was pouring out of the place where his right arm became his right shoulder, and I spun around, ripping off my clerical shirt and tying it tightly around his wound.

Billy Ray looked up. "I was gonna do it."

"I know," I said. "I'm glad he didn't let you."

He closed his eyes and remained silent.

"I can help you," I said.

He shook his head. "Too late."

"It's never too late," I said.

Later, after Billy Ray had been rushed under armed guard to the hospital by ambulance, Merrill and I sat on the sidewalk in front of the control room, talking.

"How'd you get them to give you a gun and keep the gate locked?" I asked.

He smiled his broad smile, his bright white teeth contrasting with his gunmetal-blue skin. I looked up into the control room. Standing there with a grin of her own was Robin, a model-tall woman with an athletic build and beads in her braids that matched the color of her full lips.

"You *do* have a way with the women around here," I said.

"*Shee-it,*" he said. "Women everywhere."

"Hell of a shot, too," I said.

"*Shee-it*," he said again, smiling. "I's tryin' to kill his racist ass."

I laughed.

As we sat there in the warm, but waning glow of the setting sun, I thought about the afternoon's events and my role in them. Sometimes I functioned as a chaplain and sometimes as a cop. Some days I worked on saving souls and other days I was happy just to save lives.

A Taint In the Blood

I was drinking again.

I told myself that every burning swallow would be my last, that I would once and for all quench the insatiable thirst of the simian creature lurking inside me, but I knew when I was being lied to.

Until just recently, it had been a long time since I had been drunk, and the last time I drank I climbed right back up onto the wagon the next day, so I had convinced myself that maybe I wasn't a drunk after all. I had stopped going to meetings—hell, I had stopped going much of anywhere besides work.

I was on my way to the warehouse to pick up supplies for the chapel when five white inmates, each with teardrop tattoos, emerged from behind the PRIDE building and surrounded me.

With each one touching shoulders with those on either side, their leader, an inmate everyone called Bush because of his dark wiry hair and eyebrows, stepped forward, his face an inch from mine.

I could have yelled for security. I could have tried to fight them. But I wanted to hear what they had to say. They were members of a gang known as Southern Comfort. Recently, I had been involved in an investigation that landed their previous leader in a cell full-time. Based on their body language, I'd say they weren't happy about it.

"Cut off the head of *some* snakes," Bush said, "he grows another one."

"What kind is that?" I asked.

"Southern Comfort kind," he said, gesturing to the group surrounding us.

The sour smell of the groups' body odor was almost as bad as their rancid breath.

"And we never forget any bastard dumb enough to do us harm," he said.

"So there's no point in me asking you guys to let bygones be bygones?"

"Not only that—" he began.

"But I better watch my back," I said.

He smiled, his crooked, cigarette-stained teeth looking like dried kernels of corn dangling from a rotting cob. "Blade," he said to one of the other inmates. Blade, a tall, thin, pasty boy with adolescent peach fuzz and a permanent scowl on his face, flashed the blade of a shank in front of me. He did it so fast, the blade exposed for such a short period of time, it didn't register until after he had concealed it again.

"You're alive 'cause we allow you to be," Bush said. "Do all within your power to make things go well for Southern Comfort and stay the fuck outta our business. That clear enough for you?"

Before I could respond, the small group dispersed, and I was left standing alone. I took a minute to make sure I understood their cryptic message—inmates could be so enigmatic—then proceeded through the south gate.

When I emerged from the compound, I realized I'd been so distracted by Bush and his boys that I hadn't noticed the Federal Express truck parked near the warehouse. Now that I had, my heart rate quickened and my mouth grew dry.

The truck driver was Laura Matthers. We had dated for a short while and I had not seen each other since.

I was about twenty feet from the truck when Laura stepped down from it holding a small box and an electronic clipboard. When she saw me, she set the package down on the bottom step of her vehicle and the clipboard on top of it, and waited for me to reach her.

"Hey, you," she said.

Laura Matthers looked like a beautiful, gentle deer with a broken nose. Her eyes were deep brown and her breast-length brown hair was a couple of shades darker than buckskin. Summer had not officially begun yet she already had a tan her Fed Ex uniform shorts displayed nicely.

Ever the smooth talker, I said, "Hey."

We embraced awkwardly, lingering a moment too long.

After an intense, but brief summer romance, Laura and I had decided to stop seeing each other, each for different reasons, many of them concealed, and, until now, we had managed to avoid each other until now.

Her taut body felt good and vaguely familiar, and the sweat-tinged perfume rising in the heat emanating from her skin smelled of sex, which was funny because the two of us had never had it.

"How have you been?" she asked.

"I'm okay," I said. "How about you?"

"Me, too," she said.

"You look great," I said.

"You, too," she said.

We grew quiet a moment.

Behind me, I could hear the gate opening, and I turned to see the Restricted Labor Squad, or chain gang, marching out, the cadence of their boots and rattle of their chains sounding like the percussion section of a college band taking the field. Periodically one of the inmates would call out a jailhouse cadence and the others would repeat it: "They say that Florida girls are fine, their kiss as sweet as brandy wine, but that sweet thing'll never be mine, 'cause all they'll let me do is time."

The officers escorting them were dressed in gray fatigues that made them look like military special forces more than correctional officers, the black shotguns propped against their shoulders adding to the effect. The RLS was the result of a political attempt to appease the public's desire to get tough on crime. However, if the public realized that almost all prison escapes happened when inmates were already outside the fence, they'd probably reconsider their position.

When the RLS had rhythmically shuffled by, I turned back to face Laura.

"You think we could talk sometime?" she asked.

"Sure," I said, nodding. "Is everything okay?"

She shrugged. "I'm sure it will be after we talk."

"What is it?"

She hesitated. "I think . . . . We'll talk about it when we get together."

"Laura," I said, my voice sounding as if I had a right to insist.

"Someone's harassing me," she said, "and I don't know what to do."

By the time Laura arrived at my trailer in the Prairie Palm II, I had already downed several drinks.

When I opened the door, Seven and Seven in a lowball glass in my hand, her eyes widened momentarily, but then she smiled warmly—perhaps even adoringly.

Her royal blue sleeveless summer dress hung loosely, hiding her hard body and sharp curves. A row of saddle-brown buttons ran the length of the dress, matching her leather thong sandals. Just beneath the top button, a keyhole opening revealed a small cross necklace and the fact that she sunbathed in the nude, for the slightest hint of breasts hiding there were as dark as the rest of her.

"Would you like a drink?" I asked.

She nodded. "I'll have what you're having."

Walking over to the couch, she lowered her shoulder and shrugged off the long strap of her purse, then dropped down beside it.

As I prepared her drink, I considered her again. Why had we given up so soon? What was it about her that made me willing to do that? Seeing how nervous and awkward she was now, I was reminded. At times, she walked in beauty that was truly sublime, but they were seldom, and most often she seemed uncomfortable with herself, like someone experiencing the first long days of sobriety.

Still, she looked so good.

I walked back over to her and handed her what for me would always be unlucky number sevens. She tasted it and tried to smile, but the drink was too strong, too bitter.

"You want something else?" I asked. "Maybe something with fruit in it?"

She shook her head. "This is good," she said.

The trailer was quiet, seeming more so now than before she arrived. I grabbed a remote off the couch, clicked a few buttons, and a CD of Gram Parsons began to play.

"What's *that*?"

I dropped down onto the lumpy couch beside her, the slip cover bunching beneath me, and told her.

"Are you drunk?" she asked.

I shook my head. "But you better go ahead and tell me what you need to sooner rather than later."

"I feel a little silly," she said, "and embarrassed—especially asking for your help after all this time, but . . . I just don't know what else to do."

I should have reassured her, but I just waited.

"I'm being followed," she said, "and harassed."

"You know who's doing it?"

She nodded. "I think I do, but I haven't actually seen him. If it's not him, I have no idea who else it could be."

"Old boyfriend?"

"Actually, he is," she said. "He was rebound guy after you broke up with me. It was intense, very sexual, but fun and sweet, too. I thought he might be the one."

"Very sexual?" I asked.

When Laura and I had dated, she had been a virgin, and though tempted, we had managed to avoid changing that. Until I was certain we had a future, I hadn't wanted to do anything I'd later feel guilty about. I already had enough of that.

She nodded. "I wanted you to be my first," she said. "When that didn't happen . . . well, I was just ready. And it was amazing. I discovered that I really, *really* like sex."

"Really?"

"*Really*," she said. "My mom and sister can take it or leave it, so I figured I'd be the same way, but . . . wow."

When we were together, I had assumed that being a thirty-two year-old virgin meant Laura was carrying an entire suitcase—perhaps even a steamer trunk—of sexual hang-ups. I even imagined that she had been molested as a young girl, but we weren't together long enough for me to find out.

"You really missed out," she said.

"Obviously," I said.

"Back when we were seeing each other," she said, "why didn't we—I mean, we saw a lot of each other and I just thought we were heading toward that type of intimacy. Why didn't we?"

"A lot of reasons," I said.

"I did make it clear to you that I thought I was ready, didn't I?"

I nodded.

"I seem to remember offering myself to you and you rejecting me," she said.

"It wasn't rejection," I said.

"It was gentle and kind and you did it for me, but it was rejection."

"It sounds corny, I know, but I was honestly trying to figure out the best way to love you," I said. "To do what was best for you."

"Do you think it's a sin?"

I shook my head. "I'm no Puritan," I said, "but it certainly solidifies emotional entanglements. I didn't want you to end up getting hurt."

"But I did."

"I'm sorry," I said. "But wouldn't it have been worse if we had become that intimate?"

She shrugged. "I can't know, can I?"

"And you never were really specific about your past," I said.

"Why I was still a virgin in my early thirties," she said.

I nodded.

"You're a good man," she said.

"I'll drink to that," I said, holding up my nearly empty glass.

"Seriously," she said. "And I'm glad to see you loosening up a bit. You put too much pressure on yourself. What you did was sweet, but you can't go through life avoiding emotional entanglements—and not truly connect with anyone."

She was right. I certainly needed to be more open, more willing to get down in the sometimes messy pit of personal relationships, but that wasn't the issue here.

We were silent a long moment, Gram Parsons and Emmylou Harris singing a duet in the background.

"How sure are you it's him?" I asked.

"Who?" she asked. "Taylor? I don't know who else it could be."

"What has he done?"

"He's following me," she said. "It's more a feeling than anything, but I know he's there—not all the time, but a lot. Especially at night. He spray painted the words 'cunt' and 'bitch' on my car. He calls and hangs up in the middle of the night. And I think he killed my dog. I didn't suspect him at the time, so I didn't think anything of it, just buried him, but he was young and healthy. I don't know. I just think he did it."

"Did he stay outside?" I asked. "Bark when someone came into the yard?"

She shook her head. "He was an inside dog."

I nodded, thinking about what she had said.

"What is it?" she asked.

"If he did it," I said, "it'd be one thing if he was trying to get the dog out of the way so he could come into your yard to watch you, but it's another if he really had no utilitarian reason to do it."

"Why?"

"Makes him far more dangerous."

Jack Jordan's annual birthday party at Potter's Landing was the social event of the year in Potter County. He was a popular sheriff and there was free food and booze for as long as there were people to consume it.

Laura, who was sticking very close these days, accompanied me this year. Merrill and I were taking turns following her during the day and she was spending most nights at my place. We had tried on a couple of occasions to have a little chat with Taylor Price, but he was proving elusive.

Nearly a thousand people had crammed into the small landing, which was little more than a boat launch into the Apalachicola River. Dad's deputies, one of whom was my younger brother, Jake, had set up large halogen lights at the four corners of the landing, and built a large bonfire at the center. On the back of a yellow low boy trailer, a local band was covering country tunes, in front of them, the end of the gravel road had been swept to make a dance floor.

Light from the work lamps pierced the rising smoke from the bonfire and barbeque pits illuminating the undersides of pine, cypress, and magnolia trees casting foggy shadows onto the gray night sky. In the silence between songs, the sweeter songs of crickets could be heard against the rhythm track of the flowing river, the cool currents rising off of it delivered the fragrance of magnolia and gardenia blossoms.

People swarmed around the landing the way bees did in this same location during tupelo season—twenty-five couples or so were on the dance floor, the deputies and their families were preparing food over barbeque pits and portable gas grills, and another couple of hundred sat or stood around the pavilions. The others wandered around lazily as if floating down the river beyond them on innertubes, with a bottle of beer in hand, greeting each other with the warm familiarity of friends who were just a little loaded. All the others sat on their tailgates and in the back of their trucks they had parked in the landing for just such a purpose.

Upon arriving, I was greeted by the friendly citizens of the county who had been known as Dad's since he was elected sheriff the first time nearly thirty years ago. All the people of my dad's generation greeted me as, "Jr." while those from mine called me "JJ."

When Dad saw us, he motioned us over.

Ordinarily a quiet and reserved man, Jack Jordan became attentive and charming the moment he saw Laura.

"Son, why don't you go fix this lovely lady a drink, while I introduce her around to everyone?"

"Sure," I said, as if I didn't have a drinking problem and needed to avoid the bar.

The people I encountered on my way over to the bar were as eclectic as north Florida itself. Beach people in colorful tropical shorts and shirts with deep tans and sun-bleached blond hair moved among small-town people in faded jeans and t-shirts, many of which sported beer-logos. County officials, like Dad, with khakis and button-down oxfords, kept their distance from the river people in halter tops, Daisy Dukes, and soiled wife beaters.

When I neared the food tables, Jake yelled, "Hide the liquor. The whiskey priest is here." It got a laugh, but only from Jake's redneck buddies who didn't get the reference any more than he did. He had heard me use the term in a vulnerable moment of reflection on my identification with the weakness of Graham Greene's character from *The Power and the Glory*. He had used it against me ever since.

"You didn't bring your nigger, did you?" he added. "We all left ours at home."

Again, the laughter was only from his friends.

Though openly and unapologetically racist, Jake's comments were said for my benefit. He knew how much even subtle forms of racism bothered me.

I walked over to him.

"Were you talking to me?" I asked.

"You been drinkin'?" he asked. "Hell, I can smell it on your breath," he added, his own breath smelling like the beer he was drinking.

"Were you talking about Merrill?"

"If the color fits," he said.

"Why don't you and I ride over and ask him if he's a nigger?" I said.

"He's not supposed to know it," he said. "You are. Why does he fight all your fights for you anyway?"

"He doesn't," I said, and punched him square on his obnoxious, racist mouth.

The punch was all a punch should be. I had pivoted my hips and slung my shoulders into it. It was hard and it connected well. Jake went down. And didn't get up.

As his friends started gathering around me, Jack Jordan, the man of the hour, stopped the band and, using the microphone said, "John, wherever you are, could you come up here, please? I want to thank all y'all for comin' to my party. I consider myself to be a very fortunate man, indeed, to have so many fine friends and to have the honor of keepin' y'all safe. Thanks again for comin'. Now, as you know, one of my boys is a preacher and he's moved back down here from the big city, and I sure am glad. I want him to say a blessing over our food before we start eating."

As I climbed up on the trailer and took the microphone, the noisy crowd grew quiet. I noticed several of the men taking off their baseball caps and cowboy hats. I felt out of place and unworthy of this honor, guilty for punching Jake and drinking so much lately, but as I took in a deep breath and let it out slowly, I felt the calming presence of grace—unexpected, unbidden, undeserved.

"Let us pray," I said. "Father in heaven, thank you for giving me such a good earthly father. Thank you that he has been able to be a father to our entire community. I ask that you continue to bless his life with health, happiness, and fine friends. And help us all find a way to thank him for taking the life you gave him and giving it to us. Please be with us all tonight. Keep us safe and bless the food and our time together. . . . "

When I finished, the noise started again, and I found it comforting. I looked over in Jake's direction. He was on his feet again, heading my way. I stepped off the trailer to stand with Laura and Dad.

"I think we better go," I said.

"So soon?" Laura asked.

Dad nodded, then turning to Jake, held up his hand. "Not here," he said.

Jake glared at me. "This ain't over," he said. "Not by a goddam long shot."

I nodded. "I look forward to resuming our conversation," I said.

When Jake walked away, Dad said, "I told Missy here that I'd be happy to help take care of her, so just let me know what you need."

"Thanks," I said.

"Thank you, Jack," she said, hugging him. "And happy birthday."

"Sorry about . . ." I said, nodding in Jake's direction.

"I wish you boys would get things worked out," he said.

It was as if he couldn't see just how deep our differences and animus went, as if his love for both of us gave him selective sight and long-term memory loss.

When I slammed the door to my truck, I gunned the engine and began barreling down the landing road, racing toward the Jack and Coke that would sooth the feral beast banging on my breastbone.

But Laura had other ideas for calming the creature inside.

Unbuckling her seatbelt, she leaned over and unbuttoned and unzipped my pants, my body responding immediately. Pulling down my underwear, she grabbed me hard with her hand, then brought me to her mouth, taking me in, going down deep, the warmth and wetness of her mouth enveloping me.

With amazing adroitness, she expertly used her hand and mouth to quickly, if temporarily, satiate my hunger and calm my rage. When she raised up to whisper what else she wanted to do to me and what she wanted me to do to her, I could smell myself in her mouth.

By the time we reached my place, I was ready to go again, and we didn't waste time getting out of the truck or our clothes.

The next afternoon, while I was still a little hung over, Merrill and I played in a two person charity golf tournament at the Killearn Country Club in Tallahassee, and though both of us were athletic, neither of us were golfers, a fact we were often reminded of as we attempted not to surrender all of our dignity to the tiny white ball.

On the third hole, Merrill sliced the ball on his drive and it ricocheted off a pine tree near a house before splashing into the swimming pool.

"Tell me why the hell you signed us up for this again?" he said.

He was wearing long navy Sean John shorts, a long, untucked, light blue shirt, white socks blue Nike flip-flops and a white Miami Heat had on backwards, and receiving more than a few stares.

"Seemed like a good idea at the time," I said.

He shook his head.

"It's a good cause."

"I'll give'em a donation," he said. "Hell, they can have my entire check. Anything but my pride."

When we reached the house where the ball had bounced into the pool, an elderly white couple was out on their patio looking as if we had dropped an olive in their champagne.

Merrill walked up as if they weren't there and dropped another ball just inside the fairway.

"There goes the neighborhood," I said to the couple, as Merrill swung the club as if he were playing baseball rather than golf. This time he hooked it in the other direction, but it managed to stay on the fairway and land just this side of the green. He then turned to face the disapproving couple and bowed deeply, sweeping his arm in exaggerated fashion.

The lady began shaking her head as she eyed Merrill with even more disdain. Her husband looked away. "Y'all not even safe out here no more," Merrill said. "Tiger Woods done opened up the door and all us darkies're pourin' through it like they's free fried chicken at the end of every hole."

He slung the club back into the bag and walked toward the green.

"Caddies these days," I said, when I walked past the couple. "Don't know their place anymore."

When Merrill reached the green, he didn't stop. When I caught up with him in the lounge of the country club, he was draining a cold beer out of a bottle, a glass of orange juice sat across from him.

"Not feeling very charitable anymore?" I asked.

He laughed.

A slim girl with a dark complexion and straight black hair that hung to her bottom set two bottles of beer and two glasses of orange juice on the table between us. Her enormous breasts bounced around as she moved, and she leaned over and put them in my face as she served us.

"You got some vodka you can pour in these?" I asked.

"Sure, sweetie," she said, turning and giving me the titty treatment again.

"That'd happen more often, you leave your collar at home," he said when she left.

I shrugged.

"This where we should've been all along."

"Can't argue that," I said.

Of the three other people in the lounge, only one was a woman, and I noticed that the waitress didn't put her breasts in her face.

"Seems sort of sexist to me," I said.

"Uh huh."

The woman, a white lady who looked to be in her mid-fifties, was seated at the bar having oral sex with a martini while a tall, skinny white man in his twenties, with greasy black hair plastered to his skull, was obviously trying to pick her up. Greasy looked desperate, and she looked disinterested, but not just in Greasy. In life. She wore heavy makeup, but even in the under-lit lounge it couldn't hide the deep lines and harsh boredom on her face.

An elderly man with a round paunch both above and beneath his belt line was slumped in a seat at a table near the bar with his pants undone and laid open. When the waitress gave him the boob treatment, he actually wiggled his head like a new born trying to find a nipple.

"Why can't they do a charity wet T-shirt contest?" Merrill asked. "Lotta money in T and A."

"Always has been," I said. "Of course it depends on whose T and whose A it is."

The waitress made her way back over to us, placing a couple of vodkas on the table in front of me, then giving Merrill the boob job.

I sighed deeply. "I thought we had something special," I said.

She smiled, but didn't say anything, then walked away.

I mixed the OJ and vodka and started in on the first one.

"Been a while since I seen you do that," he said.

"Tired of drinking alone," I said.

He nodded.

I knew he was concerned, but he didn't let on, and I felt no judgment from him.

"You need help climbing back up them steps," he said, "let me know."

Taylor Price moved in the self-conscious manner of a man being watched. It wasn't that he was aware that Merrill and I were following him. It was his belief that everyone in his vicinity would want to watch him. He scanned the crowd the way some celebrities do, expecting to be recognized, paid attention to, desired, envied.

We had been following him for less than two hours and I knew everything I needed to about him except his arrest record—which Dad should be calling with soon.

As Taylor stepped off the escalator and into the parking garage beneath Governor Square Mall, he was carrying bags from stores that specialized in expensive clothes and the self-indulgent gadgets of the good life.

When he used his keyless remote to unlock his feminine-looking sports car and pop its small trunk, the noise it made was loud, showy, and annoying.

"This is going to be fun," Merrill said. "Five Franklins says he wets his pants before we finish with him."

I knew how Merrill felt. The kind of guy who would stalk and harass a woman was only slightly above a child molester on my list of least favorite people, but I wouldn't take his bet. The Taylor Prices of the world could commit some cruel and inhumane acts on people physically weaker than them, but in a fair fight would fold faster than a good gambler with a bad hand.

We followed as he sped out of the parking garage, through the mall parking lot, and out onto Apalachee Parkway. Thankfully, we were in Merrill's truck, not mine, and would have no trouble keeping up.

As we turned onto Monroe, my phone rang. It was Dad.

"Christopher Taylor Price, the third, has been arrested for aggravated battery, rape, and assault," he said, "but he's never been convicted of so much as a misdemeanor. Somehow witnesses against him change their story or don't show up for court at all. He's got a juvenile record, but it's sealed, so I don't know what's in it but I'd bet more of the same."

"Thanks."

"This the guy bothering Laura?" he asked.

"Yeah."

"Be careful," he said.

"Merrill's with me," I said, "but this guy's a—"

"I meant make sure you have an alibi and don't leave any evidence," he said.

Price pulled into Lake Ella Park, carefully maneuvering his car into a spot as far from the other two vehicles as he could.

"He loves that car," Merrill said.

I nodded, though I suspected Taylor didn't love anything, that the closest he got to anything resembling love was for himself.

"I'm gonna fuck it up," he said.

Stepping out of his car, Taylor stripped down to his silk boxers, slowly, showing off his time at the health club and tanning salon, and put on his running clothes.

He then began to prance around the cement sidewalk surrounding the small lake.

It was a dark night, and it was getting late. Only three other people were on the track—a middle-aged dog walker and two college girls with FSU shorts and sports bras, their ponytails bouncing in sync as they jogged.

As he made his rounds, Taylor stepped off the track for the two coeds, saying something to them every time they passed, but made the dog walker choose between jumping out of his way or getting run over.

Merrill and I were beneath a large oak tree near Taylor's car, watching.

When the dog walker finally left, he made his move on the coeds, and though they giggled and flirted a bit, they weren't interested in anything more and told him so. But in Taylor's world, "no" means "I want you to make me," which was what he was beginning to do when Merrill and I lifted up one of the loose parking pavers and tossed it through the windshield of his car, setting off the alarm and bringing Taylor running.

"What the *fuck*?" he said as he ran up.

"We just tossed this paver here through your windshield," I said. "Turn off your alarm and we'll tell you why."

Behind Taylor and up a small hill sat the Tallahassee Police Station. He turned and glanced in its direction, seeming to calculate whether he could make it.

By the time he looked back at us, Merrill had closed the distance between them and was ripping the car keys from the side of his shorts where they dangled loosely. Pressing a button on the remote, Merrill stopped the alarm. He then pivoted and drove an uppercut into Taylor's stomach that doubled him over, dropped him to the ground, and had him making that breath-knocked-out-of-you noise that meant he was doing his best to replace the air that had just been forced out of him, but his body wasn't cooperating.

"Taylor," I said.

He didn't look up at me.

I slapped him across the face, my open hand smacking him hard, stinging his pampered skin.

He looked up at me.

"You get off on harassing women," I said.

He shook his head.

I slapped him again, harder this time.

"It wasn't a question, but a statement of fact," I said.

He shook his head again, and I drove my knee into his nose, blood spurting out, covering his face and shirt, my pants leg and shoe.

I knew when I was sober again, I'd feel guilty about what I was doing—not for doing it to someone like Taylor, but for how much I was enjoying it, and how easy it was for me to betray everything I believed in.

"You like harassing women," I asked.

This time he didn't shake his head, just continued holding his nose.

"We're gonna show you what it's like for them," I said.

Merrill smiled, his bright white teeth lighting up the area around us. "He sayin' we gonna make you our little bitch," Merrill said.

Obviously a slow learner, Taylor shook his head and said, "You some cunt's boyfriend or somethin'? If your slut strays she should get the beating not the guy who obliged her with a little cock."

"I heard it was little," Merrill said. "Big of you to admit it."

Merrill then kicked Taylor's balls so hard it had to have driven them up into his body cavity. After a few moments of excruciating pain, Taylor passed out.

Dragging Taylor down to the lake, we dropped him in the water. When he came to and pulled his head up, gasping and choking, we let him have one quick inhalation and then shoved him back under.

We repeated the process a few times before letting him up for good. After he finished coughing up water and was breathing again, he began to cry, a long string of snot from his left nostril nearly touching the ground.

"Taylor, you listening?" I asked. "Do we finally have your attention?"

He nodded.

"If you ever harass or force yourself on any woman again or even look in Laura Matthers direction, we'll be back," I said. "And if we come back, it'll be to kill you."

"No warnings," Merrill said. "No questions. No chances. No mercy. Just a little noise, searing pain, and lights out."

"Understand?" I asked.

He nodded.

"Let me hear you say the words, Taylor," I said.

"I understand," he said.

We turned and began to walk away.

"But I never did nothin' to that Matthers bitch she didn't want me to," Taylor said.

Merrill looked at me. "He tryin' to set some sort of record?" Glancing back down at Taylor he said, "You really that slow or you one of them masochist motherfuckers?"

I withdrew the empty .38 from my pocket, stepped over to Taylor, pressed the barrel to his forehead, thumbed back the hammer, and pulled the trigger.

Taylor began to cry again when he realized he heard the dry fire of the empty cylinder. He began to beg, too, pleading and promising and praying, and in the process, he wet his pants.

"Told you," Merrill said. "How much you owe me?"

"Didn't take the action," I said. "I knew putting stock in Taylor's fortitude was a sucker bet if there ever was one."

"It won't miss-fire next time, Taylor," I said. "I promise you that."

The next day I was just returning to the chapel from visiting the infirmary, when my phone rang.

"So far," Merrill said loudly above the background noise, "Price keepin' his distance. In fact, I the only bastard been followin' our favorite delivery girl."

"Delivery person," I corrected.

He was calling from a cell phone near a highway. I could hear vehicles speeding by, and somewhere in the distance, the warning beeps of a commercial vehicle backing up.

"Well, whatever she is, she alone."

It was his day to follow her. We had been taking turns, but neither of us had yet to spot anyone.

"You sound disappointed," I said.

"Well, I *was* hoping," he said, and I could hear the smile in his voice.

"You think we scared him away?"

"Oh, we scared him," he said, "but was he the one doin' the stalkin'?"

"Didn't seem like it, did it?"

"Hard to tell with these pansy-ass mama's boys."

We were quiet a moment, as I thought about Taylor Price and the likelihood of him having been the one following Laura.

"Word on the street is you and Jake play a little Cain and Abel at the landin' the other night."

"Uh huh," I said. "What else is new?"

"I hear it involved me," he said. "He tell you why?"

"No."

"I took April out Friday night," he said.

"As in his ex-wife, April?" I asked.

"Uh huh."

"Well now," I said, "that makes it all worthwhile."

He laughed. "I'm glad you feel that way," he said. "'Cause we goin' out again this weekend. Anyway, I just wanted you to know that everything is everything. The delivery girl, ah, person, is safe."

"Never doubted that," I said.

"Let me rephrase that," he said. "She safe from whoever was followin' her, but I on the case now, so she not safe from me. I one charmin' motherfucker. I've tried to tone it down some, but only so far it can go."

"I understand," I said. "You *could* tell her about my wonderful qualities. Might deflect some of her attention."

"Yeah," he said. "I should. Remind me what they are again."

"She knows," I said. "Why don't you have *her* tell *you?*"

He turned his mouth away from the phone slightly. "Well, it would appear that Blockbuster now has all they new releases. Time for us to roll up on Victoria's Secret."

"Victoria's got no secrets left," I said.

"That's what I'm hopin'," he said and hung up.

I opened my door to find Laura holding a package, completely naked except for her FedEx cap.

"Special delivery," she said. "For your package."

Though mine was the only mobile home in the failed second phase of the Prairie Palm, it was still a brave thing to do, and it made me want her even more.

I ushered her into my trailer and closed the door behind her.

Her body was lean and tan—the look on her face somehow innocent and seductive. Her small firm breasts trembled slightly from the force of her beating heart and her belly beneath them looked to have been sculpted by an artistic and meticulous God. And even lower, between two muscular legs, was a dark, thick, triangular garden that promised sweet and tender fruit.

She handed me the package. The address read: John Jordan, 69 Sex Drive, Pottersville, FL 32412.

"What's inside?"

"A tube of KY," she said, "but we don't need it. I'm practically dripping. See."

She put two fingers inside herself, moaning as she did, then brought them up to my lips. I kissed her fingertips, took them in my mouth, tasting her, then pulled her to me and kissed her hard and long.

When we had finished kissing, she dropped to her knees, unzipped my pants and took me in her mouth. I tried to undress, but as I did, her teeth scraped me, and I stopped.

"Here, let me help," she said, standing again, and undressing me.

When we were both naked, I led her over to the couch, sat her down, and knelt between her legs. She moaned as I licked along her inner thigh, arching her back and tilting her head toward the ceiling as I made my way up her leg.

After we made love, I had too much to drink, and we made love again, repeating this process until I blacked out at some point.

When I regained consciousness, we were lying on the couch together beneath a blanket.

"Welcome back," she said.

"How long was I out?"

"I'm not sure," she said. "A while."

I didn't say anything and we were quiet for a long moment.

"Taylor sent me flowers today," she said.

I raised up and looked at her.

"He apologized for any misunderstanding," she said. "What'd you do to him?"

"Just let him know what it's like to be afraid," I said.

"Well, I wouldn't know anything about that," she said. "Not anymore. Thanks to you."

"I don't think he'll bother you anymore," I said, "but if he comes around again, just call us."

I was alone in the chapel praying when the phone rang. The sanctuary was dim and cool, and I didn't want to leave it but I didn't have a choice. Most of the calls that came into my office were crises.

"Chaplain Jordan," I said.

"Hey, handsome," Laura said. "Whatcha doin'?"

"Tryin' to climb out of the bottle before I drown," I said.

"What?"

"What're you up to?"

"Just wanted to see if I could come over and cook dinner for you tonight," she said.

"Thanks," I said, "but I can't tonight."

"Got a date?"

I laughed. "With destiny," I said.

"Huh?"

"I'm going to a meeting."

"I think you've got a good handle on things," she said.

I didn't say anything.

"Aren't you more relaxed?" she asked. "Having more fun? Aren't you just as good of a chaplain? Can you name one way drinking is detracting from your life?"

"How many times have I passed out?"

"Just a few," she said.

"That's a few too many," I said.

"Can we get together after your meeting?" she asked.

"Not tonight," I said.

"But—"

"I've got to go," I said.

"Okay," she said, "but be careful. Don't mess around and lose me."

"You avoiding me?" Laura asked.

I had nearly a week of sobriety, and I hadn't seen her within that time.

"Not at all," I said. "Just been busy."

"I miss you," she said. "And the things you do to me."

"I'm finding that, at least for now, solitude helps me maintain my sobriety."

"I understand," she said. "I just miss you so much. But I'm proud of you and support what you're doing. Sorry if I wasn't sensitive before."

"Thanks," I said. "That means a lot."

"Well, I mean it," she said. "I'm here. Anything you need. And when you feel like we can get together again, let me know."

"I will."

We were quiet a moment, and I could tell she had something else to say.

"Are you okay?" I asked.

"Yeah," she said, but it wasn't very convincing.

"What is it?"

"Nothing," she said. "Really."

"Laura," I said. "It's okay. Tell me."

"I know you've got a lot on you," she said. "I didn't want to say anything, but I really don't know who else to turn to."

"What's wrong?"

"I'm being followed again," she said.

"You let me cap his ass, we wrap this thing up," Merrill said.

"It's not him," I said.

"I's wondering if he that stupid," he said.

We were sitting in Merrill's truck, a black Toyota 4 x 4, on Pensacola Street in Tallahassee across from Laura's apartment watching a man watching her through one of the rear windows. Merrill had called me shortly after I got home and said that, at last, someone was actually following Laura besides us.

The man who was not Taylor Price was young and thin, and wearing all black. He was standing near a small grouping of Bradford Pear trees near the fence behind her apartment. He'd probably chosen black attire to help conceal his presence, but it had the opposite affect, drawing attention to both the outfit and his pale face.

"He a stalker or a cat burglar?" Merrill asked.

I laughed.

"This his first time followin' Laura since we started," he said. "We wouldn't a missed his ass."

"I know."

"You think ol' Taylor was innocent after all?"

I shook my head. "Nothin' innocent about him," I said.

The young man, though partially hidden by the pear trees and the darkness, was easy to watch. He moved around a lot, as if cold or nervous, and nearly all of his gestures were exaggerated. He appeared to be stretching, as if preparing for a race.

"Not very good at this, is he?" Merrill said.

"Stalkin's harder than it looks," I said. "He'll get better."

"Less we put his ass in a wheelchair permanently," he said.

"Don't see many of them," I said.

"What?"

"Wheelchair-bound stalkers," I said.

"Let's go talk to his inept ass," Merrill said, opening his door. "I'm hungry."

When we got out, Merrill looped around to the back of the apartment building and came up behind the cat burglar/stalker. The moment Merrill got close, the guy took off, heading straight for me.

He was quick, his agility showing as he darted through the yard, dodging trees, chairs, and grills. He was fast, too, reaching me far sooner than I expected.

Now that he was closer, I could see that he wasn't wearing the outfit of a cat burglar, but an athlete. He wore long, black shorts over black athletic tights, black running shoes, a black sweat shirt and a black beanie with gray skulls and crossbones on it.

I jumped out from behind an SUV as he came up beside it, and I was able to see his face for a moment before he reversed his direction and ran around the vehicle, out of the parking lot and down Pensacola.

I followed.

Eventually, Merrill caught up with me.

"Fast bastard, ain't he?"

I nodded.

We chased him down Pensacola toward the college, running as fast as we could, but the gap continued to grow. In addition to speed, he had great stamina, showing no signs of tiring, seemingly able to maintain his current speed indefinitely.

"When we gonna admit defeat?" Merrill asked.

"Any moment," I said. "My side's about to explode."

"It wasn't Taylor?" Laura asked.

I shook my head.

We were inside her apartment. Merrill had gone home. I was staying with Laura, who would take me to get my truck at some point.

"You're sure?"

I nodded. "Even if I hadn't gotten a look at him, I'd have known," I said. "I've seen Taylor jog around Lake Ella."

"And?"

"He prances," I said. "This guy flies."

"Do you think it's been him all along?" she asked. "Taylor really was innocent?"

I shrugged. "I don't know," I said, "but we'll figure it out."

"I've got to get out of here," she said. "Let's get out of here."

"Where you wanna go?"

"Anywhere," she said. "Just out. Let's go for a drive."

Tallahassee at night is as peaceful as it is beautiful—rolling hills, spreading oaks lit from beneath, Spanish moss waving in the breeze, the nocturnal energy of a college town coupled with the easy flow of the light traffic. We rode around for a couple of hours, stopping to complete sex acts begun while moving.

An irrepressible insomniac, it was my time and I was wired— and it wasn't just the night or the dark energy but the chase earlier and our libidinousness.

And before long, it was also the drink.

The longer we drove around, the later it got, the brighter the lights of the liquor stores became, the thirstier I got, and eventually I could resist temptation no longer.

We pulled into a package store on Thomasville Road.

When we pulled out, Laura drove and I drank.

Our plan was to drive to my place and spend the night, but we never made it.

When I woke up the next morning, I was in Laura's passenger seat, fully dressed, with scratches on my neck and blood on my hands. Laura, naked in the driver's seat beside me, bloodied and beaten, was dead.

Stumbling out of the car and falling onto the ground, I crawled a few feet away and began to throw up.

The surroundings were familiar, but it took me a few moments to realize that I was at Potter Landing in the very spot where Dad's birthday party had been. The early morning was cool, though sunlight streamed through the oak and pines, dappling the dew-damp ground.

My brain felt so swollen that I thought it might burst through my skull, its throbbing ache so severe it made me nauseous. Pressing through the pain, I stood and examined what was surely a crime scene, taking in the area surrounding the car, the car, and Laura— blinking my stinging eyes as I did.

The sand of the landing was imprinted with so many tracks— both vehicle and human—it was difficult to imagine they'd be useful. None seemed any fresher than the others.

The exterior of the car held no obvious physical evidence—no tool marks or bloody palm prints, and I was certain that any physical evidence inside the car or on the body would point to me.

There was nothing I could do but make the call.

My alcoholism had been threatening to destroy me most of my life and appeared to have finally succeeded, my self-destructive actions claiming Laura as well.

"Son," Dad said.

I looked up at him.

I was sitting on the ground about ten feet from the car, head in hands, waiting for his arrival.

"You okay?"

I shook my head.

He had come alone, honoring my request for privacy during the initial moments of the investigation—an investigation *his* department would have to conduct on one of *his* sons.

"What happened?" he asked.

"I have no idea," I said. "I must have blacked out. I was drinking."

He nodded, trying to be understanding, but I could see the pain, betrayal, and disappointment in his eyes.

"What do you remember?"

I told him.

"Okay," he said. "I'll take you home so you can shower and sleep. We'll process the scene and question you later this afternoon."

"Dad," I said, "you know I have to be processed before—"

"You let me worry about that," he said.

"I can't," I said. "You're gonna take a big enough hit for this as it is. You've got to treat me like any other suspect found in similar circumstances."

"I can't do that," he said.

"But—"

"I'm gonna take the hit anyway," he said. "And I know you **either didn't kill that girl or didn't mean to.**"

As I showered, I tried to remember what had happened the night before, but no matter how hard I thought, I just couldn't come up with anything. It was frustrating, like trying to recall a name or title I should know but just couldn't retrieve, and it made my head hurt worse.

Eventually, I gave up.

And that's when the bits of memory, unbidden and unformed, flashed in my mind—the angry words of an argument. A slap. Clawing. A scratch. Tears.

What happened? I asked myself. *Think!*

Laura's face lit up in laughter, then contorted in pain.

Crying. Anger. Sadness. Shock.

Why couldn't I remember? Or was it that I *wouldn't?* Did I not really want to? Was I suppressing memories so bad, so incriminating that my subconscious was attempting to protect me from what I had done?

Whatever secrets my mind held, I was unable to wrestle them free from its grasp.

When Merrill arrived, he tapped lightly on the door and stepped in.

I was on the couch, hair wet, partially dressed, unable to move.

He sat down in the old chair at the end of the couch without saying anything, and we were silent a while.

"Your dad asked me to check on you," he said. "Told me what's goin' on."

I nodded. I had yet to look at him.

"You need anything?"

I shook my head.

"I know you been through a lot," he said, "probably in shock, but we don't have a lot of time here."

He paused a moment, but I didn't say anything.

"Who you think did it?"

"Can't think of anybody else it could've been," I said.

"Price?" he asked.

"Me," I said, looking at him for the first time, searching his eyes for how he really felt about what I had just said.

He shook his head. "No way it was you."

His eyes didn't betray him.

"Don't see how it could be anybody else," I said.

"They's a reason why they call it blacking out," he said. "Your ass is unconscious."

"But before," I said.

"Don't care how drunk," he said. "You couldn't—"

"You haven't been around me at my worst," I said. "Most of the violent things I've done, I did in Atlanta."

"Any of it against women?" he asked. "Check that," he added. "I know the answer to that. Any of it toward anybody other than predators, pedophiles, and hardcore criminals?"

"Still," I said.

"Just for the hell of it, let's say it wasn't you. Who then?"

"But to find us at Potter Landing," I said. "How—"

"Who?"

"Taylor Price," I said. "Though I thought we had scared him straight. And the guy that smoked us last night."

"I wanna rematch with that fast bastard in a little more confined space."

I thought about the guy who had outrun us and how we might find him.

"What about some evil bastard coming up and finding Laura asleep and you passed out?" he asked.

"Pretty unlikely," I said.

"More so than it bein' you," he said.

"Why not kill me, too?" I asked.

"Lettn' you take the fall for it."

I thought about it.

"We need the sheriff to have his boys canvas the area around the landing," he said. "Camps, stores, houseboats—see if anyone saw anything. While he havin' that done, we talk to some of Laura's friends and family. We go at Price again, and we find the runner from last night. Either that or sit here until they come to arrest you."

"You're John?" Anne Gaskin asked.

I nodded.

"Laura's crazy about you," she said.

I attempted a smile.

Word of Laura's death was not yet public, so we had told Anne, one of her best friends, that she was missing.

We were standing outside an orthodontist office off of Thomasville Road, not far from I-10, where Anne worked. She had long, straight, natural-looking blonde hair, pale blue eyes, and an unvarnished, wholesome beauty. If she wore makeup, I couldn't tell.

"I mean, big bad mad love," she said.

"Any idea where she might be?" Merrill asked.

"You check work?"

He nodded. "She didn't show up this morning," he said.

"Her apartment?"

"Not there."

Anne's dental hygienist-type uniform looked to have been designed by kindergarten students. Above purple pants, her white top had dancing purple toothbrushes, their arms and legs formed from floss. The name tag pinned to it was in the shape of a large molar.

"What about her parents?" I asked.

"Her mom lives over in the sticks," she said. "Near Pottersville. You might check with her, though they're not very close."

"What about her dad?"

She shook her head, her blond hair whipping from side to side. "She doesn't even talk to him."

"She mention anything to you lately?" Merrill asked. "Anything out of the ordinary?"

She looked up and seemed to think about it. "No, I don't think so," she said. "John here's about all she could talk about."

"Anybody harassing her?" he asked.

"Not that I know of," she said.

"She didn't mention any problems with anyone?" I asked.

She shook her head. "Aren't you guys overreacting a little?" she asked. "I'm sure she's fine."

"Probably so," Merrill said. "We're just sort of silly that way."

"It's sweet," she said. "I should be so lucky. You kidding? Have someone looking out for me like that."

"Anyone else we should talk to?" I asked.

"Fritz," she said. "He's really Laura's best friend."

"Fritz?"

"Didion," she said, and rattled off his phone number. "They're very close. She hasn't mentioned him to you?"

I shook my head.

"If anyone can help you, it's him."

Fritz Didion didn't answer his phone.

I left a message for him, and while we waited for the return call we went in search of the guy we had chased out of Laura's yard last night.

Based on the way he was dressed and the way he moved, my guess was that he was a marathon runner and perhaps a track coach at the college.

We drove over toward the football stadium and turned on Chieftain Way, passed the baseball stadium and circus complex to Mike Long Track.

We found him jogging around the track, urging on his fellow runners, who looked to be part of the college track team.

"Better to be lucky than good," Merrill said.

I nodded.

The guy had on the same black outfit as the night before—black athletic tights beneath black silk shorts.

"We can't let him see us coming," I said. "He runs, we'll never catch him."

Merrill nodded.

"Any suggestions?"

"Sneak up on him, knock him down, and hold him there until we're done with him," he said. "'Course, we do that out here, it'll draw attention."

"We could corner him in the locker room," I said.

"Mean we'll have to wait 'til he finish," he said. "He look tired to you?"

I looked over at him again. Almost the moment I did, he broke off from the pack and jogged beneath the stands and into the Men's restroom.

Merrill shook his head. "Like I said, it ain't about bein' good."

"It's a good thing, too," I said.

"Remember us?" I said.

He looked up from the urinal at us, confusion at first, then recognition dawning on his face.

"Probably look different today," Merrill said. "Last night we just a blur."

"You're John Jordan, right?" he said.

I was taken aback, but I nodded.

"I'm Fritz Didion," he said.

Fritz Didion looked like a runner—that or an anorexic, but unlike a person with an eating disorder, his thin frame held well-defined muscle, and his tight clothing made sure everyone could see it. Beneath closely cropped hair, he had bright blues eyes and a sun-burned face.

"Two birds," Merrill said. "One visit."

"This is Merrill Monroe," I said.

Fritz leaned back and nodded. "I'd shake your hand, but . . . it's kind of busy at the moment."

The bathroom was a lot smaller than the ones in the football stadium, but it was built the same: a row of urinals on one wall, sinks in the middle, a row of toilet stalls on the opposite wall. Like most of the facilities at athletic complexes, the bathroom was hot, moist, and had that same lingering smell of human waste.

"Shake it and wash your hands," Merrill said. "We on a dead-line."

After he flushed, he stepped over to the sink, and washed his hands.

Merrill moved to block the door. "Let's see you outrun me in here," he said.

Fritz smiled. "Sorry about that," he said. "If Laura didn't mean so much to me . . . ."

"Anne said that you're Laura's best friend," I said.

"I was," he said.

"Was?" I asked.

"'Til you came along again," he said.

"Then what the fuck you stalkin' her for?" Merrill asked.

"*Stalking?*" he said, then looked from Merrill back to me. "You really should talk to Laura," he said.

"She's missing," I said.

"*Missing?*"

"Fritz," I said. "This gonna take twice as long if you repeat everything I say."

"Are you sure?' he asked. "Have you checked—"

"We've checked," I said.

"Tell us what you were doing in her backyard last night," I said. "Or tell the police."

He hesitated a moment, then sighed heavily. "This is embarrassing," he said.

"Fritz," Merrill said. "You're among friends."

Fritz nodded as if he really were. "I was doing Laura a favor," he said.

"Bet you do lots of women favors, don't you?" I said.

"It's not like that," he said. "She asked me to come over and hang out in the back, then take off running when you approached me. She knew y'all couldn't catch me. She wanted to get your attention again. She thought you were getting distracted—maybe even thought she had never been followed in the first place. She knew if she told you someone was actually at her apartment, you'd come running and," he jerked his head toward Merrill, "bring the cavalry."

He paused and I considered what he had said. In the silence, the constant sound of dripping water seemed magnified, each drop echoing through the room, bouncing from tile surface to tile surface.

"I swear it's the truth," he said. "You can ask her when you talk to her. She told me she was going to tell you eventually."

"Let's say for the moment that what you're telling us is true," I said. "Why would you do that?"

He hesitated, then said, "Honestly, because I know what it's like to feel like you're losing the person that you love. Truth is, I'd do anything for her. Plus, this gave me the chance to see her, to spend a little time with her. I haven't gotten to much lately."

"You say you know what it's like to feel like you're losing the person you love, but we just started seeing each other again."

"Dude, she's been carrying a torch for you since the first time you dated."

"Was there really ever anyone harassing her?" I asked.

He nodded. "That prick, Taylor Price," he said. "To be honest, I don't think there was much to it. I mean, I think she saw it as an opportunity to ask for your help, but the guy's an asshole, so I wouldn't be surprised if he fucked with her some once he was finished fuckin' her."

I nodded.

"From what I hear, he's had a hard on to hurt somebody ever since you two made him piss his pants. Fact, he's probably more danger to her now than he was before. It's part of why I was willing to play decoy for her. Somebody needs to be watching over her."

"Bastard may want to take out his frustration on someone, but I doubt it'll be Laura," Merrill said.

The way we were talking, I could almost imagine that she was alive.

"You gonna keep an eye out for her this time?" Fritz asked. "Not get distracted or whatever?"

"We gonna take care of everything," Merrill said. "Don't worry your pretty little head about that."

He held up his hands in a placating gesture. "Hey, I'm not the problem here," he said. "And the first thing you need to do is find her. Where do you think she is?"

"We were hoping you could tell us that," I said.

"Wish I could," he said.

"Where'd you go after you smoked our asses in the eight-hundred meters?" Merrill asked.

"Actually did some more running," he said. "My roommates and I are training for a marathon. We met here, ran for several hours, went to Waffle House for a very late snack, then went home and crashed. If Laura really is missing, I didn't have anything to do with it."

"It's about to go public," Dad said.

Merrill and I were in his office, each of us holding stacks of glossy 8 x 10 prints.

The crime scene and autopsy photographs were graphic, every detail captured from every possible angle. Wide shots establishing context, showing everything in relation to everything else, while close-ups provided the specific horrors.

Laura's once beautiful body, now beaten bloody and disfigured, sat rigid behind the steering wheel of her car. Streaked with dark red and black blood, the strands of her light brown hair were dirty and matted.

As I looked, I found it hard to breathe. Had I done this? Was I capable of such savagery?

I could only look at the pain-filled pictures a moment at a time. Her sweet deer-like face was now purple and puffy, her right eye black and swollen shut.

"No way you did that," Merrill said. "I'd bet my life on it."

Dad nodded. "But we've got to find out who did," he said. "As soon as it comes out that you were with her last night, FDLE will take over the investigation."

I nodded.

Dad's office looked like it had for as long as I could remember, perhaps a little more cluttered, a little more dusty, but not much else had changed in the thirty years he had been on the job. Not one for change, he even had the same desk and filing cabinets.

"Any progress?" he asked.

"Guy I thought most likely is a good friend of hers and was just helping her out."

"Whatta you mean?"

I told him.

"What about the canvas?" Merrill asked.

"Nothing so far," he said.

"Everything we're learning makes it look more and more like it was me," I said.

Merrill shook his head. "All the evidence in the world could point to that, and I still wouldn't believe it."

My eyes stung and I blinked several times. His belief and support were keeping me going. I nodded my thanks to him, not trusting myself to speak.

We were all quiet a few moments.

"You got the prelim?" I asked Dad.

He nodded. "But you don't want to hear it."

Dad looked older already, as if realizing he had raised a murderer had aged him even more.

"I wouldn't have asked if I didn't," I said.

"She was raped and beaten," he said. "It looks like she was choked and took a hard blow to the head. They're not saying for certain yet which one killed her."

I shook my head, picturing what she went through, imagining myself as the one who put her through it.

"Raped as opposed to had intercourse recently?" I asked.

He nodded.

"So there was evidence of violence?"

Dad nodded again, and I could tell he was holding back, careful not to reveal everything the prelim contained, and since what he had told me already was so horrific I was inclined not to press him.

"He raped her," Merrill said, "DNA'll catch his ass and clear yours."

"Only two different types of blood on the body," Dad said. "Hers and another."

I reached up and touched the scratches on my neck. They didn't seem very deep, but I had certainly bled, and if Laura had scratched me, at the very least my blood was beneath her nails.

"They say how much of the foreign blood they found?" I asked.

He shook his head, but he seemed to know more than he was saying.

"Whether I actually killed her or not," I said, "I should've never been in the condition I was, which has put you two in the position you're in now."

They both began to wave off my apology, but my phone rang before they could say anything.

"Hello."

"John?"

"Yeah."

"It's Fritz," he said, sniffling. "I just heard about Laura. Is it true?"

"I'm afraid so," I said. "I'm very sorry."

He broke down, but quickly regained his composure.

"Do they know who did it?" he asked.

"Not yet," I said.

"Swear to me you didn't have anything to do with it," he said.

"What?"

"Did you kill her?"

"No," I said. It came out before I realized what I was saying, and I wondered how convincing it was.

"No, I know you didn't," he said. "I know enough about you from what Laura told me. Sorry I even mentioned it."

"It's okay."

We were quiet a moment.

"I'd bet my life on it being one of two people," he said. "I knew it the minute I heard something had happened."

"Who?"

"That Taylor bastard or her dad."

"Her dad?"

"Ever wonder why she was a virgin until her early thirties, then became like this major nympho?"

"He molested her?" I asked, not surprised, but disappointed I hadn't been more aware of all the signs.

Deep down I knew she was acting like an addict more than someone who just really loved sex, but I didn't want to believe it. I ignored the warnings, suppressed the signs, and exploited her weakness.

"Most of her childhood," he said. "Now he's like this raving, jealous lunatic, like he's a spurned lover or something."

"She was an addict," I said, "but instead of helping her, I exploited her."

"From where I sit in the cheap seats," Merrill said, "you had sex with a consenting adult who pursued you."

I didn't say anything.

We were in Merrill's truck heading back toward Tallahassee to talk to Taylor Price while Dad and his department searched for Laura's father.

"She tell you she's a sex addict?" he asked.

I shook my head. "But I knew something wasn't right."

"She ask for your help?"

"Still," I said, "exploiting someone with a weakness makes me a predator."

"You sure you weren't the prey?"

I turned in the seat and looked at him.

"She try to get you to stop drinking?" he asked. "Or encourage you to?"

I thought about it. She certainly hadn't discouraged me. "She's not responsible for my actions," I said.

"But you responsible for hers?"

"Guess who didn't show up for work this morning?" Dad asked.

"Besides me?" I said.

Merrill and I were outside a warehouse in Railroad Square Art Park not far from FAMU when Dad called. Taylor Price was inside the warehouse, rock climbing.

"Teddy Matthers," he said. "Laura's father."

"You think it's because he was up late killing his daughter and framing me?"

"It crossed my mind," he said.

"Thanks again for all your help with this," I said. "I'm so sorry I—"

"Don't thank me or apologize again," he said.

"Sorry," I said. "And thank you."

He laughed. "How are things on your end?"

"Taylor went out and bought himself some security," I said.

When Taylor Price walked out of the rock climbing gym in his black too-tight silk short shorts and tank top, he did so with the escort of a bodyguard and a bulldog.

The large white bodyguard was wearing black jeans and tennis shoes and a leather jacket over a T-shirt. Given the warm weather, the jacket was no doubt intended to hide his shoulder holster and the semi-automatic it held, but it could be seen when he moved. The huge man, whose neck was the size of a tree trunk, looked like a former NFL linebacker. Obviously a professional, the man moved like money, which Price had to be paying a lot of for the pleasure of his company.

As if the giant wasn't enough, at the end of Taylor's leash was an American pit bull terrier of probably twenty-two inches and eighty pounds, trained to be mean, pulling against the taut leather leash, looking for a fight.

As the three creatures neared their black SUV, Merrill and I stepped out and greeted them.

Fear danced across Taylor's face when he saw us. The pit bull began a low, gravely growl. The bodyguard smiled.

"How can the Fundamentalists look at you two and say that a sacred marriage is only between a man and a woman?" Merrill said.

"The three of you do make a great-looking family," I said.

"How'd you adopt a child that looks so much like your husband?" Merrill asked Taylor, then to the bodyguard, "Or are you the wife?"

"You'll find out when he makes you his bitch," Taylor said. His strained, quivering voice undercutting his threat.

Professional, detached, unflappable, the bodyguard's expression remained placid. Though he didn't show it, I was certain he was sizing us up, evaluating the situation, figuring out his best moves should the balloon go up.

"Zippin' up the bottom of that cool Fonzy jacket probably seemin' like a bad idea 'bout now, don't it?" Merrill said.

Amazingly enough, Merrill didn't seem small next to the man the way the rest of the world did.

"He doesn't need his gun," Taylor said. "Won't be much left for him when Killer gets finished with you."

"You named your kid Killer?" Merrill asked. "Isn't having you for a dad stigma enough?"

"Where were you last night?" I asked.

"Nowhere near where you killed Laura," he said. "Wherever that was."

"We can do this if you want," the bodyguard said, "but he's telling the truth. I wouldn't lie for anyone—no matter how much they pay me—and I can give you references, but you don't have to take my word for it. He was in Jacksonville. We drove in very early this morning. There are dozens of witnesses."

I considered him.

"I protect clients from harm," he said. "Not while they do harm." He held up his hands. "I'm going into my right front pocket for one of my cards." He did, then handed it to me. "I can also give you hotel, restaurant, and gas receipts. You can even ask the keynote speaker—the governor—who had a couple of drinks with Mr. Price following the conference."

"The more we learn, the more guilty I look," I said.

With just a few calls, Dad had confirmed that Taylor Price had been at a conference in Jacksonville and had not returned before Laura had been killed.

"Still the father," Merrill said.

I shook my head. "I've got a feeling he'll be my third strike."

"Then there's the random serial killer stumbling on the scene," he said. "Odds still better than it being you."

My phone rang and I answered it.

"John," Dad said, "remember the scenario we talked about earlier."

"FDLE finding out about me and taking over the investigation?"

"It's just happened," he said. "Special Agent Scott wants you here as fast as you can or he says he's coming after you."

"I'm on my way now," I said.

When I stepped out of Merrill's truck in front of the Potter County Court House, two FDLE agents were waiting for me. I could tell who they were because of their caps and windbreakers, both of which had FDLE printed across them in large block letters.

I walked toward them.

As I did, a man carrying a small revolver jumped out of a car and rushed me. With only a quick glance, I knew it was Teddy Matthers, Laura's father.

"You murdering cocksucker," he shouted. "You think you gonna kill my little girl and keep breathing? You sick motherfucker."

He began firing the gun, rounds ricocheting all around me.

Unable to move, I just stood there. He obviously hadn't killed his daughter, which meant I had.

The two agents turned and pulled their weapons.

"No," I yelled, and stepped in front of them.

One of them pushed me aside, knocking me to the ground, but before they could fire at Teddy, Merrill had come up behind him and wrestled him to the ground, relieving him of the revolver in the process.

"You keep saying you don't remember what happened," Special Agent Fred Scott was saying.

He was a middle-aged white man with a toughness about him. He hadn't spent his career in a classroom or behind a desk, but on the street. His balding head reflected the dull light of the florescent bulbs and his cold gray eyes were in a state of perpetual squint.

"I don't," I said.

"But you had the presence of mind to bring her into your dad's jurisdiction before you finished her off."

I hadn't thought of it that way, but he was right. The fact that we wound up in Potter County made me look all the more like a cold-hearted, calculating bastard who had committed premeditated murder.

"You were smart to bring her here," he said. "And if we hadn't gotten involved in the case, who knows, you might have gotten away with it. But we are involved and we're gonna fuckin' fry your fuckin' ass if you don't come clean and admit what you did."

We were in an interview room in the Potter County Sheriff's office. We appeared to be alone, but I knew we weren't. I wasn't sure who was beyond the plate glass mirrored window, but I knew we were being observed and recorded.

"Come on," he said. "We got your blood and cum and prints. The evidence is overwhelming. We'll get a conviction. Piece-a-cake, **but be a man and tell us in your own words what happened. Don't make her family suffer through a long, drawn-out trial. At least give them that.**"

"I wish I could," I said.

After letting me sit in a holding cell for a couple of hours, they had dumped me in here where I sat for a while longer. My head throbbed. My eyes stung. I was weak and weary, and felt like I might fall over any moment.

"I want you to see what you did to her," he said, stepping over to the door. Opening it, he yelled, "Why's it taking so long to get the goddam crime scene photos down here. . . ? What. . . ? Why the hell not. . .? Who the fuck—?"

Slamming the door, he took three quick steps and bent down in my face.

"Why'd you take your dad's copies of the crime scene photos?" he asked. "Couldn't stand for him to see what his son had done to a sweet, innocent, kind, vulnerable, beautiful young woman?"

"I didn't—"

"She wasn't beautiful when you finished with her, was she?" he asked.

I didn't say anything, images of Laura's bruised and beaten face flashing in my mind.

"After you strangled and sodomized her," he continued. "And beat her until her own mother couldn't recognize her. Hell, she's still hoping her little girl's gonna come home to her, but she's not, is she? Her parents and her little sister are gonna have to have a closed casket funeral for her, aren't they? You made good and goddam sure of that, didn't you? You piece of shit. How could you do such a thing? What'd she do to you? Tell me. I want to know. She make fun of your little pecker? She tell you she was fuckin' other men? She tell you' No' when you told her you wanted to fuck her up the ass?"

I took a very deep breath and let it out slowly, reminding myself to remain calm. "I honestly don't know what happened," I said.

"Bullshit."

"Give me a polygraph," I said. "If it proves I'm not lying, then hypnotize me to see if what happened is locked inside my head somehow. I want to know as much as you do."

Before he could respond, there was a tap on the door and it was opened by another FDLE agent who asked to speak with him.

He was gone a while, and as I sat there in the small cold room alone, I became overwhelmed and began to cry.

It was embarrassing. I knew people were watching, but I couldn't stop. When I thought about what I had done, I just couldn't imagine it. How could I live with myself? How could I not do to myself what Laura's father had failed to do? My life was over. Everything was gone. Nothing would ever be the same again.

The pressure bearing down on me was crushing. Until this moment, I had hoped I might find out that I hadn't done it after all, that I really wasn't capable, but now I knew. Now, confronted with the man I was, I just couldn't take it.

I thought about Anna, about Mom. What must they think of me?

I couldn't blame this on alcohol. This was me—who I was.

The door opened, and Scott walked back in.

"I'm very sorry, Mr. Jordan," he said. "I was just doing my job. I hope you can understand."

I didn't say anything, just wiped the tears from my eyes and sniffed.

"You're free to go," he said.

"What?" I asked. "Why?"

"Think I'll let your friend tell you about that," he said. "And again, I'm very sorry."

When I stepped out of the interview room and started down the hall, I saw Merrill standing at the end of it in a dark suit and tie, a detective shield on his belt, a .45 clipped on the side.

I walked toward him.

"What's going on?" I asked when I reached him.

"Told you," he said. "You didn't do it."

He turned and began to walk toward the door, and I fell in step with him.

"You impersonating an officer?" I asked.

"I made an arrest," he said.

I nodded.

"At the time, it was false arrest and imprisonment and I's impersonating an officer, but your dad backed me up and even deputized me eventually—which was good of him considerin' I stole his crime scene photos."

"You solved the case?"

"And got a confession," he said.

"How?"

"It was easy," he said. "All I did was WWJJD. What Would John Jordan Do?"

I smiled.

"I thought about how obsessed Laura was with you," he said. "By the way, found out some more about that. You really was the prey, not the predator. She never was followed or harassed. Only thing Taylor did was break up with her."

I nodded.

We reached the door and walked outside into the darkness and over toward his truck, but didn't get in.

"In my WWJJD mode I realized that Laura wasn't the only one obsessed," he said.

"There are other women obsessed with me?"

He shook his head. "All other women obsessed with me," he said. "But there was a cat obsessed with Laura."

"Fritz," I said.

"You good at WWJJD," he said.

I laughed.

"He killed her?"

"Looped back around after we chased his ass," he said. "He's hoping for a little gratitude, maybe he finally get to tap that ass like she been hinting and what does he see but you two back together. He follows the two of you, his rage building. At the landing he finds you passed out and her asleep and decides to collect on what she owes him. Says he didn't mean to kill her, that she hit her head on a cypress knee, but I ain't buying that."

"You're truly amazing," I said. "I know I don't mention it too much."

"*Can't* mention it *too* much," he said.

"I'll step it up," I said.

"I remember him saying he *was* her best friend," he said. "He covered by saying he meant he was until you came along, but he already knew she was dead 'cause it was his fast ass self that killed her."

I thought about Merrill being in his CO uniform the first time we met with Fritz. "Did he really think you were a detective?"

He nodded. "Told him my CO uniform was a deputy uniform," he said. "And that I had just been promoted to plainclothes detective."

"He confess to you?"

"I brought him into one of the conference rooms, made sure it was being recorded," he said. "Acted like I knew just what the fuck I was doin'. Felt like Denzel playin' a cop—'cept I look better. Told him we had his DNA—blood, semen, saliva—then I laid all the crime scene photos out on the table in front of him and sympathized with him about what a faithless slut she was and how she had no taste in men and pretty soon I couldn't get him to shut up. Hell, I thought he was gonna confess to being the gunman on the grassy knoll."

I smiled. "You're a good cop," I said. "Dad could partner you and Jake up and—"

"I just saved your life," he said.

"You really did," I said.

"You've done it for me a time or two in the past," he said.

"Did he say how I got the scratches on my neck and the blood on my hands?"

"Say she was grabbing for you as he pullin' her out the car," he said.

My heart ached, my stomach sank as I thought about Laura reaching out to me for help. I had been unable to help her only because I had gotten drunk.

"When he put her back in the car he grabbed your arms rubbed your hands in her blood," he continued. "Tryin' to set you up."

We were quiet a moment as I thought about everything.

"Thank you," I said. "I'm really—"

"Once is enough," he said. "Don't mention it again."

"That'll be difficult," I said.

"Your dad said to tell you he'll come by your place later," he said. "He's booking Fritz and givin' Scott hell for messin' with his son."

We got in his truck.

"Come on," he said. "I'm droppin' your ass off at a meeting while I go get some WWJJD bracelets printed up."

Image of Blood

My mother had drunk herself to death. She just wasn't dead yet.

As if a metaphor of her life, the room Mom was spending her final days in was dark and depressingly empty, and she had resisted all attempts on my part to change it.

"There's something I need you to do for me," she said.

Her pale, once beautiful face flickered in the light from a cable channel on an old television at the end of her bed.

"Anything," I said.

"I want you to solve a mystery for me," she said.

"What?" I asked.

"I just watched a special on the Shroud of Turin," she said. "I've got to know if it's real. I want you to investigate it for me."

For a moment, I didn't say anything, her request so bizarre as to render me speechless. "What?" I asked. "Why?"

"A woman in Turin was healed as she gazed upon it," she said.

"The Shroud?"

"Yeah."

I shook my head.

I thought we were past this. Over the last several months, I had witnessed my mom, in nearly textbook fashion, pass from denial to anger to bargaining to depression to what I thought was a place of acceptance. Either I had been wrong about where she was, or she was reverting to an earlier stage.

"If it's real," she said. "I mean really the burial cloth of Christ, then I believe I can be healed by gazing into Jesus' face at the moment of his resurrection. It's being displayed next month. If you find out it's real, I want you to take me to see it."

I found myself still unable to respond.

Never particularly religious before, lately Mom had become increasingly and desperately superstitious. It depressed me to think that I had failed to help her, finding myself awkward and impotent with her where I was usually confident and helpful with others.

"Do you know anything about it?" she asked.

"Just what makes the headlines."

"Don't you want to know?" she said. "Why haven't you ever studied it?"

I shrugged.

"Really," she said. "I want to know."

"I'm not sure," I said, though I was. "I guess I've just always assumed it wasn't real, but even if it is, it's not really relevant to my faith."

She shook her head in incomprehension. "What does that mean?"

"I'm always very leery of anything that claims to prove—especially scientifically—matters of faith. Matters that by their very nature cannot be proven."

"But still," she said. "I don't understand why you wouldn't want to know if it's real."

"It's not that I don't want to know," I said. "It's—I guess I really think we *can't* know. But like I said, either way, it's not relevant to what I believe. If it's real, it won't increase my faith. If it's not, it won't decrease it."

Talking about faith reminded me of just how much I had been questioning mine lately—not from a belief or doctrinal perspective, but from one of meaning and usefulness. I was finding it increasingly difficult to feel fulfilled in my work as a prison chaplain and wondered if I might make a greater contribution by doing something else with my life.

"Not everyone has faith as strong as yours, John," she said.

I laughed. "Nothing about me is strong," I said. "Especially my faith."

"You can't really believe that," she said. "You're so strong. So . . . you help so many people."

"Thanks," I said, "but you're obviously looking through the eyes of love."

"They're the only ones I have," she said.

We were silent a moment, I, wondering if I could really do what she was asking of me.

"Will you investigate the Shroud for me?"

I nodded. "I'm not sure what I can do," I said, "but I'll look into it and let you know."

"And if it's authentic, will you take me to Italy to see it?" she asked.

"Sure," I said, believing I was merely making an empty promise to a desperate and dying woman.

On my way home, I stopped by the public library and checked out the only three books they had on the Shroud of Turin. When I got home, I looked it up on the Internet as I ate the pizza I had ordered from Sal's.

I was surprised to find so much information and interest about the Shroud online, but I guess I shouldn't have been. It seemed that in the last several years, interest in the Shroud had increased and intensified. There were hundreds of books, journals, and articles, many of them new, and thousands of web sites. There would be no lack of evidence in this case, no shortage of clues.

As I read, I was surprised and a little amused to find that I was almost immediately caught up in the mystery of the most studied relic in human history, and the more I learned, the more the enigmatic image on the shroud began to haunt me.

Was I looking into the face of God?

Was I a fool even to ask such a question?

When I finished my preliminary reading, I knew a lot more about the world's most famous textile.

The Shroud of Turin is a well-preserved oblong linen cloth over fourteen feet long and nearly four feet wide. One side of the cloth bears the front and back images of a man appearing to be laid out in death. The fact that there are two views, both front and back, seems to indicate that the man of the Shroud was laid upon it, his head coming roughly to the center. Then it was folded to cover the front of his body. The faint sepia image appears to be scorched or lightly burned onto the surface of the off-white linen.

In addition to the scorched images, brownish and carmine-colored marks throughout, said to be blood stains, are heaviest at the wrists, feet, and a wound on the right side of the body. There are also many smaller stains covering the front and back of the image believed by many to be evidence of blood resulting from the beating, whipping, and thorn-piercing of the body.

According to the gospels, Jesus was removed from the cross and placed in a tomb, where he was wrapped in cloth in accordance with Jewish custom. But few, if any, records exist from that time to detail the burial cloth's whereabouts.

The Shroud of Turin became public in 1349, when a French knight named Geoffrey de Charny was said to have acquired it in Constantinople and brought it to the attention of Pope Clement VI. The Shroud was held in a church in Lirey, France, and was first shown publicly in 1355.

Since that first exhibition, many have questioned the Shroud's authenticity since forging religious artifacts was big business during medieval times.

After reading a description of the shroud, I carefully examined the best picture I could find of it.

I recalled reading a headline several years ago about the carbon-dating tests administered on the Shroud, but decided to treat this like any other investigation—taking the evidence as it came and maintaining an open mind.

I decided to start with the substance on the Shroud. Was it paint or blood? Even if blood were present, it still might not be the blood of Jesus, but if it weren't blood, then all other questions and evidence were irrelevant.

My next question was about the body image—not only how it was made, but also if there was any dimensionality to it, and were the wounds it depicted anatomically correct?

A whole pizza and most of a book later, I looked up and punched in a number I hadn't used in a very long time.

"I need to know about the Shroud of Turin," I said into the receiver.

If the Shroud of Turin had paint instead of blood and drawing marks rather than unique scorch marks on it, my investigation would be complete, my life less complicated. Still, I wasn't sure that's what I wanted to hear—and not just for Mom. I, too, was beginning to feel the powerful pull of the irresistible icon.

"John Jordan?" Paul asked. "It couldn't be. I heard he was dead. Who is this?"

Paul Roberts and I had gone to seminary together at Candler and after graduation, he had remained behind to work on a Ph.D. He was now a full professor and noted scholar. He was also an expert on the Shroud of Turin.

"The rumors of my death were greatly exaggerated," I said.

He laughed.

After catching up for a few minutes, he said, "What do you need to know?"

"Is it real?"

"Of course it's real," he said. "Haven't you seen the pictures?"

Same old Paul.

"But is it authentic?" I asked.

"Ah, now that *is* the question, isn't it? Are you asking if it's really a burial shroud or *the* burial shroud of Jesus?"

"Tell you what, professor," I said. "I'll ask the questions and you answer them, okay?"

"Okay."

"Do you harass your students like this?"

"Is that one of your questions?" he asked.

"It depends on how many I get."

"Well, I'm a very important academician and I have to give a speech at a dinner in about an hour," he said. "You do the math."

"Okay, I'll just ask you a few questions about the image of the body and the stains of blood and call you back as I continue my study."

"You promise?" he said.

"I'm glad you decided not to become a pastor," I said.

"Bedside manner is overrated," he said. "You want a doctor who knows what he's doing or one that's nice to you?"

"You think the same is true of clergy?" I asked.

"How the hell would I know?" he said. "I didn't go into pastoral ministry. You tell me."

"Tell me about the Shroud first," I said.

"Whatta you wanna know?"

"Is it a painting?"

"You're asking: Does it have paint on it or is it a painting?" he said.

"What's the difference?"

"It has paint on it," he said. "It's not a painting. In 1978, the Shroud of Turin Research Project or STURP, examined the Shroud with the most sophisticated equipment available at the time. They discovered that there are no pigments, paints, or dyes present in the formation of the image. They also found that there are no brush stokes or directionality of any type which would be characteristic of an artist's painting."

"But—"

"I'm not finished," he said. "Also, renowned artist Lisa Picket of San Francisco said that 'the practiced arts come to the conclusion that the Shroud is definitely not a painting or the result of manipulation by a medieval artist. While the technology of our own age has mastered outer space exploration, we are still at a loss to explain the image on the Shroud or make another Turin Shroud. It is not the result of invention.'"

"I'm impressed," I said. "Was that all off the top of your head?"

"I give over a hundred presentations on the shroud a year," he said. "My wife says I say this stuff in my sleep."

"How exciting for her," I said. "Now, can I have a straight answer? Is there paint present or not?"

"There is an incidental amount of artists' pigments on the surface."

"And?"

"And, this led some, including Dr. William McDaniel to conclude that the Shroud was a forgery made with paint," he said.

"But you don't think so?" I asked.

"No," he said. "I agree with McDaniel's fellow members of the STURP, Holt and Allen, who said that it had nothing to do with the body image."

"Then how'd it get there?" I asked.

"I don't know," he said.

"But you have a theory," I said.

"We're talkin' about the most holy icon in history," he said. "Think about it. There's only one. It can only be in one place at a time—until, presto-copyo, they traced and copied it."

"So the paint came from attempts to reproduce it."

"That or some senile old monk used it for a drop cloth when he was re-doing his abbey."

"What?"

"I'm saying it's the most widely recognized and reasonable theory. The truth is we're talking about somethin' that could potentially be several centuries to thousands of years old. It's come in contact with everything imaginable during that time, so a little paint shouldn't surprise anyone. The bottom line is the image is not paint."

"But is it blood?"

"No."

"No?"

"It's scorch or burn marks of the body and *some* blood stains."

"I'm amazed you're not a literalist," I said.

"Just tryin' to be precise."

"Tell me about the scorch marks," I said. "What made them?"

"We don't know," he said. "There's nothing else like it in the world. No other body has ever left such a mark on anything. And if it were a painting, then it's the first outline-less painting in existence. Every artist uses an outline—especially when working on something fourteen feet long, but there's not one on the shroud. And another thing, the color of the image is nearly indistinguishable. I mean it's one color, yet the image is almost three dimensional, and the closer you get to it, the more the image disappears into the cloth. You really have to be a least six feet away from it to see it, so if an artist did it, he'd have to have used a six-foot brush."

"What about—"

"I'm not finished," he said. "The image seems *not* to be the result of something being added to the linen, but something being taken away. It's a chemical change. The marks seem to be the result of those areas aging faster. Like a newspaper yellowing in the sun-light. The STURP concluded that they were created by a phenom-enon, as yet unknown, or a momentous event that caused a rapid cellulose degradation oxidation of the very top linen fibrils of the cellulose fibers of the Shroud, thereby creating a straw-colored im-age similar to that of a scorch. And one last thing, when STURP flooded the Shroud with transmitted light from behind, the blood stains showed up very well—presumably because they're substantial and solid, but the body image barely showed up at all."

"So there *is* blood on the shroud?" I asked. "Not paint or pigment or dye?"

"Yes," he said. "The late Dr. Joseph Hellen identified the blood on the Shroud as being mammalian, primate, and probably human. Dr. Peter Lowenstein, professor of forensic medicine at the

Turin University, has stated that the blood on the Shroud is human with characteristics appearing to belong to type AB."

"So, there's scientific evidence that there's actual blood on it," I said, excitement filling my voice.

"Yeah," he said. "But that doesn't mean it's the blood of Jesus."

"Yeah," I said. "That's true."

"But it is a shroud that wrapped a real human body that had undergone a real-life crucifixion. There are blood stains and post-mortem blood spillage to indicate injuries caused by severe whipping, various incidental abuse, such as a crown of thorns and beatings, piercings of the feet and wrists, and a bladed weapon being driven through the side of the chest. Ring any bells?"

"Just one."

"Have you seen pictures of the Shroud?" he asked.

"Yeah."

"Did you notice the two blood flows near the visible wrist?"

"Yeah."

"Those trickles could only have been made by the arms being stretched out sideways at a sixty-five degree angle."

"In other words," I said. "A crucifixion position."

"Exactly," he said. "And, it depicts the nails having been driven through the wrists, not the hands, which is the way most artists have erroneously painted them for thousands of years. And did you notice you can't see his thumbs on the Shroud?"

"Yeah."

"That's because the nails were driven through the wrists, which means they severed the median nerve, which triggered a motor reaction—the thumbs snapped into the palms. That's just one way the Shroud's images and injuries are anatomically and forensically correct."

I thought about what he was saying. There was far more to this mystery than I realized.

"And get this," he said. "Whatever made the image, what-

ever precipitated this rapid aging, affected only the very top fibrils—
the images are a surface phenomenon, but the blood stains seeped
down into the fabric. And, the blood stains were on the shroud
before the image was formed, and there is no image in the area of
bloodstains. The blood somehow impeded the image from forming."

"Which means?"

"That if a forger had painted or created the image and then
added human blood to make it realistic, wouldn't he have had to
make the image first and then added the blood afterward?"

The sun seemed to be trying to make up for what it had missed
during the rainy, overcast morning, steam rising from the sizzling
wet asphalt, the remaining raindrops on the hood of my S-10 bak-
ing off. Inside, in the absence of air conditioning, Mom and I cooked.

"I'm about ready to be flipped," she said. "And in another
few minutes, I'll be ready to serve."

"Sorry," I said.

A drive to the coast to get her out of her death room had
sounded like a good idea when it was still cloudy and overcast.

"It's okay," she said. "I'm just happy to be here with you.
The sun will be down soon."

The descending sun set the tops of the slash pines to the
west ablaze in front of an artist's bold splash of pink and orange
that cast elongated shadows across the road like backlit window
blinds.

"Why don't you buy a new car?" she asked. "You can afford
it, can't you?"

"I had a lot of debt after the divorce," I said. "I'm still chip-
ping away at it."

We rode for a while in silence, the monotonous uniformity
of the seemingly endless rows of pines on either side of us only

occasionally giving way to an open field or pasture where cattle nuzzled their way through the damp grass. The sound of running water from the flowing ditches mixed with the wind whispering through the pines created a lonely, empty sound in the absence of our conversation.

"I'm sorry, John," Mom said, turning away from her window to look at me. "For the kind of mother I was. For what I put you through, for what you inherited from me."

No matter how many times she apologized, it never sounded real. Not that I doubted her sincerity. I didn't. Maybe it was the way her confession lent credibility to everything I felt—the verbalization of my nightmares in the waking world. Hearing her speak aloud our secrets prevented me from maintaining my normal distance and defense when I could almost imagine I was thinking of someone else—my doppelgänger, perhaps, and his mom. Her words confirmed my fears, her acts of contrition confronted my denial, and I never knew quite what to say.

I glanced over at her.

Mom's dark brown hair was quickly becoming gray, her deep brown eyes, though finally clear, were sad and longing. Her face held no visible sign of emotion, just the too-early deep lines of a life lived hard. She was still pretty, and occasionally when she smiled, you could see just how beautiful she had once been.

When I was a child, we were very close. Far more alike than anyone else in the family, we shared an understanding nearly conspiratorial in its intimacy. I never doubted her love or adoration—until it was withdrawn from me to be lavished on her existential melancholy and the elixirs she used to mute it all too briefly.

"I don't want to die," she said. "I'm not ready."

My eyes began to sting as I nodded my understanding, glancing over at her, realizing just how unprepared for her departure I, too, was.

"Too much left to do," she continued. "I've just started living again."

"But some people never do," I said. "You've used the gift of death to—"

"No," she said, shaking her head violently. "It's not a gift. It's an enemy. It's not right. It's not supposed to be this way. This isn't natural. This isn't what God planned."

I didn't say anything. Her opinions on this subject were far more relevant than mine.   "Am I a fool?" she asked.

"What?"

"To believe I could actually be healed," she continued. "To believe that the Shroud might be a conduit of God's special grace for me? Is it just desperation? Just a last foolish act?"

I slowed down as the road ended at the Gulf of Mexico. When we came to a stop, I checked my rearview mirror and discovering that there was no one behind us, sat for a moment, and stared at the calm, key lime-colored waters as they gently caressed the brilliant white sands of the shore. The setting sun shimmered across the surface, its soft glow refracting off it like a rain of fireworks sparks.

"I don't know," I said. "I *do* know that all acts of faith involve a certain degree of foolishness. They're illogical, unreasonable, so of course they seem foolish."

She nodded, seeming to think about it, to attempt to knead some reassurance out of it.

We took a left on Highway 98 and drove slowly through the growing town of Mexico Beach. The beaches were empty, the tourists conspicuously missing from the hotels and shops with CLOSED signs hanging in their windows.

"Do you believe in divine healing?" she asked.

I nodded.

"What do you believe?"

I shrugged. "I don't have beliefs as much as openness to possibilities," I said.

"What about the Shroud?" she asked. "Can God use it to heal me? Is it real?"

I shrugged. "She can use anything," I said. "Her grace is in all things and all things can be conduits of that grace. I think it comes down to where or in what or whom we can most readily find that grace. If that's the Shroud for you—"

"It could be," she said, "but only if it's real. Is it?"

"I don't know," I said. "I've just started looking into it. It's going to take a while. I'm trying to be thorough."

"Just don't take *too* long," she said.

"I won't."

"What have you found out so far?"

I told her.

"So you think there really is blood on it?"

"It appears to be," I said. "An ancient DNA specialist confirmed the presence of male DNA on the Shroud. And every one of the wounds is consistent with a victim of crucifixion. And many forensic pathologists have confirmed that the wounds and blood flows are anatomically correct."

I could see hope beginning to expand inside her, and though I feared it was premature, it improved her countenance so much I continued.

"There's no explanation for how the image got there either," I said. "It's like a faint burn mark, almost like a picture. In fact, it shows up better as a photo negative than it does as a positive. And there doesn't seem to be any way an ancient forger could've done it. So far, no one has been able to duplicate it—even using modern technology."

"So it could be . . . ," she asked, unable to keep the excitement out of her voice.

I shrugged. "I'm still skeptical," I said. "You probably shouldn't get your hopes up just yet."

"But how can I not?" she asked. "It seems that all the evidence is pointing to it being authentic."

"Not all of it," I said. "I've just glanced over it. I'm going to try to study it some more soon, but it looks as if the presence of blood on the Shroud contradicts Jewish burial customs."

"How?"

"From what I've found, the Jewish custom was and still is to wash all the blood off a body before it's buried. And I haven't even gotten to the carbon-dating tests yet."

"I just feel like I'm giving her false hope," I said.

"Are you?" he asked.

I was sitting in Milton Warner's office on Grace Avenue in downtown Panama City. A former Episcopal Priest, he was now a licensed counselor with a private practice in a small converted house. A fellow recovering alcoholic and sometime skeptic, Milton and I had a lot in common, and I always felt better for having talked to him—which made me wonder why I didn't do it more often.

"In one sense, I'm not sure," I said. "In another, almost certainly."

"Explain."

Clear, empathic blue eyes beneath thick gray hair, Milton was kind and soft-spoken, but often very direct. The spider web of lines on his face speaking to his experience and explaining the wisdom that issued forth from his mouth.

"Part of me thinks I shouldn't be doing this at all," I said. "That it's ridiculous to even consider."

"That would be the skeptical side," he said with a smile.

I nodded, flashing a smile of my own.

"The other side of me says anything's possible, and at this stage in her, life false hope is better than no hope at all."

"Do you really believe that?"

"Obviously I'm conflicted," I said. "It's why I'm here."

He smiled. "Conflicted, huh?"

"I think her time could be spent much better than looking for a miracle," I said.

"How?"

"Preparing," I said.

"To die?"

His question hit me harder than I would have thought, and all I could do was nod.

"How do you feel about that?"

"What?" I asked, stalling, my voice sounding trapped inside my constricting throat.

"Your mom dying," he said.

"We haven't been very close," I said. "Since I was in my early teens—but the closer we get to her death, the more I feel, the more it bothers me."

"Have you talked to her about how you feel?"

"Some," I said. "Not much."

"Is it possible it's not just her time that could be better spent?" he asked.

I nodded. "It's why I'm here," I said.

"So where's the conflict?"

"I wouldn't've believed it," I said, "but there's something so compelling about the Shroud."

"Really?"

I nodded.

"You becoming a believer?"

I shook my head. "At this point, all I can say is that I'm still open," I said, "and that really surprises me."

"Could it be that you're looking for a little hope, too?"

"False hope?"

"Any kind," he said. "You still questioning what you're doing at the prison?"

I nodded.

"Are you planning on leaving?"

"Got no plans at the moment," I said. "Just trying to figure things out."

"Good luck with that," he said, smiling.

"Okay, not things," I said. "Me. I'm trying to figure out why I'm feeling the way I do."

"Which is?"

"Empty," I said. "Lonely—in an existential way."

"Like there's no God?"

"Like there might not be," I said. "I sure don't feel her like I once did."

"Yet you're open to the possibility that the Shroud of Turin could be genuine?"

I thought about it, then nodded slowly.

"Then you're not too far gone, are you?"

When I couldn't sleep, which was most nights, I found various ways to occupy my time—most often reading in a booth at Rudy's Diner.

I was seated in the last booth in the back corner next to the humidity-covered plate-glass window that looked out onto the dark night. The night sky was filled with clouds, their thick gray masses shrouding the moon and stars. Beneath them, the empty rural highway and the oyster shell parking lot were damp from a shower earlier in the evening.

On the table in front of me, I had arranged all the books and articles I had found on the Shroud of Turin, a pad on which I made notes, and a large glass of Cherry Coke.

"You want another Coke?" Carla asked.

"Thanks," I said.

Carla was Rudy's teenage daughter, and while he sat in front of the television drinking and watching reruns of old sitcoms, she worked all night in the diner. In the mornings, while he slept it off, she served breakfast and rushed off to school and made mostly A's.

Rudy's wasn't busy late at night, and after she had done her homework, Carla would lay her head down on the counter and steal brief snatches of restless sleep.

She set the Cherry Coke on the table in front of me, and I looked up at her. She was strikingly beautiful, the way her mother was before she ran off and left them. Even with a soiled apron and strands of blond hair falling down around her face she was stunning—the fact that at seventeen she wore a soiled apron and a tired face beneath falling hair, made her all the more so.

She slid into the seat across from me.

"Whatta you studying?" she asked.

"The Shroud of Turin."

"How can you stand the excitement?" she asked with a cute, slightly mischievous smile.

"I'm a trained professional," I said.

Carla's beauty wasn't model beauty, and it certainly wasn't Miss Teen USA beauty. It was a wise and tough beauty that had been forged on her face in the cauldron of hardship and pain.

"Don't grow up and marry an alcoholic," I said.

"Wait, wait, I know this one," she said. "Because being the child of one and all, I'm far more likely to?"

I smiled. "I've mentioned this before?"

"A few times," she said.

"Has it sunk in yet?"

"A couple more thousand times should do it."

"Sorry," I said.

She shook her head. "I appreciate the concern."

We grew silent a moment. She looked out the window into the night. I watched her, then followed her gaze.

As usual, the diner was cold. I could feel the frigid laminate seat beneath me through my jeans and the moisture on the glass resembled a glacier beginning to thaw.

"My mom married an alcoholic," she said, still staring out into the darkness. "But she remedied it."

"But at what cost?" I said.

"Yeah," she said, turning toward me. "Not much to her." Suddenly, her demeanor turned as icy as the diner. "Don't worry, I wouldn't do that to my kids."

"Have you thought anymore about that ACOA group?"

"And when exactly would I go to it?" she asked, glancing around at the diner.

"I can line somebody up to watch the diner," I said. "You can ride with me. I'll take care of everything."

She smiled.

"What?"

"You try," she said.

"What is it?"

"To take care of everything—of everyone. But you can't, you know. Hasn't your sponsor told you that?"

I laughed at how obvious I was, even to a seventeen-year-old with far more important things on her mind. "A time or two," I said.

The heavy pungent scent of old grease and stale cigarette smoke—even though people only smoked in the bathrooms since the law changed—still hung in the air, its presence like a dingy olfactory film on everything. In the corner, a drooping potted plant was turning brown, and I wasn't sure if it was because of the arctic climate or the thick smog. It wasn't just the customers Rudy was killing.

"They call that caretaking, don't they?" she asked with another smile. "Or is it just a messiah-complex?"

"Something like that," I said.

"There a cure?"

"Getting a life," I said. "Or just getting laid."

She smiled.

We were quiet another moment, and I watched as her gaze followed a passing car, its headlights shimmering on the wet pavement of the empty highway out front.

"Wonder where they're going," she said.

Within a moment, the night had swallowed up the tiny lights of the car into its black void again, but she continued to stare down the dark highway.

Eventually, she turned back toward me.

"So, is that thing for real?" she asked, nodding toward a picture of the Shroud on the cover of one of the books.

"That's what I'm trying to find out."

"Why?" she asked. "Why does it matter?"

I shrugged. "I guess it doesn't," I said. "At least not to me, but it's real important to my mom."

"Taking care of her, too?"

"Yes, Dr. Fraud, I guess I'm trying to," I said.

She scratched her nose slowly, a subtle way of giving me the finger.

"You considering becoming a shrink?" I asked.

"I've been leaning toward exotic dancer," she said. "But I'm keeping all my options open."

She slid out of the seat and walked back behind the counter. "I'll let you get back to saving the world," she said. "I've got to get some sleep."

I returned to my books while she straightened up, the loud clatter of plates and glasses directed toward Rudy in the back, though I was sure he had already passed out.

Previously, it had been believed that the Jewish burial custom was to wash a body prior to its burial. And this had been confirmed for me by several sources, both ancient and modern. That being the case, the body of Jesus wouldn't have had blood on it to deposit onto the Shroud.

However, there was and still is an exception to this custom found in Maurice Lamm's, *The Jewish Way in Death and Mourning*:

"The blood that flows at the time of death may not be washed away. When there is other blood on the body that flowed during lifetime, from wounds or as a result of an operation, the washing and taharah [purification] are performed in the usual manner.

Where the deceased died instantaneously through violence or accident, and his body and garments are completely spattered with blood, no washing or taharah is performed. The blood is part of the body and may not be separated from it in death.

Where blood flows continually after death, the source of the flow is covered and not washed. The clothes which contain the blood that flowed after death are placed in the casket at the feet."

So Jesus was buried in the traditional Jewish custom and his body was covered in blood. But was that what stained the Shroud of Turin?

When Carla had finished straightening up, she put in a load of dishes to wash, brushed her teeth, and sat down and put her head on the counter.

"Goodnight," she said without opening her eyes.

"Good night, sweet princess," I said.

She smiled. "I know this one," she said. "Hamlet, right?"

"With a minor change."

"Minor?" she asked. "If Hamlet had been a princess rather than a prince, none of that shit would've happened."

"So the greatest tragedy ever written is the result of testosterone?"

"Nearly all tragedies are," she said with a smile.

She then closed her eyes, and I went back to work. A few minutes later, she lifted her head up slightly and said, "Thanks for being here."

"Thanks for having me."

As I continued to read, I found an argument put forth by a number of Shroud researchers concerning the dust and debris covering the surface of the Shroud. They contended that the constituents coating the Shroud would be indicative of the environments it had been in before its discovery. For example, if it were exposed to a modern industrial area, it might have fly ash from power stations and lead from the exhausts of engines still operating on leaded fuel.

Dr. Matt Frey was the first to take sticky-tape samples from the Shroud and search for pollen. He was followed by the STURP What they found was amazing. In addition to finding pollen that seemed to confirm the shrouds authenticity, they also discovered another explanation for the presence of the various sprinklings of paint particles on the shroud.

Without ever having been touched by the hand of an artist, the Shroud could have acquired its faint residue of pigment or paint from its home in Turin. In virtually every room of the Royal Palace in Turin where the team examined the shroud, the ceilings were richly decorated with frescoes from which tiny paint fragments would fall like confetti as they worked below.

Before his death, Dr. Frey had identified pollen from fifty-eight different plant species, many of which corresponded with the Shroud's documented travels around Western Europe. However, the most startling of his discoveries were those of plant pollens that are indicative of Near East environs, most notably the Dead Sea and Jerusalem. This is significant, since the Shroud has only a documented history dating back to the fourteenth century and only in Western Europe.

Not only had the Shroud visually satisfied the criteria for everything that might be expected of the burial of a first-century Jew crucified in the manner of Jesus of Nazareth, but also its own intrinsic physical evidence was indicative of the same.

The next question I had was whether there were other burial cloths. Had other ancient shrouds been discovered?

To my surprise, they had.

A number of ancient burial cloths still existed, though none of them was from Israel, since they didn't embalm the bodies of their dead. But Egypt and other places had burial cloths as old as or older than the Shroud—even if it had covered the body of Jesus of Nazareth. However, no other shrouds had images on them.

The more I studied, the more I concluded that it was no wonder so many people found the Shroud convincing. I had much more to cover, some entire books actually written to refute the Shroud's authenticity, but there was so much that couldn't be explained, so much that seemed to suggest that the Shroud was utterly unique in the world.

Another cloth associated with Christ's burial, the Sudarium, or face cloth of Oviedo, is said to be the cloth used to cover Jesus' face when he was first taken down from the cross. Unlike the Shroud of Turin, the Sudarium of Oviedo, named such because of it's location in the Cathedral of Oviedo in Oviedo, Spain, had a documented history. It stayed in Jerusalem until A.D. 614, when it began to move from place to place just ahead of conquering Persian armies. It was moved to Alexander in North Africa, Cartagena in Spain, then to Toledo before finally reaching the Cathedral of Oviedo, where it has been safely kept without interruption since the mid-eighth century.

The Sudarium is a linen cloth measuring two feet nine inches by one foot nine inches. The most amazing thing about the Sudarium is its blood stains and their similarity to those of the face area of the Shroud of Turin. These similarities were first noticed by Monsignor Ricardo Guarmo in 1955 and further examined by Dr. Alex White using his Polarized Image Overlay Technique.

Using this technique, Dr. White laid the image of the Sudarium over the Shroud. He was able to see clearly, what Guarmo had observed. There were over seventy congruent blood stains on the face and over fifty blood stains on the back of the head and neck. He concluded that the blood stain patterns were so strikingly similar to one another that they could only have been formed by both cloths coming in contact with the same body.

In his book, *The Great Discovery of the Shroud of Turin*, Dr. White states that this was consistent with the Jewish burial custom of wrapping the face of the deceased with a small cloth while the burial preparations were being made. And since anything with the lifeblood of the deceased on it had to be buried with him, the Sudarium was placed in the tomb near the body.

Was this it? Did the documented history of the Sudarium and its similarity to the Shroud validate the authenticity of the Shroud? Were they both silent witnesses to the same truth? Were both cloths sacred? Did they contain nothing less than the DNA of God?

"According to the carbon-dating tests, the Shroud can't be the burial cloth of Jesus."

I had called Paul Roberts again and asked him about the carbon-dating tests performed on the Shroud—something I had been putting off.

"Harold Greeley, the prime inventor of the accelerator mass spectrometry, the method used to test the Shroud, said that the chances of the Shroud being authentic were one in a thousand-trillion."

So that was it. All my other findings were moot. If the linen of the Shroud didn't date back to the time of Christ, it didn't matter how the image of the body was formed on it or that it contained real blood.

"Why didn't you mention this the first time we spoke?"

"You didn't ask," he said. "We were just getting started when we ran out of time. And I figured you could read it for yourself."

"Where did they date it?" I asked.

The door to my office was closed, but I could see a steady stream of blue through the thin panel of glass as the inmates filed past it on their way to the sanctuary for choir practice. The inmates who formed the choir were some of the most religious in the institution. They were also some of the most difficult and obnoxious.

"Between 1260 and 1390," he said. "The Middle-Ages, which is about when it first appeared in the historic record."

He hesitated, but I didn't say anything. I was too disappointed—and not just for Mom, but for me, too. I had become mesmerized by the man of the Shroud. I wanted the image to be Jesus. I wanted it to be a sign of the resurrection. I wanted it to be a point of contact between heaven and earth, between my heavenly mother and my earthly one.

"Do you understand what carbon-dating is?" he asked, his voice cold and scientific.

"No," I said.

"You okay?" he said. "You sound disappointed."

Through the wall behind me, I could hear the sounds of choir practice beginning, but it wasn't music or singing. It was the sound of inmates arguing over who was going to sing which song and who was going to play which instrument. Half the rehearsal time would be spent that way.

"I am," I said. "I wanted it to be the real thing."

"The test is based on the principle that all living things, in their taking in of carbon dioxide, also take in a tiny amount of radioactive isotope carbon-fourteen, which is continually being formed in the upper atmosphere. It comes down in the air we breathe, via photosynthesis, and the food chain. It's an integral part of all plants and animals."

"So it's in the fabric of the Shroud?" I asked.

"Yeah," he said. "It's in every living thing. In all living organisms, non-radioactive carbon is maintained at about one part in a trillion. But when a living thing dies, carbon-fourteen begins to decay, reducing its proportion to the stable carbon-twelve in whatever may be left. So, the test compares the proportion of carbon-fourteen to carbon-twelve. And it can be done in anything: bone, wool, leather, wood, or linen. All along, there've been a lot of people that thought the Shroud was a fake, and they challenged it to a carbon-fourteen test. It was done by three different laboratories: one in Zurich, one in Tucson, and one in Oxford."

"And they all got the same result?" I asked.

An inmate knocked on my door and I turned to see who it was. When I did, he could see that I was on the phone, but didn't offer to leave.

"Yeah," he said. "On October 13, 1988, they all announced their results, dating the origin of the shroud somewhere between 1260 and 1390."

"Which means it couldn't possibly have been around to wrap the dead body of Jesus," I said.

"On the basis of this test, no," he said. "In fact, the head of the Oxford laboratory said on public television that anybody who doesn't believe the results they obtained ought to belong to the 'flat earth society.'"

I sighed heavily.

"What is it?" he said. "Were you thinking it was real?"

"I was hoping."

I told him about Mom and her hope to be healed through the Shroud, but only if it were authentic. "This was the last thing I could do for her," I said. "This and take her to see it."

"Oh, man, I'm sorry," he said. "I didn't know. If I'd've known I could have—"

"What?" I asked. "What could you have done?"

"I could've lied to you," he said. "Which is what you should do to your mom."

Mom looked worse than she had the last time I had seen her—a lot worse, and it had only been a couple of days. When I walked into her room, she made no attempt to sit up, merely extended her small hand over to me. I took it. And held it. And told her how much I loved her before bowing my head and praying with her.

When I had finished, she looked up at me with tears in her eyes. "How are you?" she asked. "Tell me what's going on in your life."

I did. Well, I told her the good parts. As I talked, I could tell she felt a part. Perhaps it was the first time since she and Dad had divorced that she had.

"How are you doing?" I asked.

"You know. Good days and bad," she said, between shallow gasps of breath. "This is one of the bad."

"I'm sorry. What can I do?"

I held my breath as I waited for her to ask me about the Shroud.

"Just sit here with me," she said. "You can tell me some more about yourself or what's going on in your life, or you could just sit here and hold my hand for a while."

Relief washed over me.

"Chaplain Jordan?" the voice in the receiver asked.

"Yes."

I was back in my office at the prison.

"This is Jamie Sandford. I'm a colleague of Paul Roberts."

"Yeah?"

"Well, he asked me to call you," she said.

"Why's that?" I asked.

"Because," she said. "For some very good reasons, I believe the carbon-dating tests done on the Shroud of Turin were wrong and that the burial cloth is actually the one that covered Christ."

"Really?"

"Yeah, and there's a lot of people like me," she said. "We don't believe that the earth is flat or that science is evil or that there was a conspiracy behind the dates reported. Just people who interpret the mountain of other evidence on the Shroud as being at least as valid as carbon-dating, and who don't simply write it off on the basis of the one test alone."

"I'm listening," I said. "And I could really use some good news this morning."

"Paul said you probably could."

"He's got a heart after all," I said.

"I'm not as convinced of that," she said. "Anyway, did you know that none of the STURP scientists went into their tests of the Shroud believing anything but that it would be proved to be a forgery?"

"No."

"It's true," she said. "They were scientists looking for how the image of the Shroud was formed. And what they discovered made religious men out of most of them. They could *not* prove that the Shroud was a forgery. But they *could* prove by an overwhelming degree of probability that the shroud was *not* a forgery. They could not, nor can anyone since find any chemical or physical or biological process—in any combination—to account for the properties of the image."

I found myself nodding in agreement, though she couldn't see me.

"And tests that are admissible in a court of law have proven that blood *is* present on the cloth," she continued.

I didn't say anything.

On the corner of my desk was a picture of Jesus behind bars that someone had sent me, and though I liked the concept, the execution was all wrong. For one thing, it was in a gold frame. For another, the bars looked superimposed and fake, which they were. But most of all, the Jesus of the picture was a bland, pale European, Jesus, not the radical Jewish rabbi who came to set the captives free.

"Well, don't you understand what that means?" she asked.

I shrugged, though she couldn't see me. "I guess not," I said. "What does it mean?"

"If the carbon-dating tests are accurate, and that's a very big if, then what we have is the miraculous, inexplicable image of a fourteenth-century crucifixion victim on a burial cloth."

She paused, but I didn't say anything, suspense hanging on the line between us. I knew she had more to say.

Since count had cleared, inmates had been continually trickling into the chapel. Now it was noisy and busy, and I could hear the beginnings of theological arguments already.

"Crucifixions weren't done in the fourteenth-century," she said. "Not by anyone. So, if you believe that the Shroud is a fourteenth-century piece of linen, then you believe that someone was crucified in the exact same manner as in first-century Rome. And that someone murdered a man just to produce a forgery of the burial cloth of Jesus. And that still doesn't explain how the image got onto the cloth."

I realized how impetuous I had been to write off the whole investigation based on one piece of evidence.

"*Now* who's a member of the flat-earth society?"

"Not you," I said.

Through my window, past the rose beds, two overweight correctional officers with expressionless faces stood at the back of the security building smoking. Their light brown uniform shirts, expanding to hold back the landslide of fat hanging over their belts, resembled maternity clothing. Neither of them spoke, just stared down the compound disinterestedly.

"And what about the C-14 test itself?" she said. "Each lab was supposed to get three samples without knowing which one was the actual Shroud, but they didn't. And all the samples were taken from the same place—of course the labs came up with the same date, they did the same test on the same sample. And the sample wasn't taken from a very good place. It came from the edge. Remember, how many people have handled that edge over the years. The public displays use to involve people grabbing it by that edge and holding it for long periods of time."

She took in a deep breath and began again.

"And remember, the Shroud has been repaired. It has a backing and threads in it that are from the Middle Ages. In fact, one thread was sent to a different lab for a test and it dated between 200 and 1,000 A.D. And what about the fire of 1532? It got so hot the silver of the box the shroud was in melted on it."

I thought about the burn marks I had seen, extending the length of the shroud.

"So silver, fire, and water all touched the Shroud. You don't think that changed its chemistry? Of course it did. And what about the build-up on the linen itself? Think about two-thousand years of dust and debris and organisms."

"Quit with all the ambiguity," I said.

She laughed, but only for a second and was back at it. "Carbon-dating is not an exact science. Do you know how many mistakes have been made using it? Some of them have dated things off by thousands of years. And get this. In their own reports, the labs that did the tests have to concede that all the statistical manipulation in the world can't get rid of the fact that the range of the dates is much too large to be accounted for by the expected errors built into radiocarbon dating. In other words, there's a ninety-five percent chance that the discrepancy in the raw dates means that there were variables ratios in the samples themselves. In 1988 the whole world carried the story about the carbon-dating of the shroud, but in 1990, when the Vatican publicly stated that the results of the tests were strange, nobody reported it." She paused for a moment, then said, "So, whatta you think?"

"That I broke one of my cardinal rules of investigating," I said. "I rushed to judgment without considering all the facts."

"Bottom line, the carbon-dating tests were contaminated," she said. "And they are only a small part of a very large mountain of evidence, all the rest of which points to the Shroud being the actual burial cloth of Jesus."

When we had finished talking, Jamie Sandford e-mailed some additional information on the Shroud to me, and although I printed it, I read the entire article on my monitor, eyes transfixed to the screen.

Though the most venerated relic of Christianity was declared a fake in 1988 by three independent scientific institutions, new science suggests the Shroud deserves another look.

Willis Gray, a retired physical chemist, proposes that the samples used to date the Shroud in 1988 were flawed and the experiment should be repeated. His assertion is based on a recent chemical analysis of the shroud and previous observations made during the 1978 STURP examination, of which he was a part.

In 1988, the Vatican allowed small stamp-size pieces to be cut from one corner of the shroud and distributed to three laboratories—at the University of Arizona in Tucson, Oxford University in England, and the Swiss Federal Institute in Zurich—for carbon-dating. The results, published in 1989 in the journal *Nature,* revealed that the fabric was produced between 1260 and 1390.

Recently, Gray received a sample of the shroud from a colleague who had collaborated on STURP. The sample was taken from the same strip of cloth distributed for carbon-dating in 1988. Through chemical and microscopic analysis, he discovered a madder dye and mordant and gum mixture—evidence the cloth had been repaired at some point. Even more interesting is the fact that these ruby-colored madder dye-mordant mixtures did not even reach France or England until the 16th century.

Gray also uncovered evidence that the patch he was examining had not only been dyed but also been repaired and re-woven. He posits that the dye and repair job were probably done in the Near East during the Middle Ages, which coincides with the carbon-dating results.

"The date published in 1989 of 1260 to 1390 was accurate for the sample supplied," Gray said. "However, there is no question that the radiocarbon sampling area has a completely different chemical composition than the main part of the shroud. The published date for the sample was not the time at which the cloth was produced, but the time it was repaired."

This corroborates earlier findings of STURP scientists who, using ultraviolet fluorescence, also revealed that the sampled corner was unlike any other region of the Shroud and had been excessively handled over the years.

"You reached a conclusion yet?" Milton Warner asked.

I shook my head. "I've barely begun," I said, "and there's so much evidence on both sides."

The clear blue of his eyes was penetrative as he held my gaze.

"Aren't you almost out of time?"

I nodded.

"What're you going to tell your mother?"

"I really don't know," I said.

He nodded slowly, his lined face softening some.

"How're you feeling?"

"Better, actually," I said. "And I think it has something to do with the Shroud."

"What do you mean?"

"I'm not sure exactly," I said. "It's not that I'm convinced that it's authentic—hell, I'm not even sure what I believe about the resurrection, let alone that this could be a snapshot of it—but it's such a haunting image, such a profound mystery . . . I just find it . . . inspiriting somehow."

He nodded. He rarely showed a reaction to anything I said, but he seemed pleased.

"Most people I deal with are frightened by the unknown or inexplicable," he said. "They want answers—"

"There aren't any."

"But you . . . You seem to be inspired by the mystery of it all."

I nodded, and thought about what he had said.

We were quiet a moment.

"Do you think the Shroud has the power to heal?" he asked.

I shrugged. "It's having an effect on me," I said. "I guess I think anything can become an agent of healing. Probably has far more to do with the person being healed than the object."

"Do you think if you tell your mom you're convinced that the Shroud is genuine and take her to see it, she'll be healed?"

"I just don't know," I said. "I can't say for sure that she wouldn't."

"Then why not lie to her?"

I thought about it. "I'm not sure," I said. "I've certainly lied for less noble causes, but I just don't think I can."

He nodded, but there was nothing in it except acknowledgment.

"I don't know what to do," I said.

"Then it's a good thing you're comfortable with ambiguity."

The next afternoon, in the warmth of the sun, Mom and I sat in rocking chairs on her front porch. Mom was feeling better, and the pleasant afternoon seemed to help her as much as anything had recently.

I still didn't know what I would say to her exactly. She was dying. I wanted to give her hope, to do all I could to give her every chance of prolonging her life or at least having the best life possible in whatever time she had left, but I wasn't sure how.

The afternoon was the warmest in the last few weeks, and sitting in its soft glow with Mom as an occasional pine needle floated down from the trees to the earth below, was a moving experience.

"Well?" she said.

"What?" I asked, stalling.

"Is the Shroud real?"

My pulse quickened as my stomach dropped.

I wanted to be able to tell Mom that I had solved the mystery of the Shroud of Turin, that it was the actual burial cloth of Christ, and that if anything could be used by God to heal her, this holy relic could, but I couldn't.

"I still don't know," I said. "There's an amazing amount of evidence on both sides. I think it's a mystery that can't be solved. And I don't think it should be."

"What do you mean?"

"I think it should remain an enigmatic symbol of faith," I said. "Then the question becomes not whether or not science can prove that it's real, but whether or not we believe, whether or not we allow mystery to work its magic on us."

"Do you believe?" she asked.

"I don't have an easy answer for that one either," I said. "I do believe that it's something special, utterly unique in the world. And I think it can be a sign from God if we allow it to be. Isn't that really all that matters? Not whether or not it actually covered the body of Jesus, but if it speaks to us of him. If it reminds us of his suffering, of a God who suffers with us, whose heart breaks for what you're going through just like mine does."

Tears began to trickle down her cheeks, and she reached over and took my hand.

"I'm haunted by the image on the Shroud," I said. "And like all matters of faith, or art, it doesn't matter how it came to be or if it can be authenticated or scientifically validated. Its only validity is what it does for me. In that sense, I can say it's real."

"So do you think we should go and view it?" she asked.

"Do you?"

"I don't know," she said. "I really don't."

I thought about it for a long time, trying my best to weigh everything and determine what was in her best interest, saying a short prayer for guidance.

"Yes," I said. "I think we should."

"Do you think it's possible I'll be healed?" she asked hopefully, her tears changing as her face lit up.

I nodded. "I honestly believe anything's possible."

The most venerable and venerated relic of all time had been slipped out of the silver casket that had protected it for centuries, through fire and water, doubt and blind belief, and gingerly unspooled under the supervision of Giovanni Cardinal Saldarini and a German textile conservation expert. After the top cloth, a red taffeta sewn by Princess Clotilde of Savoy in 1886, had been pulled back, the fragile, scarred length of ancient linen had been smoothed into place in a metal and glass display case built precisely to its dimensions.

We were gazing up at it.

Mom and I had flown to Turin, Italy, two days ago to be a part of the estimated three million people who would line up over the next eight weeks to view this most sacred of cloths.

The cathedral was as ornate as any building I had ever been in, the sweet scent of incense lingering thickly, an olfactory match for its opulence.

The air in the case that held the Shroud had been drawn out and replaced with argon, an inert gas. It hung horizontally at the intersection of the Turin Cathedral's nave and transept, near the center of the cathedral's magnificent built-in cross.

Beside me, Mom gazed up at the image burned into the Shroud like a woman seeing a vision, herself a vision, mouth open, head back, eyes wrinkled at the corners as she squinted to see, her face made fresh by awe and wonderment.

What she was seeing I could only guess, but I felt that what she beheld was far more than an ancient cloth bearing an enigmatic image. Perhaps she was seeing nothing less than the visible image of the invisible God.

I was.

Not that I was suddenly convinced that the Shroud was a silent witness to the resurrection, but that even if I were staring at the image produced by an artist in the Middle-Ages, it, like all art, was evidence of the divine. And like all art, what we see in it tells us as much about ourselves as the object we're beholding in hushed reverence.

What does what I saw say about me?

That I'm a believer. I believe in mystery and possibility, that nothing is impossible. Not the existence of God. Not a virgin birth. Not a God-come-flesh. Not a resurrection from the dead. Nothing. Not even a love that is stronger than death—a love that is itself an evidence of the existence of God, of the justification of the hope I felt. Hope for Mom, for me, for the world.

Mom let out a small, but audible gasp.

"Yeah," I said. "I know."

I could tell she wanted to say more, but couldn't.

Only time would tell if this had cured her disease, but I had no doubt that our holy pilgrimage had healed her. Her humanity was healed. She finally and fully accepted the fathomless forgiveness she had been offered.

And she forgave herself.

Standing there beside her, gazing up at the ghostly image, I felt newly baptized, fully submerged in the healing presence of Christ.

Our awe and reverence for the sacredness of life, of individual moments like this one, which hinted at eternity, was restored to us like when we were children.

Both of us were in some sense healed, wounded mother and son, as if in some sense reflecting the wounded son and mother of the nearby Pietà—united with them in humanity, in pain, in love, in faith, in mystery, and in hope for divinity.

Printed in the United States
62448LVS00002B/4-9